**Bet[...]
fro[...]**

To her utter amazement, a small pink fist flailed in the air. The whimper swelled to a cry, and when Bethany bent over to look, she saw a tiny baby wrapped in a print blanket.

It was crying, its face screwed up and its legs kicking emphatically under the blanket. Bethany dissolved into total bewilderment, half thinking this must be some practical joke, yet knowing in her heart that it couldn't be.

Bethany reached down and unpinned an envelope from the baby's blanket. The outside of the envelope was blank, so she opened it and unfolded the note inside.

COLT, it said in printed block letters. PLEASE TAKE CARE OF ALYSSA FOR ME. I'LL BE BACK.

It seemed that her new ranch hand, Colt McClure, had some explaining to do.

Dear Reader,

May is *"Get Caught Reading"* month, and there's no better way for Harlequin American Romance to show our support of literacy than by offering you an exhilarating month of must-read romances.

Tina Leonard delivers the next installment of the exciting Harlequin American Romance in-line continuity series TEXAS SHEIKHS with *His Arranged Marriage*. A handsome playboy poses as his identical twin and mistakenly exchanges "I do's" with a bewitching princess bride.

A beautiful rancher's search for a hired hand leads to more than she bargained for when she finds a baby on her doorstep and a *Cowboy with a Secret*, the newest title from Pamela Browning. 2001 WAYS TO WED concludes with *Kiss a Handsome Stranger* by Jacqueline Diamond. Daisy Redford's biological clock had been ticking…until a night of passion with her best friend's brother left her with a baby on the way! And in *Uncle Sarge*, a military man does diaper duty…and learns about fatherhood, family and forever-after love. Don't miss this heartwarming romance by Bonnie Gardner.

It's a terrific month for Harlequin American Romance, and we hope you'll "get caught reading" one of our great books.

Wishing you happy reading,

Melissa Jeglinski
Associate Senior Editor
Harlequin American Romance

COWBOY WITH A SECRET
Pamela Browning

HARLEQUIN®

TORONTO • NEW YORK • LONDON
AMSTERDAM • PARIS • SYDNEY • HAMBURG
STOCKHOLM • ATHENS • TOKYO • MILAN • MADRID
PRAGUE • WARSAW • BUDAPEST • AUCKLAND

If you purchased this book without a cover you should be aware that this book is stolen property. It was reported as "unsold and destroyed" to the publisher, and neither the author nor the publisher has received any payment for this "stripped book."

This book is dedicated to the memory
of my brother-in-law, Bob Grier, who loved to demonstrate
in rip-roaring fashion the wonders of the Grier Ranch.

ISBN 0-373-16874-8

COWBOY WITH A SECRET

Copyright © 2001 by Pamela Browning.

All rights reserved. Except for use in any review, the reproduction or utilization of this work in whole or in part in any form by any electronic, mechanical or other means, now known or hereafter invented, including xerography, photocopying and recording, or in any information storage or retrieval system, is forbidden without the written permission of the publisher, Harlequin Enterprises Limited, 225 Duncan Mill Road, Don Mills, Ontario, Canada M3B 3K9.

All characters in this book have no existence outside the imagination of the author and have no relation whatsoever to anyone bearing the same name or names. They are not even distantly inspired by any individual known or unknown to the author, and all incidents are pure invention.

This edition published by arrangement with Harlequin Books S.A.

® and TM are trademarks of the publisher. Trademarks indicated with ® are registered in the United States Patent and Trademark Office, the Canadian Trade Marks Office and in other countries.

Visit us at www.eHarlequin.com

Printed in U.S.A.

ABOUT THE AUTHOR

Pamela Browning is an award-winning romance author who has written for children and teenagers as well as adults. She's an intrepid world traveler and has spent "significant time" on a cattle ranch owned by her sister. Though she has never found a baby on her doorstep, she once left one on a friend's doorstep as a practical joke. (They're still friends, she thinks.)

Books by Pamela Browning

HARLEQUIN AMERICAN ROMANCE
101—CHERISHED BEGINNINGS
116—HANDYMAN SPECIAL
123—THROUGH THE EYES OF LOVE
131—INTERIOR DESIGNS
140—EVER SINCE EVE
150—FOREVER IS A LONG TIME
170—TO TOUCH THE STARS
181—THE FLUTTERBY PRINCESS
194—ICE CRYSTALS
227—KISSES IN THE RAIN
237—SIMPLE GIFTS
241—FLY AWAY
245—HARVEST HOME
287—FEATHERS IN THE WIND
297—UNTIL SPRING
354—HUMBLE PIE
384—A MAN WORTH LOVING
420—FOR AULD LANG SYNE
439—SUNSHINE AND SHADOWS
451—MORGAN'S CHILD
516—MERRY CHRISTMAS, BABY
565—THE WORLD'S LAST BACHELOR
600—ANGEL'S BABY
632—LOVER'S LEAP
786—RSVP...BABY
818—THAT'S *OUR* BABY!
854—BABY CHRISTMAS
874—COWBOY WITH A SECRET

looking for er call after 6 pm.

Wanna learn how to two-step in five easy lessons? Call Dottie at #74857

Room for Rent: 550$/m plus w&h. #99857

House for Sale: 4br 2bt, 18k sq ft. Call Mr. Rose at #88576

ANTIQUES AT THE BARN. Quality antiques. Open ...ly, Public ...nment

Housekeeping services needed for family of seven. Salary and benefits excellent. #48955

MAIL-ORDER COWBOY
Have horse, will travel. Experienced ranch hand seeks work. No job too hard, no ranch too small. Send particulars to Box 261, Higginsville, Oklahoma.

DISTRESS SALE
Everything must g...

Riding Lessons, cheap! Rockin' C Ranch, call Denise at #87906

Part-time baby-sitter needed fo afternoons. 3 tots under 5 y.o. Rate competitive. #87695

Tickets, Tickets, Who Needs Tickets! All venues availab...

Chapter One

Colt McClure pegged the gal at the Banner-B Ranch for a babe as soon as he spotted her. But it was the promise of the ice-cold beer he'd insulated and stowed in his saddlebag that made him urge his horse into a hellzapoppin' gallop down the long curving driveway.

The hot Texas wind flung a handful of grit into the five days' growth of beard bristling from his face, but Colt didn't care. He didn't care about anything now except finding a place to work and a place to live. Oh, yeah—and that beer.

Instantly alert at the hammer of hoofbeats on parched earth, the gal lifted one hand to shade narrowed eyes against the orange sun sinking its way toward the horizon. The other hand rested on a neatly rounded hipbone.

He reined his horse to a stop at the edge of a patch of dry dusty grass in front of the two-story house. As he swung down from his mount, he realized that the woman's eyes were a cool aquamarine, the shade of the sea where there was no bottom. Or at least what he thought the sea would look like—he'd never seen the ocean. And he never wanted to after having a gander at those eyes. He could drown in them if he'd let himself.

The air shimmered with heat in the space between them. "Bethany Burke?" he said.

Long golden hair fell in loose curls around her face and tumbled over her shoulders. The way she nodded her head in confirmation and the resulting ripple of that incredible hair jolted Colt with the kind of emotion he hadn't felt in a long, long time.

Or maybe it wasn't emotion. Maybe he'd been too long away from women. Well, he planned to work on that, and from the look of things, Gompers, Texas, could be the place to do it.

"I'm the mail-order cowboy," he said into the silence.

Her skin was nut-brown from spending long hours in the sun. Her eyes startled him again with their beauty. She had a soft-looking mouth, the lips full and berry-red without the aid of makeup. It formed itself into a perfect O.

"You wrote. You said you needed a ranch hand." His voice was gruff and rusty with disuse. He hadn't done much talking in prison.

"I did. I do. I didn't expect you to just—arrive," she said.

"I rode over from town. Managed to cadge a ride down from Oklahoma for both me and Buckaroo with some folks who had extra room in their horse trailer."

She was a little thing, although well-worn boots added a couple more inches to her five-two or so, and she was clearly all woman under that plaid shirt. A man's shirt, too big for her, but it had been washed so many times that the well-worn cotton clung tightly to her fully rounded breasts.

No bra. He reckoned he knew such things. She'd left

the top buttons unfastened to reveal a deep cleavage, shadowy and pretty near fascinating.

She toyed nervously with the front of her shirt, then realized he was watching. Her hand fell away. A roughly callused hand, but daintily made.

"Where do I bunk?" he said. He saw no point in wasting words. The ranch was a shambles; fences sagging, bunkhouse falling apart, who knew what else. There was work for him here.

She gestured with a thumb. "You'll—you'll find an apartment over the barn. I would have cleaned it out if I'd known you were coming." She didn't have the local accent, which had a tendency to twang like out-of-tune banjo strings.

"No matter if it's clean or not. It'll do. I'll start in the morning." He nodded his head curtly and began to lead his horse away.

"You didn't tell me your name."

He stopped and turned slowly. His shadow fell across her face. "McClure," he said. "Clayton McClure. They call me Colt."

"Well, Mr. McClure, we'll meet in my kitchen tomorrow morning at seven o'clock sharp. Breakfast. We'll talk about your duties then."

"You got it," he said.

He knew she watched him all the way to the barn, but he didn't care. As soon as he popped the top off the beer, he took the stairs two at a time and poked around the tiny apartment. *If* you could put that name to a room-and-a-half with a tiny bath attached. Everything was furred with a thick layer of dust, but that was Texas. Basic furniture, nothing fancy. It would do.

Colt wasn't daunted by the lack of suds the soap coaxed out of the trickle of alkaline water that passed for a shower in his quarters. Afterward he unfurled an old musty blanket from his bedroll and spread out naked on the bare mattress provided. The air was stuffy; not much of a window. His skin was slicked with sweat before he was half asleep.

He didn't dream. He'd trained himself not to. It was better that way, especially when your dreams had a way of slipping out from under you and catapulting you into a shaky shadowy world where nightmares woke you screaming.

BETHANY BURKE stared wide-eyed as Colt disappeared into the barn. When she'd first seen him trying to outrun the cloud of dust he'd stirred up as he galloped toward her, she'd thought he was one of those mirages conjured up out of the heat on a hot summer's day. She'd almost forgotten about replying to that peculiar ad.

But, she admitted to herself, if she'd ordered a cowboy to her own specifications, he couldn't have been better. He was lean and lithe, without an extra ounce of fat. His narrow hips sat a horse like he was born to it. Those wide shoulders meant muscular upper arms, good for roping and branding. And he had hungry eyes.

That last thought took her by surprise. Hungry for what? Or was the expression under those drooping eyelids a raw insolence unconcealed by his thin veneer of politeness? Those eyes weren't only hungry, they were hard as flint. A shiver ran down her spine in spite of the fact that it was ninety-five degrees in the shade.

"Who was that I saw go into the barn?"

Bethany whirled to see Frisco, her bandy-legged foreman, stumping toward her from the equipment shed. Jesse James, the border-collie mix, bounded along beside him.

"A guy I just hired to work on the ranch," Bethany said offhandedly.

"What guy?"

"His name's Colt McClure. I answered an ad."

"What ad?"

Bethany scuffed the ground with the toe of one boot. "It was a kind of mail-order thing."

"What," Frisco said suspiciously, "are you talking about?"

"I ordered him. Through an advertisement. He showed up. That's about all there is to tell." She turned toward the house, but Frisco caught her arm.

His expression was incredulous. "You ordered this honcho through one of them catalogs you're always getting in the mail?" Frisco always teased her about her penchant for mail-order catalogs. Seed catalogs, clothing catalogs, knickknacks, lingerie, and health-care catalogs—all found their way into the big Banner-B Ranch mailbox.

Bethany bit her bottom lip. "The ad was in the *Cattle Rancher's Journal.* It was a quarter page, with a wide border. I couldn't help seeing it."

Frisco released her arm and shot her a baleful glance out of his one eye. "Looking for trouble if you ask me."

"I didn't ask you, Frisco. We need someone around here, and we need him desperately." This ongoing conversation between them reminded her of a snake eating its tail, circling 'round and 'round.

"I try my best," Frisco said, lapsing into his defensive mode. "I know I'm getting a little worn, but I ain't about to assume room temperature yet."

Bethany slid an arm around his stooped shoulders, wishing that every successive episode of this debate didn't have to scrape away at Frisco's self-esteem, although she knew that's exactly the way it was. "I want you to take it easy because Doc Hogan said you should. I couldn't stand it if anything happened to you."

Frisco jutted his jaw out. "So you invite a perfect stranger to live in the barn. A stranger who needs a shave real bad. Hair's overlong, too. He looks no 'count."

"We've had hands who weren't razor-friendly before, Frisco." She tried not to think about Colt McClure's eyes and how they'd sliced right through her like a well-aimed bullet.

"One of them hands you're talking about took a hankering after somebody else's horse, another ran up an overlarge tab at Pug's Tavern before he lit off for parts unknown, and the last one wrecked the pickup. That's what happens when you hire people you don't know."

"No need to have a conniption fit over this, Frisco. Besides, no one we know wants to work here. Mott Findley has seen to that." Mott was her late husband's cousin, and he wanted nothing more than to see the Banner-B go belly-up.

Frisco worked his forehead into a knot, a sure sign that he was engaged in deep thought, and rammed his hands down in his pockets. "We'll see how this guy works out," he said grudgingly.

Bethany bent and scratched Jesse behind one ear. The dog immediately stopped thumping his tail in the dust and relieved himself on the sunflower seedlings she'd recently set out on the side of the house. He always did this when he was happy, according to Frisco.

It was exasperating, this habit of Jesse's. "You know, Jesse," she said, "you're a mighty expensive flea motel. For two cents I'd trade you in on a good mouser."

"Jesse eats cats for fun," Frisco warned. "He ran off all them barn cats we used to have."

"Maybe I'll get me a nice inside cat, one of those flat-faced white Persians to sit on the windowsill and lord it over all of us. Including that ungrateful mutt."

Frisco looked pained. "You really want to tick Jesse off, you go right ahead and do that. No telling what Jesse might do, you tick him off."

Bethany sighed. They'd acquired the dog to help with cutting cattle, but from the beginning he'd refused to have anything to do with such foolishness. The fact was, Jesse was untrainable. Unfortunately he and Frisco had bonded.

"I'd better go find that posthole digger. I plan to let our new hand build fence tomorrow," she said.

Frisco's one good eye regarded her with deep affection. "Don't get to counting on this mail-order guy," he said.

Bethany remained unruffled as she headed toward the shed. It had taken Frisco a few years to learn to take orders from a woman. And besides, she was the one who had promised Justin that she'd make the Banner-B a success.

She'd do it. No matter what.

THE NEXT MORNING Bethany hurried downstairs in her bathrobe to plug in the coffeemaker at precisely six-fifteen. She never set her alarm clock because this was the time she always woke up, rain or shine, weekday or weekend. But today was different. Today she would interview Colt McClure.

She sneaked an early cupful from the coffeepot and nursed the fragrant steaming mug in her two hands as she paused to fill her ears with the first warbles and trills of birdsong outside her window. Morning bathed the home place in delicate silver-gray light, unfurling a misty curtain to blur the relentless brown everything.

As usual, she turned on the radio for the early farm-and-ranch report, "brought to you by Rubye's Beauty Box, we curl up and dye for you." Down by the chicken coop, a raucous rooster greeted the slow-rising rim of the sun with a jubilant fanfare. Later the heat would be blistering, sucking precious moisture from the grass, the trees, the vegetables in the garden.

When Bethany had first arrived on the Banner-B, she'd hated west Texas with its endless wind and dust and heat and glare, not to mention its indigestible food. Later, after a rough period of adjustment and more Texas Pete hot sauce than she cared to think about, Bethany had come to appreciate the wide-open spaces and the friendly people.

Anyway, she thought with a sigh, she was here to stay. At least she'd learned to tolerate the food well enough. Some people bragged about abs of steel. Bethany was proud of her stomach of iron, forged by repeated blasting in hot-pepper sauce.

Listening to the ranch report with one ear, she mentally began to arrange the day's schedule around breaking in a new hand. First she'd make sure this McClure guy knew how to dig those postholes, and while he was working at it, she'd drive into town and sweet-talk old Fred Kraegel into letting her charge more barbed wire to her account. Later she'd tackle Sidewinder, the most ornery horse in the world.

But before she got started on any of this, she'd best get decent, which meant throwing on a pair of jeans and one of Justin's old shirts, same as she did every day. There was no need to put on airs while she interviewed a new employee. By her best recollection, the last time she'd worn a dress was to her husband's funeral five years before.

Once upon a time before she married, before she moved from Wichita to Gompers, Texas, to start a new life as Justin Burke's wife and helpmate, Bethany had worked in an office. In a tall building. With air-conditioning. And she'd dressed stylishly in suits complete with pantyhose and heels for her nine-to-five job in an insurance office. She'd been Bethany Carroll then, had belonged to a young singles' club, jaunted around town in a red convertible and had never owned a jar of moisturizer in her life.

Now she rode a horse and worked cattle, gunned a dented pickup truck through the dry arroyos and gullies of the Banner-B, and her only concession to skin care was giant jars of moisturizer that she ordered periodically from one of those catalogs Frisco was always grousing about. Her main hobby consisted of daydreaming about growing the hardscrabble ranch left to Justin by his daddy into a spread whose name could actually be uttered in the same breath with the word *prosperous*.

That time, however, still seemed mighty far in the future. So far, in fact, that maybe by the time she could afford decent clothes and makeup again, she wouldn't have the face or the figure to show off anymore.

But I'm only thirty years old! Out of sheer desperation, she reminded herself of this often. Most of the time she felt much older; the responsibility of the ranch weighed heavily on her shoulders. With no family of her own, distanced from her friends in Wichita by a life that they couldn't begin to understand, she often felt so alone.

These thoughts were abruptly ended by the unmistakable clomp of cowboy boots on the wide wooden boards of the back porch. A wild glance at the clock confirmed that it was only six-thirty, too early for Frisco and certainly too early for Colt McClure. And Mott Findley usually didn't swagger onto her porch at this ungodly hour.

She edged a cautious eye around the bravely starched curtain hanging at the window. It wasn't even properly light outside.

"Ma'am?" Colt McClure peered back at her, and her coffee sloshed over the rim of her mug before she dumped it in the sink with a clatter. She was suddenly mindful that she wore nothing under her old chenille bathrobe but bare skin. Backing away from the window, she clutched the two sides of fabric together. "I told you seven o'clock," she said sharply.

He cleared his throat. "No offense, ma'am, but I'm here to work. I don't mind gettin' an early start."

"Well," she said. Her robe had never seemed so skimpy, and she wondered if it revealed anything she didn't want him to see. A sneaky peek at her reflection in the black plastic door of the microwave oven reassured her. Faded yellow chenille was not exactly titillating stuff.

She flicked off the radio. "Come in," she said. She kept her back to the door, hitched the belt of her robe even tighter and busied herself pouring him a mug of coffee until he was inside. Well, actually it oozed more than poured—she brewed her coffee strong.

When she turned around, Colt McClure, all six feet and more of him, stood to one side of the kitchen table crushing the brim of his worn black Stetson brushpopper in his enormous hands. He smelled of soap and leather and clean blue denim, and he'd slicked his dark hair back behind his ears. Today he looked much less fierce; he'd shaved the beard stubble to reveal a square, lean jaw. His eyes gleamed above the planes and hollows of his face, and she searched them for a hint of the insolence she'd noticed yesterday. If it was there, he'd concealed it.

He wasn't drop-dead handsome; far from it. The scar bisecting one cheek took care of that. But he gave off a rugged strength, and he was certainly an imposing figure, with shoulders way out to El Paso, stomach flat as the west Texas plains, and long, long legs. His jeans were well-worn and so soft that they clung all the way down. His thighs—but she had no business thinking about his thighs. Or any of the rest of him.

"Sit down, please," she said briskly, attempting a brief and impersonal smile. "Sugar? Cream?"

"Black," he said. He lowered himself onto one of the kitchen chairs, the woven cane seat creaking under his weight. Even sitting, he blocked a good deal of light from the door.

She slid the coffee in front of him and clapped a spoon down on the table beside it. He kept his eyelids lowered, which she found respectful until she realized that he was staring at her bare feet. Her toes curled unwittingly, and she felt a slow heat work its way up from her chest to her neck to her cheeks.

She turned away in embarrassment, so fast that the bottom part of her robe flipped open. In exasperation, she yanked it closed. She'd give anything to be able to stuff the fabric between her knees and clamp it in place with her kneecaps, but she couldn't. She didn't want to appear undignified.

She'd intended for the new hand to take her seriously,

which was perhaps a futile hope at this point. Nevertheless, she tried.

"I believe your ad said that you've worked on a ranch before," she ventured primly as she assembled eggs, flour, milk and bacon on the counter beside the stove.

"Yes, ma'am," he said in that grating voice of his, rusty as an old door hinge.

If she wanted more information, obviously she'd have to dig.

"What kind of work?"

"Everything."

"Could you be more specific?"

"Ropin', brandin', workin' cattle. Fences, barn repair, cleanin' out ditches. Balin' hay, trainin' horses—"

"Are you good at it?" She slapped cold bacon into the warming skillet.

"At which, ma'am?"

"Breaking horses."

"I think so."

"What's your philosophy about it?" she shot back. She began to cut out biscuits with the top of a jelly glass the way Dita, Frisco's wife, had showed her years ago when Bethany had arrived at the ranch with no more idea of how to bake biscuits than how to rope or brand or ride fences.

He watched her punching out floury circles of dough, narrowing his eyes as if he suspected a trick question. Which it wasn't.

"Philosophy, ma'am?"

"Please don't call me ma'am. You can call me Mrs. Burke. Or Bethany, if you prefer."

He didn't say anything.

"I asked your philosophy about breaking horses," she reminded him.

He paused before answering. "I don't like to think of it as breakin'. I like to think of it as buildin'. I think if you've got a horse to train, it's like bringin' up a kid. Your future relationship with the horse depends on how well you do it."

She was surprised at this easy, unexpected flow of words and risked a quick look at him out of the corners of her eyes. "You've trained a lot of horses?"

"A fair number. Even some tough ones."

She turned around and studied him. His deep-set gray eyes were thoughtful and clear, with silvery motes swimming in their depths.

"And how do you go about training a horse that doesn't cooperate?" She was thinking of Sidewinder, the two-year-old quarter horse who had, of late, appointed himself the bane of her existence. Or so it seemed.

Colt's eyes, those marvelous eyes, met hers with a crinkle of amusement. There was nothing hard about them now. "You have to train an uncooperative horse like porcupines make love. Very gently, ma'am—Mrs. Burke."

She whipped back around, not wanting him to see that she was charmed as well as embarrassed. She shoved the biscuits into the oven and slammed the oven door. The noise it made reverberated into an awkward silence. Well, perhaps it was only awkward for her. She didn't dare look at him.

"Mr. McClure, how many eggs can you eat, and how do you like them cooked?" she blurted.

"You better call me Colt. And I can eat five eggs. Or six. Sunny-side up."

"I don't usually cook for the help. From now on, you'll eat with the ranch foreman at his house." She was setting boundaries now; she discouraged familiarity with the hands.

"That's fine."

She drew a deep stabilizing breath. "Maybe I'd better explain things. Frisco's my foreman, and he's been here since my late husband was a boy. Dita's his wife, a hard worker. She does the work of a man around here. Eddie's their nineteen-year-old son, and he cooks, handles odd jobs and works in the garden." She didn't tell him the rest about Eddie; Colt would figure that out for himself.

"This Dita—you mean to say she's a regular hand?"

"That's what I mean to say, all right. She's in her forties and as strong as an ox. She's also solid and dependable, which is more than you can say for some."

"I see," Colt said, although she knew he was puzzling over a forty-something-year-old woman being employed as a hand. Well, Dita was a blessing, and you had to take help wherever you could get it. Also, Dita and Frisco and Eddie were her family. They weren't related by blood, but they were all she had now that Justin was gone; her own parents had died when she was a teenager.

"You have any objection to hard work, cowboy?" she asked Colt.

"That's what I'm looking for," he said evenly.

"I'd say you've found it at the Banner-B."

"Looks like it, all right. Speakin' of which, what do you want me to do today?"

"Dig postholes," she said. "You'll find the posthole digger in an empty stall in the barn, and my foreman will show you where to start."

She caught him eyeballing her breasts, but he quickly glanced away when he saw that she noticed. Still, she felt her nipples pucker under the soft robe. And in response to what? A cocky attitude, a penetrating gaze?

Colt McClure wasn't her type; he was a drifter, no doubt, and there was something hard about him. Something tough. And something dangerous enough to set off wild alarms inside her head.

She'd meant to ask Colt where he'd worked last, and she wanted him to supply references, but her physical response to him was getting way out of line. It embarrassed her and made her feel guilty—she hadn't even looked at another man since Justin. She'd figured that sex was something she'd never experience again, like wearing suits to work and drawing a regular paycheck.

Fine, but then why was she feeling something breathtakingly akin to lust simmering just below the surface of her skin? Why had her heartbeat gone all aflutter under the chaste folds of her robe?

And the man who was responsible for her turmoil was totally unaware. Colt McClure wolfed down eggs and biscuits as if there were no tomorrow. He had a sensual mouth and big hands, and for an instant she imagined that mouth exploring hers and those hands caressing her breasts.

No!

The man was an unknown quantity with nothing to commend him but the right physique for the job and a willingness to work at the Banner-B. Bethany probably shouldn't have hired him, but what else was she to do? She'd promised Justin to make the ranch a success, and she couldn't do it all alone even with Frisco and his family's help. And maybe she wouldn't be able to do it at all if cousin Mott succeeded in snatching the place out from under her.

Oh, why had she thought of that? Sudden tears welled in her eyes, and she blinked them away. If Mott succeeded—but she'd already made up her mind that she wouldn't allow it, no matter how powerful he was, no matter what his political connections.

"Anything wrong, Mrs. Burke?"

Bethany couldn't let herself seem vulnerable to this man. Or to anyone else for that matter. Vulnerability was too often seen as weakness. But oh, sometimes she felt her loneliness like a vise around her heart, and sometimes she thought she couldn't stand the pain of it.

She tossed a spatula into the sink with a distracting clatter and made a blind beeline for the hall stairs. She called out over her shoulder, "Any questions about the job, ask Frisco."

"I thank you kindly for breakfast," he called after her. "And do you have any sheets for my bed?"

She pretended that she hadn't heard, but she wished she'd thought of that. Of course he'd need sheets. And maybe some other things, too.

It was the other things that she didn't dare to contemplate. Felt guilty for even thinking about. But she was sure that they also had something to do with bed.

Chapter Two

By one o'clock in the afternoon, the day was rolling along full blaze ahead. Colt swiped at his forehead with one sleeve of the shirt he'd tied around his waist in an attempt to tan away some of the prison pallor. He hadn't been out in the sun much for the past three years—inmates were allowed only one hour a day exercise in the pen.

He squinted for a moment at the line of dust rolling toward him from the horizon, then threw himself into the task at hand—digging holes. It wasn't an interesting job, but it gave him time to think.

Thinking was a pastime he'd cultivated in prison because there hadn't been a whole lot else to do except explore the prison law library for information that would win him a new trial. New information had surfaced, finally. And he'd been sprung, thank God. The trouble was, he hadn't thought out what he wanted to do with the rest of his life. When you didn't think you were going to be able to have a real life, you didn't plan for it. At least, he hadn't. All his plans went down the drain when the judge handed down that prison sentence.

He moved on to the next spot. Now he could see the

dilapidated ranch pickup at the head of all that dust, and he figured it was probably Frisco checking to see if he was working. The old guy didn't think much of him. Colt had figured that out the first time they set eyes on each other. Or eye, in the case of Frisco, who wore a black patch over his left one.

The pickup jolted over a rise and pulled to a stop just short of where he stood. Colt worked stolidly, knowing he had to prove himself. To his surprise, the person who slid out of the truck wasn't Frisco but Bethany Burke.

"Greetings, cowboy," she said. "How's it going?" She seemed cautious and so solemn. He wondered what it would take to make her bust loose and let go of that cool reserve.

He straightened and leaned on the posthole digger. A runnel of sweat trickled down his back. "It's going okay," he said.

"I brought you something to drink." She looked deceptively delicate as she hauled a large thermos and a mason jar out of the pickup and poured him some iced tea. It was sweetened already, the way he liked it. He thanked her and gulped it down before holding out the jar for more.

Even in this miserable heat, Bethany looked so cool that butter wouldn't melt in her mouth or on any other place, either. She stood close enough for him to inhale the warm sweet fragrance of her skin, and it reminded him of the scent of wildflowers borne on a prairie breeze. Colt's eyes were inadvertently drawn to her cleavage, or rather to where her cleavage had formerly shown. Today her shirt—big and blousy like yesterday's—was buttoned higher.

His eyes roamed elsewhere, taking in the paler skin of her inner arm, the glint of sunlight on blond curls, the way she stood with one hip canted to counter the weight of the big thermos. He felt a rush and a stirring somewhere south of his belt and bolted down the second jar of cold tea in an attempt to quench the fire.

He made himself look somewhere, anywhere, which was why he happened to notice that over on the highway, a small light-colored sedan had slowed to armadillo speed. That in itself seemed unusual, since when people hit a lonely stretch of road in isolated parts like these, they tended to floor the accelerator. The car stopped briefly, then sped up. Bethany kept her eye on it the same way he did before turning back to him.

"Did you talk to Frisco about supper?" she asked.

"Yes, ma'am," Colt said. Then he remembered. She didn't like to be called ma'am. And somehow Mrs. Burke didn't fit her. He'd call her Bethany, but it seemed overly familiar to call her by her first name. Okay, so from now on he'd call her nothing. Though he did think Bethany was a good name for her—soft and feminine, just like her.

"And did he tell you what time to show up?"

"Six o'clock," Colt said. Because he didn't include the ma'am, he thought he sounded too abrupt. "Dinner today was delicious," he added.

"Eddie cooks at noon. He's good at it." She watched him carefully for his reaction, but he wasn't going to give her one. Sure, he knew about the kid. The signs were unmistakable. Eddie had Down's syndrome, born with an extra chromosome. Mentally challenged, as some put it. That didn't bother him. Eddie had been polite, friendly and interested.

"Can't say I've ever had a better meat loaf," Colt said.

Bethany's face lit up with a smile. Clearly the kid

meant a lot to her. "You'll eat well at the Neilsons'," she said.

He nodded, bedazzled by the shimmer of her when she smiled like that.

"I'm going to leave this thermos of tea with you," she said, setting it on the ground. "There's salt tablets in the barn, and you'd better take them in this weather. You can keep the thermos. You'll need something to drink when you're working far away from the home place in such heat."

"Thanks. I appreciate it," he said.

Without saying anything else, she marched back to the pickup and got in. When the engine turned over, she backed and wheeled around, leaving him standing at the edge of a spurt of dust.

Colt watched her go, thinking that a high-class babe like her was wasted 'way out here in no man's land. Bethany Burke should be someplace where there were palm trees waving in the breeze, balmy nights and a passel of admiring men flitting around her in appreciation of her spectacular beauty.

Come to think of it, he could appreciate it well enough, but he didn't think she'd like it. She'd made it clear that her relationship with him was to be businesslike.

He wondered about her, wondered how long she'd been struggling to make a go of this place. There was something valiant about Bethany Burke's refusal to do the obvious with the Banner-B. Many an experienced rancher would have packed it in by this time. But she didn't seem of much of a mind to give up. She wasn't a quitter. That was one thing the two of them had in common.

The pickup merged with the horizon where it flattened under the weight of the sky, and Colt put his back into his work and dug another posthole. He thought about his new employer, pictured her reclining under a palm tree in one of those tiny string bikinis, a demure come-hither glint in those remarkable blue eyes.

He might have sworn off nighttime dreaming, but there was no reason why he couldn't indulge in a few daydreams now and then.

COLT HEARD THE RUCKUS as he was storing the posthole digger in the corrugated equipment shed where he thought it belonged, not in the barn where he'd found it. A horse squealed in panic, the heart-wrenching sound echoing back and forth between the barn and the shed. A horse's terror was one thing Colt couldn't stand to think about. He knew what it was like to feel that way— no damn good.

He ran out of the shed and around it. A red roan galloped around the perimeter of the corral behind the barn, bucking every once in a while for good measure. Whatever else was going on wasn't any clearer than his vision, which was normally 20/20 but presently obscured by the ominous cloud of dust billowing in the air.

Then he saw Bethany Burke clambering up on the fence, displaying the pert curve of her backside in the process. She dragged a leather halter behind her.

"What the—?" he hollered.

"This horse is meaner than cuss," she hollered over her shoulder. The halter caught on the fence post, and then her foot slipped and she fell back into the corral.

Colt was over the fence in an instant. The roan, a thousand pounds or so of muscle and sinew, was wild-eyed and galloping straight toward Bethany. She realized the danger and rolled over twice to fling herself away from the onslaught of thundering hooves. Colt planted his two feet firmly in the dust between Bethany and the horse and fixed his gaze on the horse's eyes. Not surprisingly, the horse fled to the other side of the corral and stood panting, sides quivering.

"Get up," Colt said tersely into the sudden quiet. He didn't dare take his eyes off the horse.

Behind him, he heard Bethany climb on the fence, up and over. Colt backed away, still holding the horse with his gaze. Then he vaulted over the fence and jumped down, landing lightly beside her.

Bethany's face was ashen. She was scared. He couldn't blame her; she could have been trampled.

"You all right?" he asked sharply.

She nodded and closed her eyes for a long moment. "I'm okay. Thanks."

"What were you doing?"

"Trying to put a halter on him."

"Who spooked this horse? Not you, I take it?"

She lifted a shoulder and let it fall, but she wasn't as nonchalant as she seemed. A slick of perspiration beaded her forehead, and he thought he detected a slight trembling of her upper lip—a very sensual upper lip, it seemed to him.

"You'd have to ask Mott Findley."

"Who's he?"

"My neighbor. I took Sidewinder from Mott in trade believing I could help him, but I'm thinking he's hopeless. Sometimes I'll be making progress, then something sets him off. If he can't catch on to what a good horse is supposed to do on a ranch, I'll have to get rid of him."

Colt knew what that meant. The roan was well on his

way to becoming poodle food. With a marginal operation like the Banner-B, a horse wasn't worth the feed and vet care it took to maintain him if he couldn't pull his weight.

He moved closer to the fence, leaned on it. The sinking sun felt good spread across his shoulders. The roan, a gelding about fourteen and a half hands high, had the powerful hindquarters and deep chest of a good quarter horse, a breed developed for cutting cattle and roping steers. To say this horse was skittish was an understatement—he was downright dangerous. Colt hadn't seen a horse in such bad shape in years, not since Ryzinski's. He didn't have to think about it for more than a moment.

"You mind if I have a try at him?"

Bethany chuckled mirthlessly. "Not if he's going to kill a perfectly good ranch hand."

"I know what I'm doing." Colt turned around and looked at her. She was covered with dust, but she didn't seem to mind. She'd bundled her hair into a barrette at her nape and tucked her thumbs inside the waistband of her jeans. It drew them tight around her belly. *Nice.*

"You think you can calm him down, go ahead. Just don't take any chances."

"I figure I can help him some," he told her. She didn't say anything, so he climbed up on the fence and studied the roan. The horse was blowing air in long huffs and eyeing Colt with trepidation, his ears laid back along his neck. His sleek coat gleamed in the sun.

"What's his name?"

"Sidewinder. Like the rattlesnake."

Colt wasn't sentimental about animals. He wasn't sentimental about anything anymore. But Sidewinder was an animal caught in a prison, and Colt identified with that. Worse, the animal had no one to help him get out. And a horse only knew to run when threatened. A horse didn't fight. Block his flight, and you terrified the animal. The horse was beside himself with wanting to be free.

Trouble was, this horse would never be free. He was expected to work. If someone didn't show him how to work, he'd soon be a dead horse. Nothing free in being dead.

Colt's shirt was sweaty and stuck to his skin; he stripped it off in one swift motion and flung it over the fence. He alit from the fence, dropping into the corral. Bethany moved closer, but he didn't look at her. The only power that would hold Sidewinder was the strength of his gaze, and this wasn't the time to waste it.

The horse rolled his eyes, shook his proud head and took off at a trot, but that was what Colt expected. He strode to the center of the enclosure and kept his body turned fully toward Sidewinder, maintaining eye contact. *What has someone done to you?* he said silently. He'd never known if horses knew what people were thinking, and he wasn't sure it mattered if they did. He didn't need any special ESP with Sidewinder because his body language would do the job. It had never failed yet.

Sidewinder took off at a gallop, and Colt let him run off some steam, facing him all the while, finally allowing himself to break eye contact. Soon he noticed that Sidewinder kept the ear on Colt's side still, and Colt knew that the horse was trying to understand the situation. In Sidewinder's world, Colt was a new person presenting a new scent and a new attitude; Sidewinder was intelligent and wanted to know what was going on.

The horse made several more revolutions of the corral. He was amazingly beautiful as he ran, a magnificent horse. Bethany looked on doubtfully from the other side of the fence. Colt couldn't blame her for being skeptical.

It took a while, but Colt finally recognized the signs. Sidewinder licked his lips and pretended to chew. The horse was ready to calm down.

"Maybe you'd better come out of there," Bethany said behind him. "He's looking agitated."

She'd misread the signs. Lots of people did. Bethany clearly thought that Sidewinder was gathering himself for an attack. Well, her thinking was not unusual.

"He's fine, just fine," he said. To his satisfaction, Sidewinder dropped his head and kept trotting. This was a signal.

Colt now broke eye contact and changed his body position. Sidewinder stopped running. The roan stood, his flanks heaving, watching. Colt didn't move.

"Colt—" Bethany said urgently.

Colt shook his head slightly and she knew enough to keep quiet. The horse took a tentative step forward, then another. He stopped again. Colt waited.

Then Sidewinder, the horse that had almost trampled Bethany Burke less than a half hour ago, walked slowly to him and stood submissively at his side.

Colt spoke to him then. "Good boy," he said as he reached out and stroked Sidewinder's nose. The horse remained alert, but allowing himself to be stroked was an admission of trust. Colt kept stroking, moving his hand downward to rub the horse's neck. This horse was no problem horse. He just hadn't been handled right.

"Never have I seen anything like that. It's incredible," Bethany said from her perch on the fence. She sounded awestruck.

"Tomorrow we'll try a saddle," Colt said. He patted Sidewinder's neck and made a slow turn. The horse followed him when he headed for the gate.

Bethany met him on the other side and waited while he closed and latched it. "Lordy, Colt, what is it you do?" she said.

Colt was feeling pretty good about what he'd accomplished. "Secret," he said. He didn't let on how psyched he was.

"Will you really try a saddle tomorrow?"

He peeled his shirt off the top rail of the fence. It had dried stiff, and he didn't want to put it on so he crumpled it into a ball.

"And maybe more." Until those final moments, he hadn't realized how exhilarating it was to be doing what he did best. He'd been aware of Bethany Burke. He'd wanted to impress her. But that wasn't the main thing.

Bethany studied him, and he wondered if she was assessing more than his resolve. Her gaze dropped to his bare chest, a movement that looked involuntary. Or was he reading too much into this? Maybe he'd better stick to reading horses.

"Well, cowboy, that was some show. I'd like you to tell me how you do it. I mean it."

"I can show you much better than I can tell you," he said. "Meet me here tomorrow afternoon at the same time."

"Is it okay if Frisco watches?"

"How about just you?" So far Frisco had been all hiss and vinegar, and the idea of the old guy's spectating held no appeal. Colt was determined to cement his place here before setting himself up for criticism. A job was a job, and he intended to keep this one. It was far enough away from Oklahoma, for one thing, and there was plenty to do and no competition. The Banner-B suited him.

"All right, then, just me." Bethany smiled at him.

Smiles from beautiful women had been few and far between in the last few years, and it was all Colt could do not to turn his considerable charm on her.

Bad idea. He'd save it for the horse.

"I'll be out planting posts tomorrow early," he said. He deliberately tacked a gruff edge to his words.

"Fine."

With a curt nod, he left her. Next, supper with the Neilsons. Maybe he could soften up the old coot by being friendly with the kid. Eddie liked him, he could tell.

COUNTRY MUSIC WAS PLAYING on the radio, something whiny and sad that made Bethany feel mopey just listening to it. She rattled around in the kitchen, cobbling a meal together from leftovers because she didn't feel like cooking. To make things even worse, she was nursing a bruised shoulder, an unpleasant souvenir of her dust-up with Sidewinder.

While her food warmed in the microwave, she wondered what was going on around the Neilsons' supper table. Frisco was probably whittling invisible notches in that chip on his shoulder, and Dita would be making cheerful table conversation. Eddie—well, Eddie was Eddie.

What would Colt McClure add to the mix? He wasn't exactly Mr. Personality. And anyway, why did she care?

Well, she did care. She desperately wanted the new hand to work out. Not to prove Frisco wrong, but to make life easier at the Banner-B for all of them. After she'd left the corral that afternoon, she'd ridden out to the new fence line and checked on the work Colt had done. He'd dug more fencepost holes than she'd imagined one man could do in a single day. And what he'd accomplished with Sidewinder was nothing less than phenomenal.

Bethany was glad that the old system of breaking a horse's willpower and creating subservience through fear had fallen into disrepute. She hated pain and cruelty of any kind. These days, the trend in horse training was to use more humane methods than trainers had employed in the past.

She and her own horse, Dancer, worked as a team, and next to Frisco, Bethany considered Dancer her best friend on the ranch. Consequently when Sidewinder first arrived in trade from Mott Findley for some extra bales of hay that she'd grown last year, when the horse had turned out for some reason to be skittish and afraid, she'd thought that teaching him was a mere matter of showing him love and thereby developing trust. So far, all her high-minded theory had achieved for her was a near-death experience courtesy of a terrified horse that was worth less than spit.

But Colt McClure knew something she didn't, something that would save Sidewinder. He had a rare gift. And Bethany was eager to learn his secret.

She'd been so preoccupied with all she'd had to do today that she'd clean forgotten that Colt needed sheets for his bed. After supper, she loaded the dishwasher and then rummaged in the linen closet until she found what she was looking for. Colt would probably still be eating with Frisco and his family, so she'd drop the sheets off and afterward take a long walk the way she often did late in the evening.

That rascal Jesse roused himself from his spot alongside her old slat-bottomed porch rocker and followed her as she headed toward the barn, her arms full of neatly folded sheets and an extra pillow.

"Dumb dog," she said to him, nice as pie even though she didn't feel it. "Trying to ruin my sunflowers. Seems like after all I've done for you, you could show respect for the things I love. How am I ever going to get flowers started around the house? What am I going to do with you, Jesse James?"

Jesse, outlaw that he was, wagged his tail enthusiastically and lifted his leg on the truck tire.

Bethany, thoroughly put out, kept walking. "Like I said, Jesse, you're a dumb dog. But maybe not so dumb. You've got Frisco on your side at least." When he saw that Bethany was going nowhere more interesting than the barn, Jesse wandered away toward the bunkhouse, which was so decrepit and rundown that it wasn't in use anymore.

The barn was big and more ramshackle than Bethany would have liked, but repairing either it or the bunkhouse was out of the question as long as she continued to have serious cash flow problems. Still, the barn was comforting in its familiarity. As she wrinkled her nose against the dust motes swimming in the last rays of the dying sun, Colt's horse stuck his head over the door to his stall and pricked his ears. He was a beautiful black quarter horse, sleek and well-kept.

Her own horse, Dancer, nickered and blew in recognition at the sight of her, but her arms were full and Bethany couldn't get to the carrot she'd stashed in her back pocket. "I'll be back soon," she promised. Dancer snorted and bumped her nose against the gate to her stall.

All was quiet overhead in Colt's apartment. Her footsteps echoed hollowly on the wooden steps as she made her way upstairs. The door hung wide-open, which didn't surprise her much. Anybody would want to get a cross-draft going in such airless quarters.

"Colt?" she called.

No answer. Inside the tiny room, an oscillating fan positioned on a table blew air across the top of a chipped enamel pan heaped with ice cubes. A primitive air conditioner? It made sense, but not when Colt wasn't there. And where'd he get that much ice? The apartment refrigerator was the small square kind college kids used in their dorms, and it made minuscule ice cubes.

She stepped into the room, thinking to leave the sheets on the bed. But before she could set them down, she saw a photograph resting on the mattress. It was tattered around the edges, as if someone had repeatedly taken it out of a wallet for a closer look.

The picture was one of those glamour photos. It was of a young woman with dark hair teased into what Bethany thought of as Mall Bangs and deep soulful eyes made comical by too much eye makeup. Despite the hair, eyes and the studded leather jacket with the collar turned up, there was something arresting about the girl's expression. She looked as if under all that bravado she was hiding an underlying sorrow. Then again, it might be the photographer's lighting. Whatever it was, she was very pretty.

Bethany was so absorbed in the photograph that she didn't hear Colt until he entered the room. She wheeled around, startled. And then she saw him.

Her new ranch hand was buck naked and dripping from the shower. His hair was slicked back, darker wet than it was dry, and the water had curled the hair on his chest into tight little burrs. He looked as startled as she felt—thank goodness, certain strategic body parts were modestly hidden by the towel he held in front of him.

She dropped the sheets. Also the pillow. She was totally unprepared for the wave of lust and helplessness that washed over her at the sight of him. Colt McClure was magnificently built, from the solid muscles of his arms and chest to the hard rippling ridges of his abdomen. And below that—she looked away, refusing to speculate on what was behind the towel.

Their gazes caught and held. Bethany could not pull her eyes away. Colt, completely unabashed, merely quirked his eyebrows and said, "Hand me the jeans on that hook behind the door, would you?"

The spell broken, Bethany groped behind her, felt cloth and yanked blue denim. She tossed the jeans to him and bent over to gather up the sheets. When she straightened, he'd wrapped the towel around his waist.

"I—um—well, I brought the sheets," she said, swallowing hard.

Colt cleared his throat. "I think you better excuse me for a few seconds," he said, and he disappeared into the bathroom.

She wanted to run, but that would betray her embarrassment. She told herself that the thing to do was act as if nothing unusual had happened. This was a ranch. She was accustomed to stallions mounting mares, to bulls servicing cows, to misguided but amorous female dogs seeking out Jesse James.

But she wasn't used to naked men.

When Colt emerged from the bathroom, she was nonchalantly shaking dust off the previously clean sheets and pillow.

"These got a little messed up," she said, wondering

if her cheeks were flushed. They certainly felt that way, and the air blowing across the ice cubes in the pan didn't help much.

Colt wore only jeans, and his hair was still wet. It was wavy, something she hadn't noticed when it was dry.

He reached for the sheet she was folding, and the fragrance of fabric softener and dried lavender wafted up from the soft percale. The scent brought back memories so sweet that they pierced her to the heart and left her aching inside. Justin had always liked the way she folded dried lavender sprigs from her little garden into the sheets, and they had spent many, many nights making love on those sheets in their double bed beneath the eaves of the bedroom they'd shared in the ranch house, the same room where his father had been born.

She surrendered the sheet. "I'd better be going," she said as she watched Colt's big hands smooth wrinkles out of the fabric. Thankfully she heard footsteps on the stairs and backed toward the door. She knew it wasn't Frisco because the tread was too even to fit his unsteady gait, and for a moment, Bethany thought it might be Dita. But it was only Eddie, toting a bucketful of ice cubes.

"Mom sent these," he said, holding out the bucket.

Colt grinned at him, man-to-man friendly. "Much obliged, Eddie. Set the bucket by the table."

"Anytime you want ice or company, Mom says hang your red bandanna out the window." Eddie brushed fine pale hair out of his eyes and turned to Bethany. "Hi, Bethany. Dancer wants a carrot and I don't have one."

Bethany was flooded with relief. Eddie had provided a rescue of sorts. She pulled the carrot out of her back pocket. "You're in luck," she said, dangling it in front of him.

Eddie grabbed at it, eyes asparkle. "Can I give it to her?" He was like a child, all enthusiasm. It was one of the things Bethany loved about him.

"Of course you can."

She turned to say goodbye to Colt, but he had scooped the photograph up from the bed and was sliding it into his wallet. He looked preoccupied, thoughtful.

Bethany didn't speak after all, just high-footed it out of there. Colt called out a goodbye, but not until she and Eddie were most of the way down the stairs.

AFTER THEY'D FED DANCER half of the carrot and given the other half to Colt's horse as a kind of welcoming present, Eddie started back toward the Neilsons' and Bethany headed for the stand of tall cottonwoods beside the creek. There she sank down on the mossy bench Justin had built for her during her first year at the Banner-B.

Sometimes she'd had to get away from the heat and dust and cattle and the rowdy hands they'd employed in those days, and this was where she'd sought refuge. Here, where the Little Moony Creek meandered slowly around slippery boulders and purled over shiny rocks; here where she could pull off her boots, spraddle her legs in unladylike fashion and dabble bare feet in the cool, refreshing water. In the spring, cottony seeds drifted down from the trees and caught in her hair, and in the summer, shiny triangular leaves cast welcome shadows across her upturned face. At night, myriad stars peeped through the lattice of foliage above, and now they were winking at her against the backdrop of a velvety blue sky. Winking seductively, it seemed to her tonight.

"Well, now what?" she said out loud. Frisco would have called it dingbat behavior, but sometimes Bethany talked to Justin in this special place. It kept her from getting too broody, too introspective. And it was a way to think over the pros and cons of a thing, like the time early on when she'd gotten it into her head to sell the ranch to Mott. She'd been disabused of that notion when Mott came to call and suggested that *he* could warm her on cold nights, which was when she had worked herself into such a hot temper that she'd thrown him out.

She was much too young for all the responsibility the inheritance of this ranch had placed on her, and she was the first one to admit it, though she excelled at putting up a brave front. After Justin died, she hadn't thought she could go on without him. She'd had to grow tough and hard in order to cope. Sometimes she got tired of being tough and hard, she longed to be soft and sweet the way she used to be. That sweetness was what Justin had loved about her, and she wondered if he'd still love her now that she was a different person. But then, love didn't die, Justin had always said. He had been positive of that, and because Bethany was the one he'd loved, she'd been sure of it, too. That undying love was why she liked to think that maybe Justin heard her out when she had a problem.

The problem was Colt McClure. Maybe she should have known better than to resort to the mail-order method of hiring, but what was she to do? Mott Findley was telling everyone that she couldn't pay her bills. No hand worth his salt dared to take the chance of not being paid for services rendered at the Banner-B when there was plenty of work available on nearby ranches. It further complicated matters that she was a woman and Frisco was a grouch.

Whatever, she'd be better off not thinking about it, not talking out loud when no one else was present, and not allowing herself to be fascinated by Colt McClure. She'd be better off watching TV, which functioned as her mind-numbing drug of choice on nights when the stars seemed too near and her body seemed too deprived. This was definitely one of those nights.

Steady, said the voice in her head that she sometimes heard when she sat here. *Steady.*

That was all it said. She didn't know for sure if the voice came from Justin or not. Maybe it was merely her own thoughts rattling around inside her brain. Whatever it was, it gave her heart. It gave her the will to go on.

After a while she stood and followed the path along the creek until it bisected the driveway about a half mile from the house. She was walking along, hands in pockets, mulling, when she saw a small car cut out of the driveway onto the blacktop highway. They'd had a visitor, then. She didn't recognize the car at first, but as she watched it she thought it resembled the light-colored sedan that she'd seen moseying past when she was talking to Colt that afternoon out in the far pasture.

The car's presence made the pit of her stomach feel hollow, which was ridiculous. It was just a car, perhaps someone visiting the Neilsons or lost on this remote stretch of highway after taking a wrong turn from town. She squared her shoulders and ignored the feeling that something was wrong.

Chances were that the car was driven by one of Mott's minions, who might be checking out anything from the new hand to the line of fence posts going up along her property line. Well, let Mott look. She wasn't ready to declare bankruptcy yet. Or to sell. He and his vultures would have a long wait.

She strode forward, head down, preoccupied with calculations. She'd ship cattle to the feed lots later in the month, and she'd be able to pay her bill at Kraegel's after they were sold at auction. Fred Kraegel had thrown in an extra bag of feed today, she thought because he liked her and wanted her to succeed. Or maybe he just didn't like Mott, which was not all that unusual in these parts.

She'd left the house before dark, so the porch light wasn't on. When she started up the porch steps, lost in her musings, she almost tripped over the wicker basket.

Bethany's first thought was that Dita had left her laundry on the front porch, which was a natural assumption because Bethany and the Neilsons shared one washer and dryer located in the utility room off the kitchen. But the kitchen was in the back of the house and had its own porch, so it was highly unlikely that Dita had left her basket in the front of the house.

And then she heard the whimper. Something inside the basket moved.

To her utter amazement, a small pink fist flailed the air. The whimper swelled to a cry, and when Bethany bent over to look, she saw a tiny baby wrapped in a print blanket. No, it must be a doll. It couldn't be a baby. People didn't really leave babies on peoples' doorsteps. Certainly they didn't leave them on *her* doorstep.

But it wasn't a doll. It moved. It was crying, its face screwed up and its legs kicking emphatically under the blanket. Bethany dissolved into total bewilderment, half thinking this must be some trick of Mott Findley's, yet knowing in her heart that it couldn't be.

Jesse, who among his many failings never bothered to bark at strangers, loped over from the barn, tail wagging, tongue lolling, and looking doggily curious. And, ominously, much too happy.

Before the dog could proceed with his self-appointed mission to water the world, Bethany yanked the basket out of harm's way. She nudged the front door open with the toe of her boot and carried the baby inside, letting the door slam in the perplexed Jesse's face.

"Mercy me, what on earth!" she said to the baby, which only wailed more loudly.

Bethany pushed aside a stack of catalogs to set the basket on the narrow hall table and unpinned an envelope from the baby's blanket. The outside of the envelope was blank, so she opened it and unfolded the note inside.

COLT, it said in printed block letters. PLEASE TAKE CARE OF ALYSSA FOR ME. I'LL BE BACK WHEN I GET SOME MONEY. I LOVE YOU,

MARCY

Chapter Three

"Well, I'll be," said Frisco.

"Is the baby going to live with us?" Eddie asked. "Like a sister?"

"I don't know, son," Dita said as she slid an arm around his shoulders. Though she was a native of Mexico, her voice bore little trace of an accent; she'd lived in the States for more than twenty years.

"Colt?" Bethany stood with her arms folded across her chest, reminding herself to be tough. As soon as she'd realized that this baby wasn't about to be leaving the premises right away, she had summoned Frisco and Dita and Eddie with a quick phone call. Eddie, goggle-eyed, had hurried to get Colt, who ran all the way from the barn. Now the five of them hovered over the wicker basket, and the baby was cooing and laughing up at them, putting on a show.

"I—well, I sure didn't expect this," Colt said. His voice rumbled deep in his throat, prickly as a cocklebur.

"The note was addressed to you." In Bethany's mind, Colt had some explaining to do.

Colt frowned at the bit of paper, then folded it and stuffed it down into his jeans pocket. He wore only jeans, a T-shirt, and boots, and the T-shirt was wrinkled as if he'd just pulled it out of his bedroll. "I don't know what to say," he admitted.

"It's a very nice baby," Eddie said.

"Yes, it is. But it's not our baby," Bethany replied firmly, her irritation building.

Colt cleared his throat and looked from one of them to the other, his gaze stopping when it reached Bethany. The pause lengthened, stretched, hung there. "I know whose baby it is," he said finally.

"Would you mind telling *us?*" Frisco growled.

Colt seemed to stew over this before shaking his head. "I can't," he said.

"What do you mean, you can't?" Bethany asked, sharp as all get-out. She recalled the well-worn photo on Colt's bed and figured that the girl in the picture was Marcy.

"I just can't say right now, ma'am. Mrs. Burke." Colt had the good grace to look embarrassed, but he met her gaze squarely.

"Call me Bethany," she said.

"Bethany," Colt repeated. He drew a deep breath. "I'm afraid I'll have to ask your patience. And your understandin'. I'll look after the baby." He looked away for a moment as if considering. "The baby can stay in my apartment for tonight," he added.

"There's barely room in your apartment for one, much less a baby, and there's no air," Dita said. She tended to have a blunt manner, which people sometimes misunderstood.

"She could stay with us," Eddie suggested, looking hopeful.

"Absolutely not," Frisco huffed. "We ain't set up for a baby."

At that the baby puckered up her face and began to wail.

Frisco pounced on this development. "You see? Babies cry, and they make messes. Babies are a lot of work. We can't have the baby at our house, and that's that." He stumped over to the door and stood looking out toward the barn.

The baby's squalling roused a maternal instinct in Bethany. She found herself absolutely incapable of listening to the baby's screams. Before she'd even thought about it, she had slid her hands beneath the tiny body and lifted Alyssa out of the basket. She halfway expected the child to fill her arms like a minisack of feed grain, but she wasn't at all like that. Alyssa had less heft to her, and bones. Not only that, but the baby stiffened every time she screamed, clutching her little fingers into wildly brandishing fists and contorting her face into a tight red knot of anger. Instinctively and with only a slight hesitation at first, Bethany rocked the baby back and forth.

"Shh," she crooned softly. "It's all right. We won't hurt you." Her motherly instinct, or whatever it was, billowed full-blown. It took only a moment to decide what she had to do. She looked around at the others and spoke over the baby's cries. "Alyssa can stay with me tonight. In the extra bedroom."

"Great," said Frisco. "Peachy. I'm going home to watch TV. Too much noise around here." He slammed outside and down the stairs.

The noise of the door's banging distracted Alyssa so that she suddenly stopped screaming. Dita touched the baby's cheek. "So soft," she said. "So sweet. Look, Eddie, at her little fingers. Have you ever seen anything so perfect?"

"Never," Eddie breathed in awe.

"Dita, how old do you think she is?"

"A month or two, I'd guess."

Colt rummaged under the blankets in the basket. "There's canned formula and a bottle here," he said, setting them on the table. "And enough disposable diapers until I can get more. And a pacifier."

"Eddie and I can bring the old family cradle over," Dita said. "It's stored in the attic. Oh, and you'll want cornstarch. I have that, too."

"Cornstarch?" Bethany said blankly.

"It prevents diaper rash," Dita told her.

"Goodness gracious," she said, embarrassed. "I guess I don't know much about babies."

"No reason you should," Dita said. She chuckled and patted Bethany on the shoulder. "I'll dig out that cradle right now," she said, and then she and Eddie left, Eddie chattering excitedly all the way out the door.

When it was quiet, Bethany stopped rocking the baby, who in turn regarded her solemnly. The baby's hair looked like downy dark chick fluff, and her breath smelled milky. Bethany thought about how it might have been to hold her own baby like this, to have someone to care about more than anything in the world. More than the ranch, even.

"All this time I've been learning how to run the Banner-B while other women my age are having children," she said, half to herself.

"Sounds like that bothers you."

Colt's words startled her. She had momentarily forgotten that he was there.

"My husband and I always wanted kids," she said. The baby was staring intently up at her, searching her face for—what? Its mother? What kind of mother would leave a baby on someone's doorstep?

Bethany found herself growing angry on the baby's behalf. A baby deserved parents who cared enough about it to keep it safe. A baby deserved better than being dropped on someone's doorstep, prey to anything that came along, like abusive kids or coyotes or—well, peeing dogs.

"Here, why don't you let me take her," Colt said. Wordlessly she let him lift the baby from her arms. Although his hands were big and rough, he was surprisingly gentle. Bethany thought, *maybe Colt McClure has the same feeling for babies that he has for horses.*

For some reason, this was a disturbing thought. Or was it the way Colt's hands adjusted the baby's blanket, or maybe the unaccustomed softness of expression that flickered brief as heat lightning across his rough-hewn face? Or the way he offered the pacifier and his look of relief when the baby accepted it?

Maybe none of this was so surprising. The baby was his. *Had* to be. Why else would this Marcy, whoever she was, be leaving a baby here?

Her anger burgeoned to include Colt. And yet there wasn't much she could do if he'd earlier abandoned this Marcy and their baby to come to the Banner-B. It wasn't her fault. She reminded herself that Colt was the one who'd advertised for work. She'd only answered the ad. It wasn't as if she was the one responsible for his irresponsibility.

She thought if she didn't get away from him she might say something she'd regret. "The baby's probably hungry. I'll go pour this formula into the bottle," she said through clenched teeth. She pivoted abruptly to go into the kitchen, the air in her wake sending a picture of Justin clattering to the floor. Quickly she bent and picked it up, carefully examining the frame to see if it was broken. The picture had been taken during the first year of their marriage, and Justin was smiling into the camera lens. Smiling at *her*. Bethany had taken the picture.

She carefully returned the picture to its hallowed place on the hall table. "Your husband?" Colt said.

"Yes." She didn't want to talk about Justin with this man, but when she went into the kitchen, Colt followed.

"I reckon it's none of my business, but how long have you been a widow?" he asked in a conversational tone.

"You're right. It's not your business." *Any more than it's my business how a baby came to be left on my doorstep for you. Or who Marcy is,* she almost added.

"Sorry," Colt said.

Suddenly it seemed important to her to let this drifter, this man who'd abandoned his own child, know exactly what responsibility was. "Justin died five years ago after a tractor accident, and I've been running the ranch ever since."

"That's no easy job."

"Right," she snapped. "The most important things in life aren't." She could have told him plenty about how hard it was, how she'd had to learn computer management programs and read up on cattle breeding and deal with creditors and, of course, fend off Mott—but she wouldn't.

If he felt the sting of her words, Colt gave no sign. He didn't reply, but sat down on a kitchen chair and hoisted Alyssa so that her face rested against his shoulder. The baby was alert, sucking vigorously on the pacifier. Colt looked pensive for a moment and drew a deep breath before he spoke.

"I want you to know that I'll do my best to find Alyssa's mother, and as soon as possible."

"And if she can't take the baby back?"

"I don't rightly know whether she can or not."

"There's always foster care," Bethany said.

"No!" Colt said forcefully.

Bethany hadn't expected her casual and matter-of-fact suggestion to provoke such an outburst. She swiveled and looked at Colt in ill-concealed surprise. His expression had gone all dark and forbidding.

"Never. No matter what. I'd leave and take her with me before I'd let her go to a foster home," Colt said fiercely. His arms tightened protectively around the baby.

Bethany hid her dismay. He could have talked from hell to breakfast and not said that part about leaving when the last thing she needed was to lose a ranch hand.

It took a moment for her to recover. "All right, then. We'll manage for now," she replied in a level tone, not wanting him to know he'd rattled her. She ran hot water into a pan and set the bottle in it to warm.

When she heard Dita and Eddie outside, she opened the back door and they came in. They presented the cradle for inspection by depositing it in the middle of the kitchen floor and setting it to rocking. "It's a family heirloom Frisco and I brought from Mexico," Dita said. She grinned at Bethany. "Frisco's not half as hardhearted as he seems, you know. He already had the cradle out and was cleaning it when Eddie and I walked in the house."

"I'll take it upstairs," said Eddie. He was strong and proud of it.

"Put the cradle in the blue bedroom, Eddie," Bethany told him.

"Blue bedroom. Okay." He lifted the cradle and departed.

"Here's the cornstarch," Dita said as she set the small yellow box on the kitchen table. "Anything else you need?"

"No, Dita, I think we're all set."

They heard Eddie clattering down the stairs. "I put the cradle by the window," he said.

"Thanks, Eddie," Bethany told him.

"Well, Bethany, I'll see you in the morning. Eddie, let's go. Your dad's about to pop a movie into the VCR." Dita kissed Bethany briefly on the cheek and left, Eddie following close behind.

When they had gone, Bethany turned her attention back to Colt. Cowboy and baby made an incongruous sight; Colt was concentrating on his task, his brow furrowed slightly, and Alyssa slurped hungrily at the bottle, her tiny fists curved like pink seashells against Colt's broad chest.

Bethany thought how pretty the baby was, and how helpless. And she still couldn't understand how anyone could have left such a beautiful child on a strange doorstep. Or how the father of such a lovely child could leave her behind somewhere to take a job on a ranch like this one.

"She's stopped drinking," Colt announced, interrupting Bethany's thoughts.

"I think that means she's had enough."

He looked up at Bethany, his eyes troubled. "I won't let the baby be a problem. I'll look after her tonight. She'll have to be fed and diapered, and I can get up with her and do it. You need your sleep."

He was right about that, because suddenly she felt very tired indeed. It had been a long day. Her bruised shoulder ached. But he had worked hard, too.

She must have looked hesitant because he said, "I mean it. I'll be the one to get up with Alyssa."

Reluctantly she decided that it was only fitting for Colt to do the honors. Plus, she didn't want to get overly attached to the baby. She was already feeling little tugs of her heartstrings over the way Alyssa looked and felt and smelled.

"Bethany?"

At least he hadn't called her ma'am again. Colt was looking at her inquiringly, and she knew he wanted her to show him where the baby would sleep. And where he would sleep, too, in order to be near. Well, she had wanted him to accept responsibility, and now he was doing it. Still, she hardly knew him. Did she really want him in her house all night long?

Bethany had sensed something dangerous about Colt McClure from the beginning, and certainly something about him didn't quite add up. She was well aware that this man could have found work on any of a couple dozen ranches, and she didn't know why he had chosen to work for her. And, adding even more uncertainty, she knew Frisco didn't like him.

He waited for her answer, and she detected a challenge in him—or maybe it was a dare. It was almost as if he knew what she was thinking. His eyes filled with concern as he looked from the baby to her and back to the baby again. No—what she saw in Colt McClure was more than mere concern. It was that hunger again, that longing that she had interpreted as insolence when he rode up to the house yesterday.

She briefly considered sending Colt and the baby

back to the barn, but she thought again how bare Colt's rooms were, and how stifling hot. The smells of the animals in the barn below penetrated the thin boards of the apartment's floor.

Now, as he stood before her holding the baby in his arms, he didn't seem at all threatening, only worried. She reminded herself that she was doing this for the baby's sake. The kid already had a couple of strikes against her, and Bethany didn't want to make things even worse. Being responsible, she told herself, meant doing things you didn't want to do sometimes. That was what finally made up her mind.

"Okay, come with me," she said into the loaded silence. She heard Colt let out his breath as if in relief. It surprised her, that release of tension, but then he'd been full of surprises ever since he appeared, galloping his horse up the driveway.

She led Colt, who was still carrying the baby, through the quiet and dark house, into the hall with its picture of Justin staring at her reproachfully from its embossed silver frame, past the seldom-used living room full of well-worn but cherished furniture, up the stairs and past the door of her own bedroom.

Across the hall from hers, the guest room was occupied by a four-poster double bed, which was covered with the quilt that had been given to Justin's mother by her best friend on her wedding day. An antique washstand held a matching china pitcher and wash basin, and rag rugs hooked by Justin's grandmother adorned the hardwood floor.

Bethany turned on the small candlestick lamp on the bow-front dresser. It bathed the room in dim golden light. "Here's where you both can stay. The bathroom's near and you'll be comfortable enough. In fact, you can put Alyssa in the cradle now. Wait—we'd better check to see if her diaper is wet. I'll get a towel."

Bethany hurried into the bathroom next door. When she returned with the towel and spread it over the quilt, Colt laid the baby on the bed, opened the blanket and felt the diaper.

"Soaked," he said. "Looks like I'd better be fixin' to change her."

"Do you know how?"

"I've never changed a diaper before," he conceded. "Have you?"

"No, never. It can't be too hard," she said. Reluctantly, because she didn't want to have anything more to do with this situation than absolutely necessary, she picked up one of the clean disposables and unfolded it. Colt had already removed Alyssa's wet diaper.

"Hand it over."

She gave him the diaper and Colt slid it under Alyssa's plump bottom. He fumbled with the adhesive tabs. "Wastebasket?" he said.

Bethany nudged it closer to him with her foot. "Here."

Colt tossed the pull-off strips into the basket and tentatively sprinkled on a smattering of cornstarch. Alyssa bicycled energetically, her plump little legs pumping the air. Colt's enormous hands fit the fresh diaper around her hips, and even though he stuck it together lopsided, Alyssa didn't seem to mind. If she hadn't been so tired and so angry with Colt, Bethany would have smiled at the sight of the big rawboned ranch hand turned nanny.

Those same hands lifted Alyssa tenderly, readjusted the sacque she wore, and laid her carefully in the cradle. For a moment the baby stared curiously up at them, two large strangers looming over her with concern. Then she uttered a soft little sigh, and slowly her eyelids became heavier and heavier until they closed.

"You can sleep on the bed," she said to Colt. She leaned over him and pulled the quilt down to expose the clean sheets underneath.

He stopped her with a hand on her arm. His touch was so unexpected that a warm tremor swept through her, and she stepped away from him as far as the narrow space between bed and wall would allow. "I'll do that. You've done enough. Thanks, Bethany. Thanks for not flyin' all to pieces over this."

His appreciation sounded heartfelt, and she was bewildered at the confusion she felt. She was still angry with him, but she was beginning to respect the way he was rising to the challenge of this baby.

In that moment it struck her that he was standing so near and the setting was so intimate she could have reached over, twined her fingers together behind his neck and pulled his head down to hers. And kissed him.

Heavens! She would *never*.

"Good night," she said, pushing past him so that her thigh brushed his, so close that she could smell the clean male scent of him, so close that the hollows under his cheekbones lost their shadow. All grace had left her, had drained clean away, and she felt awkward and ungainly. She stumbled over the toe of his boot, and his arm whipped out to steady her.

"You all right?" he asked.

"I'm okay. I'll see you in the morning." She made herself walk past the cradle and out the door.

In her own room, she closed the door with a firm click and locked it for the first time ever. Then she leaned against it, wearily circling a hand under the damp collar of her shirt and thinking that Texas summers had surely grown hotter than they used to be. After a minute or so, she removed her clothes and pulled on a nightgown, any gown, from her dresser drawer. The gown smelled of old cherry wood and fabric softener and, faintly, of lavender. Its soft familiarity soothed her.

She lay awake for a long time that night, listening to cicadas chirring in the shrubbery and to Jesse James yodeling at the moon. She never heard the baby cry, not even once. But she did hear Colt's footsteps pacing back and forth, back and forth on the creaky oak floor. If he slept at all, she couldn't tell it, and she didn't fall asleep herself until past midnight.

MORNING. PALE LIGHT. A baby fussing. The scent of coffee.

Colt struggled out of a deep sleep. For a moment he was confused. Where was he?

Then he remembered. Marcy's baby was waking up. He'd fed her and diapered her during the night, and now she was probably hungry again.

He forced himself to slide out from beneath the smooth sheets, marveling at the fact that he no longer slept in a prison bunk. As he pulled on his jeans and shirt, he thought that never again would he take a real bed with a comfortable mattress for granted.

He bent over the cradle. Alyssa was squirming, screwing her face into an expression that he'd learned meant she was about to let loose with big-time bawling. He poked around under the blanket and found the pacifier.

"Here's your stopper," he said. Alyssa opened her mouth and accepted it, her eyes wide as she took in the looks of him.

"I know I'm not much to look at with this scar and

all," he whispered as he gathered her up from the cradle, a family heirloom carved with initials and angels and roses. Eddie had probably slept in this cradle, and maybe Frisco, too. Colt smiled to think of the crusty Banner-B foreman as a baby.

He changed Alyssa's diaper, getting the hang of it now. It wasn't an unpleasant job, exactly. Cleaning up after horses was much worse, though he'd heard tell of horses that wore diapers, carriage horses in touristy towns, and he thought it was a travesty. Babies, now, that was a different thing altogether. Trouble is, the person who should be dealing with this baby's diapers was Marcy.

"Well now, I *am* goin' to find your mommy," he told the baby. "Goin' to bring her back."

Not that it was so hard to understand the desperation that had brought Marcy to the point where she'd left her baby with him, but he couldn't imagine what she'd thought he would do with a baby. Just out of prison, trying to make a life for himself—well, he could think of better things than dealing with somebody else's problems. But then he'd always been a sucker for Marcy no matter how sorely she tried his patience, mostly because he knew how unhappy she was. Poor kid, she'd never had a chance with Ryzinski for a father.

"We'd better get you something to eat," he said to the baby. He lifted her in his arms and studied her features for a moment. She had Marcy's dark hair and eyes, and the set of her chin was pure Marcy.

A voice materialized outside the door. "Colt?"

Colt caught a glimpse of himself as he passed the mirror over the dresser. He looked rumpled and unshaven with one lock of hair falling over his forehead and his eyes rimmed by dark circles. He'd hardly slept at all.

He swung the door open with his free hand. Bethany stood there smelling of soap and shampoo, and he felt a little current of pleasure quiver through him just to see her. She'd showered and washed her hair, he could tell from the fresh clean scent of her. And she was wearing a T-shirt today. It was big, though, and left plenty to the imagination. He had no trouble imagining, none at all.

"How is the baby? I didn't hear her cry during the night."

"I didn't let her cry. Didn't want her to wake you." He'd jumped up out of that comfortable bed at the slightest whimper from the cradle, and he'd rocked and fed and changed diapers like he knew what he was about.

Bethany sallied forth into the room. There was a sashay to her walk, but he'd bet she was completely unaware of it. "I'll fill her bottle with more formula." She looked at the baby, and the focus of her eyes softened. "Here," she said, "let me take her." She held out her arms and he sort of dumped Alyssa into them. He was wary of touching Bethany's breasts by mistake. Wary and aware. Today she wore a bra, but instead of enhancing her figure, to his way of thinking it minimized it. Maybe that was what she wanted.

As Alyssa began to whimper, Bethany hesitated, then, as if she couldn't help herself, dropped a kiss on the fuzzy little head. "Hush," she said, a gentle command. The baby hushed.

"You can wash up in the bathroom if you like," she said. "Meet me in the kitchen afterward." It was as if she hardly saw him. She only had eyes for the baby.

Which was a good thing. At least she hadn't demanded that he leave. In fact, she'd looked right put out last night when he'd said that bit about not letting the baby be sent to a foster home. Well, he'd meant it.

Colt went into the bathroom. It was all white tile and white fixtures with a fluffy blue rug on the floor. It was clean, real clean. To him, it seemed the ultimate in comfort and convenience. He would have liked to take a shower from a spigot with a decent flow of water, but Bethany hadn't said anything about that so he didn't. He did open the corroding mirrored door of the medicine cabinet, hoping to find a razor. There wasn't one, only a bottle of aspirin and one of mouthwash. He gargled with the mouthwash and studied his face in the mirror. No wonder Bethany wasn't more friendly.

Well, hell, why would she be? He'd arrived unannounced, taken up residence, and saddled them with a baby, all in a short period of time. Boy, would he give Marcy a real talking-to when he finally caught up with her.

And how would he do that? He had no idea. The last time she'd visited Colt in jail, Marcy had informed him that she had a boyfriend, and she'd made it clear that she'd moved in with the guy because there was nowhere else to go. The man had probably walked out on her, left her pregnant and she couldn't support the kid. End of story. Beginning of a major problem—for Colt, anyway.

He'd have to find Marcy. And he would, as soon as possible.

When he walked in the kitchen, Bethany was sitting in a rocking chair that hadn't been there before. She had the baby spread out on her lap and was crooning to her, punctuating each word with a gentle pat-a-cake of the baby's tiny feet. Alyssa seemed to like it, gazing at Bethany in rapt attention.

"You're safe with us, Alyssa, safe with us. Yes, you are, you are," Bethany said. She glanced up at the sound of Colt's footsteps and suddenly became all business.

"Give me her bottle, will you, Colt? And help yourself to the coffee." She gathered the baby in her arms, the game, whatever it was, over.

Colt handed Bethany the warm bottle, which she tested on the inside of her arm before sliding the nipple into Alyssa's eager mouth. The baby began to suck and commenced looking blissful, making little dovelike noises deep in her throat.

Colt circled around and poured himself a big mug of coffee. Then he leaned against the counter and said, "I know it's a burden on everyone, havin' a baby here. This morning I thought I'd make a few phone calls, see if I can find out where her mother is."

"Good. I'm supposed to work cattle with Dita today, and you can pick up digging postholes whenever you're through making calls. But—" her face fell in dismay "—someone has to watch the baby. We can't leave her alone here."

He raked a hand through his hair. There were so many things to think about when a baby was involved. "She can stay with me while I'm on the phone," he said. "Isn't there someone around here who can babysit?"

Bethany shook her head, and despite everything else that he was thinking about this morning, he couldn't help reflecting that she was one beautiful woman. She was talking, and he made himself concentrate on her answer to his question.

"We'll have to manage ourselves, I'm afraid. The closest people are Milt and Betty Harbison, who live on the next ranch. They're elderly and don't get around too well, and I can't imagine that they could look after a baby." Colt got the idea that Bethany Burke prided herself on her self-reliance and wouldn't ask for help with much of anything.

That decided him. "How about if I make a quick trip into town? I'll get more diapers and more formula. While I'm there I'll ask around, see if there's anyone who could help out."

Bethany tossed off a resigned look that seemed to say, *Well, okay, if that's what you want to do.* "Fix yourself some breakfast first. There's eggs and bacon, and I've set the skillet out. Bread's in the freezer, make yourself some toast. After you eat, you can use the pickup and take Alyssa with you. I don't think you'll find a baby-sitter easily, unless you make it worthwhile money-wise."

"I'll pay whatever I have to." This delivered with grim determination.

Another look, highly skeptical. "I expect you remember that I won't be handing you your first paycheck for another two weeks," she reminded him.

"That's okay. I have money."

He didn't think she believed him, but it was true. His life savings were parked in interest-bearing accounts here and there. Before he went to prison, he'd been planning to start a business.

Colt swigged the last of his coffee. One thing you had to say about Bethany—she made a great brew, plenty of muscle in it. "You want to go ahead?" he asked. "Get started with those cattle before the heat settles in?"

"I'd better. Dita's probably ready to ride out."

She stood up, setting the chair to rocking, and handed Alyssa over. "She's a beautiful baby," Bethany said, measuring each word. In that accusatory moment, as their eyes caught and held above the baby's head, Colt was reminded that Bethany believed Alyssa to be his child.

Of course she would. Why else would someone leave a baby with a man? Mothers of infants didn't just go around dropping them off with members of the opposite sex without good reason. Usually the mothers were peeved that the fathers had run off. Colt knew well and good that many parents were derelict in their duty, but he wasn't one of them. Even thinking about such parents made him feel sick to his stomach, because he'd been a victim of a father like that and it had messed up his life. If he were ever lucky enough to have children of his own, he would be the best father in the world.

"Bethany," he began, suddenly desperate that she know he wasn't that kind of guy.

She treated him to a go-eat-roadkill look punctuated by a negligible toss of the head. In her stance, in the straightness of her back and the glint of her eyes, she exhibited all the steeliness and resolve that made her capable of running this ranch under less than favorable circumstances.

"No need to edify me, Colt, because I don't want to hear about it. Just do what you have to do, and I won't ask questions."

In that moment, Colt longed for nothing more than for Bethany to ask questions and him to answer them, but if he were honest, she'd find out exactly where he'd spent the past three years and why. A certain knowledge hit him hard in the gut: A woman alone with only a lame one-eyed foreman, another woman and a special-needs kid to protect her might fire him on the spot if she knew about his past. *Should* fire him on the spot. He'd killed a man, after all.

It wasn't easy to live with despair, and Colt had lived with it far too long. He'd only recently fought his way out, accepting his new chance at life, knowing that things were going to get better from here on out.

Now he felt despair settling back in, reaming him out, tamping him down. He couldn't allow it to get him around the throat again. But he could feel it jeering at him, no doubt about it.

And so he said nothing. Instead he merely stared down at Marcy's baby and regretted, not for the first time, that he'd ever met that SOB Ryzinski.

Chapter Four

The sky was blue, the grass was green, and there was a clean, gentle breeze blowing over the prairie, but Bethany found that all she could think about was getting back to the home place.

"Looks to me like you've got too much on your mind," Dita said pointedly after Bethany failed to close a gate securely behind them as they worked the cattle. Because of her carelessness, two steers escaped, and they'd had to leave the others to graze as they rounded up the miscreants. Bethany didn't blame Dita for being annoyed with her. They'd always worked well together as a team, and today Bethany didn't have to be told that she wasn't pulling her weight.

Dita was a big woman, stocky and solid, and she rarely chastised, but now she swiveled in her saddle and skewered Bethany with a hard look. Bethany uncorked her water bottle and let a cool slide of water ease her dry throat. "I keep thinking about that baby," she said. She recorked the bottle and put it away.

"You let that Colt McClure do the worrying," Dita advised as she nudged her heels into the sides of her mount, Frypan, and set out toward the Blue Pasture, so called because a fringe of Texas bluebonnets bloomed all along the fence in season. Bethany followed along slowly, letting Dancer pick her way surely through the dusty grass. She distracted herself by studying the sky. If they didn't get rain soon, the cattle would suffer, and there wasn't a cloud in sight. Or in recent memory, come to think of it.

She caught up with Dita at the edge of the creek. The horses drank, their tails lazily switching away flies.

Leather creaked as Bethany shifted in her saddle. "It's his baby. Don't you think so?" She wasn't making idle conversation; she was hoping to verify her own thoughts on the matter.

"I can't say whose baby it is." Dita slid her a sideways glance. "Does it matter?"

Dancer stopped drinking, and Bethany reined in her mount. Dancer tossed her head impatiently, and Bethany patted her absently on the neck. "Of course it matters," she said. "His character is in question."

Dita scoffed at this. "A month ago you said you were so desperate for a ranch hand that you'd hire anything that could rope and ride. What does character have to do with it?"

Bethany shrugged and let Dancer choose her own path through the tall grass at the edge of the creek. "If I'm letting a guy stay overnight in my house, I want to know that he's not a murderer."

"Did he give you any trouble?" Dita asked sharply.

Bethany thought about the way she'd reacted when Colt's arm had steadied her last night in the moments before she'd gone to her own room. No, he hadn't done anything to frighten her. What scared her was that her own emotions seemed to have been whipped into a frenzy by nothing more than a look, a hint of something dangerous and exciting under Colt's calm demeanor.

"No trouble," Bethany said, clipping the words off sharply and booting Dancer forward in a sudden urge to limit this conversation. At the same time, she was thinking about the way Colt's forearms were covered with springy dark hair, the little space between his two front teeth, his sinewy hands curved around a coffee mug.

"Then I won't worry," Dita said.

"You shouldn't worry about me anyway."

"Well, I do. Who would look after you if Frisco and I didn't?"

"Not Mott Findley, for sure," Bethany said, pointing toward the road in the distance that bordered the edge of the property. Mott's black pickup truck bumped a tad too fast along the fence line, churning up a trail of dust. Its brakes squealed as it slid to a stop, skidding slightly before the driver regained control. Mott got out and walked around the truck toward them, pushing his hat back on his head and watching them speculatively.

"I don't want to meet up with him this morning," Bethany said, turning Dancer in the opposite direction. *Or any morning,* she thought to herself. If there was one person she wished would disappear from the face of the earth, it was Mott Findley. Unfortunately his property bordered hers.

Behind them they heard a shout from Mott, but neither she nor Dita turned around. Whatever Mott wanted to say to them, it couldn't be something they wanted to hear.

They took some time to check the fence on the east side of the pasture, then headed for home. It was almost noon, and Bethany was hungry. She hadn't eaten her usual big breakfast this morning. She'd been too preoccupied with Alyssa and the problems that she'd presented. As the shiny tin roof of the barn came into sight, she wondered idly how Colt had made out this morning, if he'd found a baby-sitter or even the baby's mother. She wanted him to get back to work, and fast.

The ranch pickup that Colt had driven to town was parked in a patch of shade beneath a large oak tree, and Bethany heard Alyssa's cries coming from within the ranch foreman's house as she swung down from her horse's back. That baby had a powerful set of lungs on her, no doubt about that.

"Sounds like she's hungry," Bethany said.

Dita grinned. "Babies are always hungry. And since when did you get to be such an authority on them?"

"Since somebody left one on my front steps," Bethany said wryly.

Dita only laughed. "I've got to go over to the barn. Need to check on Mocha's hoof." Dita was the closest thing they had to an on-site veterinarian and tended to all the animals when they were ailing.

Bethany slapped Dancer on the rump to signal that she could go back to the barn for a rest and a long drink at the trough. With Dancer trailing Dita and Frypan, Bethany hurried up the winding walkway. She called out as she opened the door. "Frisco? I'm here." She tossed her broad-brimmed hat on the deer-antler hatrack in the hall.

"Damned good thing, too," Frisco said. As Bethany's eyes adjusted to the light inside the house, she saw that Frisco sat in the shadowy living room on his recliner, which was in the upright position. He was rocking the baby and looking as if he felt very foolish. "Maybe you can get this kid to stop hollering. I sure ain't been able to."

"Where's Colt?" Bethany asked as Frisco dumped Alyssa into her arms.

"In the kitchen helping Eddie get dinner on the table," Frisco said loudly over the din. "Judas Priest, but that kid can holler." No sooner were the words out of his mouth, however, than Alyssa stopped crying.

Frisco spared Bethany a sour look. "I told you babies are a sight of trouble. I patted her and talked to her and she wouldn't give me the time of day. You pick her up and she clams up. I never will understand babies. Thank goodness you're here so I can wash up." He disappeared abruptly into the bathroom.

All kinds of feelings rushed over Bethany as the baby settled into her arms. Alyssa smelled like baby powder, and her hair rose into a little peak at the top of her head. Bethany had been thinking about this baby all morning, but even so, she had forgotten how very tiny she was. How sweet and soft and helpless. She smiled down at the baby, who was studying her with wide eyes. She wanted to tell Alyssa how cute she was and how utterly fascinating to her, but she didn't say anything because maybe you weren't supposed to talk to babies that way. Babies were something of a mystery, especially this one.

Bethany's boots clicked on the cool Mexican tile underfoot as she made her way along the center hallway of the house from which all the other rooms opened. Alyssa seemed to notice the colorful folk art arrayed on the walls, blinking curiously at it as they passed. "Pretty, isn't it?" Bethany asked. She loved this house, which Dita had so painstakingly decorated; it had become a second home to her, a place where when she went there, they had to take her in. And moreover, they wanted to. Frisco and Dita were like surrogate parents to her, and Eddie—well, Eddie was special.

At the back of the house was the kitchen, Eddie's noontime domain. Judging from the scent of things, they were having tacos today.

"The food smells wonderful," Bethany said as she rounded the corner into the kitchen. Dita was coming in the back door.

"Well, you know I'm the taco king," said Eddie, his eyes sparkling as he spooned meat sauce into taco shells.

"Eddie, you want both hot and mild sauce on the table?" Colt glanced over his shoulder at Bethany, his eyes softening when he saw her holding the baby.

"Hot for most of us, but Bethany likes the mild kind. Don't you, Bethany?"

"You know I do," she said, spellbound at the sight of Colt McClure acting like one of this family. That boded well for the ranch—she'd wanted someone who would fit in. But she'd judged Colt to be a misfit, standoffish, self-contained. She hadn't realized that in the short space of time he'd lived here, he'd taken to Eddie and that Eddie had also taken to him. She wasn't sure how she felt about that. She'd always been Eddie's favorite, and perhaps she wasn't ready to relinquish that status to the likes of Colt McClure.

"Did you make any progress in finding Alyssa's mother?" she asked Colt abruptly.

He slid two bottles of taco sauce across the polished tin top of the kitchen table. "Not yet," he said. "It may take a while. I found a sitter, though." His gaze was steady.

"A baby-sitter? Who?"

"She says she knows you. It's Loreen Thaxler, she's

the daughter of the woman who owns the beauty parlor in town."

"I thought Loreen had a summer job at a discount store over in Lubbock."

"I guess she got laid off or something. She says she can use the baby-sitting money for school clothes."

Loreen was about to start her senior year in high school, and she was dependable and trustworthy. Her mother, Rubye, had been cutting Bethany's hair for years.

"When can she start?"

"Tomorrow."

"Good. That means you can finish with the fence posts."

"Yeah, reckon it does."

Bethany spared him a curt nod. She didn't want to get too friendly, but on the other hand she would have liked to ask him what he'd done so far to find Marcy, the baby's mother. Whatever she might have asked was lost in the general shuffle to sit down to their noonday meal.

Eddie slid a large salad bowl across the table. "You gonna put that baby to bed now, Bethany?"

"She doesn't look sleepy, and anyway, I'd rather hold her," she said, liking the way Alyssa curled her tiny fingers around her thumb.

"I bought a carrier for her," Colt said. He jerked a thumb over his shoulder, indicating a child seat on the far counter.

"You better put that baby down," Dita said to Bethany. "You need your food. If you don't eat right, you'll lack energy this afternoon, and I need my partner to be one hundred percent."

Bethany sighed and got up. She knew that Colt's eyes

followed her as she fastened Alyssa into the child seat. "I guess she can stay up on the counter and watch us," she said.

"Just what I need, someone looking down my throat while I shovel in the food," said Frisco, but no one paid him any attention. They were used to his complaining.

Dinner was tacos, salad, fresh green beans from the garden and sweetened ice tea. Colt was lavish in his praise for Eddie's cooking skills.

"I'm the taco king," Eddie said, getting up to get more shells. "What do you expect?"

"Maybe you could teach me how to make them," Colt suggested.

"Not a chance!" said Eddie. "I might have to give up my place as taco king if I show you how."

"If I could make tacos this good, I'd be satisfied to be the taco prince," Colt told him, and Eddie crowed his delight.

"Okay. Maybe," he conceded finally.

Bethany was quiet as she ate, listening to the byplay around her. Dita wanted to know if Frisco had called the vet about medicine for Mocha, and Frisco said no, but he would, and by the way, he could have called this morning except that he'd had to hold the baby for half an hour or so. Bethany wondered privately why, if there was a child seat, Frisco had had to hold the baby. She decided it was probably that he'd wanted to hold Alyssa but, true to his cantankerous nature, was loathe to admit it.

Dita reminded Eddie that he was supposed to work in the garden during the afternoon, and Bethany told Frisco not to go out in the hot sun if he could help it. Finally Eddie brought out a coconut cake that he'd bought at the church bake sale, and they all proclaimed it delicious. It was a normal noontime meal, and yet, with Colt McClure sitting across from her and hardly saying anything at all, there was something about it that wasn't normal at all.

When she had eaten, Bethany scraped her chair back and stood up. "Are you still planning to work with Sidewinder this afternoon?" she asked Colt.

"Sure," he said. "If the baby's napping."

"I'll watch her. I'll take good care of her so you can be with Sidewinder," Eddie said.

"The garden," reminded Dita.

"After I work there I could watch the baby," Eddie said, looking to Colt for help.

Colt stood up, too. "You come over to the house after you're through in the garden, Eddie. Maybe we can work out a deal."

Eddie brightened. "Maybe," he said.

Bethany was on her way out of the house when Colt caught up with her in the hall. "I want to thank you again for being so nice about all this," he said.

She looked at him, at his earnest face, at the scar that curved along the edge of the hollow in his cheek. "We all pull together at the Banner-B," she said. "When one has a problem, we all pitch in to solve it." She didn't add that they hadn't needed any more problems; she figured he knew that. But somehow, as much as she wanted to harden her heart to this man, she couldn't.

"I'll see you later today. At the corral," he said.

"At the corral." Bethany turned and walked out into the hot bright afternoon, dazzled, she knew, by more than the sun. She didn't know why this cowboy attracted her. It was another thing she figured she didn't want or need to know.

After supper, Colt turned Sidewinder out into the corral and let him work off some steam before he went in with him. He saw Bethany approaching from the direction of the house, looking all cool and fresh from another shower. He'd seen her ride in earlier with Dita and had deliberately avoided them. He was pretty sure Dita didn't approve of his spending time with Eddie, and as for Bethany, well, his thought processes didn't seem to work right when she was around.

The horse was rambunctious today, and even more so when Bethany hitched herself up on the fence and sat solemnly watching as Colt latched his gaze onto the horse's. Sidewinder resisted at first, tossing his head and pawing the ground as he circled the pen. Colt wished the corral's fence had been constructed of solid boards; they would have limited Sidewinder's vision and made it easier for him to concentrate.

Finally the horse cocked his ear toward Colt and rippled his jawbone, exposing a brief flash of teeth.

"What does that mean?" Bethany asked in a low tone.

"He's showin' me that he's ready to talk," Colt replied, but he didn't let up on the horse. He felt good when Sidewinder let his head drop. "That means he's ready for the next step, which is for me to let him know I'm the lead horse. This is how I do it." Colt set his body at a forty-five-degree angle to Sidewinder's, and sure enough, Sidewinder stopped and moved toward him. Soon he was standing at Colt's side.

"So it's a matter of body language?" Bethany said.

"You could call it that."

"Is that what they call horse whispering?"

"Some do." He stroked Sidewinder's face. "I'll take

care of you, boy. I won't let anything happen to you." The horse nickered gently.

Colt made several revolutions around the corral with Sidewinder walking docilely behind him. "You see what he's doin'?" he asked Bethany, who still watched intently from her spot atop the fence. "A horse is a herd animal. By my body language, I've let him see that I'm the leader. He's joined up with me."

"He trusts you. You're the first person who's been able to get near him since he arrived at the Banner-B." Bethany sounded awed, and Colt guessed maybe she was.

"We'll try something new now." Colt walked through the cloud of dust they'd stirred up and yanked a saddle pad off the fence where he'd put it earlier.

"He's not going to stand for that," Bethany predicted, but Colt tossed her a grin and said, "Wait and see."

Sidewinder stood calmly as Colt gently slid the saddle pad and then the saddle across his back. Speaking to the horse in a gentle voice, letting him know what a great working horse he was going to be, Colt tightened the girth. When it was done, Sidewinder rolled his eyes a bit and danced away, flicking his ears around until Colt deliberately changed his position.

"Why are you letting him run?" Bethany asked as the gelding started to trot around the corral.

"I want him to get comfortable with the idea of a saddle on his back. He has to know he's safe wearing it before a rider tries to mount him."

They watched as Sidewinder bucked a few times. By now, however, the horse seemed to be bucking without much enthusiasm.

"He's doing that thing with his jaw again," Bethany

said after Sidewinder had made a few more circuits of the corral.

"You're ready to deal, aren't you, boy?" It was almost as if he could read the animal's mind; the method never failed. That was because Colt based his actions on what he'd observed with horses in the wild, not on any rule book made up by man. He'd thrown out the old rules long ago and never looked back.

The horse quieted and soon he stood beside Colt, allowing himself to be stroked.

After a few more minutes, Colt introduced the bridle. Sidewinder acted as if wearing a bridle was no big deal. In fact, Bethany could scarcely believe that this was the same horse who had nearly killed her when she'd tried the same maneuver only days ago.

Finally Colt rubbed his hands across the saddle and the girth, whispering sweet nothings to Sidewinder the whole time. He told him what a beautiful horse he was, too good to give up on, and how he could be a real help to them on the ranch. He told him how he had a home now where no one would hurt him intentionally. He said that all Sidewinder had to do was learn a few more important things, and then he and Sidewinder would be riding together across the wide Texas plains, cornering steers, policing the fence lines and having about as good a time as a man and a horse could have together. He all but promised him his own Stetson and a couple of margaritas, although if he'd thought that would help, he might have thrown those in, too.

When Colt finished talking to him, Sidewinder stood quietly, almost as if hypnotized. The gelding's confidence in him was growing, he could tell.

"Good horse, Sidewinder. Good job." Colt started to remove the saddle.

"Is that the end of the session?"

Colt had become so absorbed in Sidewinder that he'd almost forgotten Bethany, but when he glanced up and saw her perched on top of the fence, her clean shirt all starched and white, her hair caught back in some kind of clip, he wondered how he could have.

"Yep. Tomorrow I'll ride him."

"Tomorrow? Oh, no." She sounded unduly alarmed to his way of thinking.

"That bother you?"

"I'm afraid he's not ready."

"Oh, he's ready. He's tired of being such a worthless critter, aren't you, boy?"

Bethany slid down from the fence. "I hope you know what you're doing," she said doubtfully.

Colt hefted the saddle and turned toward the barn. "It'll be all right."

"Colt?"

"Yes?" He turned back to look at her.

"You're all right, too."

He hesitated, unused to praise, afraid he might even blush.

"You have a magic way with horses," Bethany said. "It's wonderful."

"I didn't think I'd ever want to work with horses again," Colt said, before realizing he'd said too much.

In response to her puzzled look, he shrugged. "Got to get this stuff put away," he said gruffly. She was still staring after him as he disappeared into the cool shadowy recesses of the barn.

Buckaroo was waiting with his head hanging over the stall door when Colt walked in with the saddle.

"Why'd I have to say that?" he asked Buck, but the horse only nudged at the stall door with his nose, his thoughts probably on something really important, like his next ration of feed.

AFTER DARK, WITH DITA and Eddie to stay with Alyssa, Bethany slowly made her way to the bench in her special place beside Little Moony Creek. She ripped off her boots and socks and, with an audible sigh of pleasure, dipped her feet down into the cool, clear water. She was grateful for the creek. It provided irrigation for the cattle, and because of it, she had peace of mind during this long drought. Other ranchers envied her the creek, including Mott. He had to depend on his wells, and it wasn't unusual in these parts for wells to run dry when there had been little rain.

But for now, the drought wasn't on her mind. She gathered her energies, tried to hone her focus down to business matters. Somehow, no matter how hard she tried, she couldn't think about anything but Colt McClure. He had invaded her space, caught her imagination, and engendered a sense of wonder for his prodigious talent in training Sidewinder. Yet the more she knew him, the less she knew *about* him.

Her experience with men had been minimal, to say the least. She wasn't sure she would ever understand how they thought or what they wanted. Frisco was a case in point; after all these years, she had barely begun to figure out what motivated him. Now there was Colt, who was even more of an enigma. At least Justin had been easy. They'd been true soul mates.

Justin. Her husband. Her lover and her friend. He had always been patient and understanding, and her welfare had ever been uppermost in his mind. That was why she found it normal and natural to speak to him when she came to this special place. She didn't have to say the words out loud, although sometimes it seemed to help. All she needed was to think her thoughts, ask his advice and heed what she heard, not with her ears but in her heart.

"There's so much I don't know about Colt McClure," she whispered. "I don't know if I can trust him."

But this time, there was no answer forthcoming. The only thing she heard was the whisper of the leaves overhead. As the breeze picked up, it skittered a few leaves across the path, and that's when she heard the footsteps. She looked up, startled.

"I thought I might find you here," Colt said. He was no more than a shape against the trees, a shifting shadow. She was surprised that he had so soundlessly invaded her private place. His approach had been muffled by the stream purling past, singing its way over rocks, bubbling in the shallows.

"Mind if I sit down?"

She had never shared this place with anyone, and it didn't feel right for him to be there. On the other hand, it didn't feel wrong. "Okay," she said.

He parked himself on a tree stump a few feet away. She couldn't see the expression on his face, but she smelled fresh-washed skin, a faint soapy scent. She knew then that Colt had taken the time to wash the dust from his face and neck, had cleaned up after his session with Sidewinder, but she knew it was not necessarily for her.

The shape of his head was a mere outline in the darkness. His voice was quiet, its tone respectful. "I wanted to tell you that I need to make a few more phone calls to find Alyssa's mom. I don't want to run up your phone bill, so I tried to buy one of those prepaid long-distance phone cards in town today. Murdock's Sundries was out of them, so I thought you could take the cost of any calls I make out of my pay. That all right?'' He held his breath, waiting for her answer. It was important to him that she not think he was taking advantage of her. He wouldn't live off any woman; he'd pull his own weight.

"It works for me." Bethany infused her words with an offhandedness that she didn't feel; she didn't want him to think she was too aware of him. But she was. Oh, she was. Aware of every nuance of his speech, aware of his rough masculinity and his voice that sounded like someone walking on rusty nails. She was also aware of his eyes, how they followed her every movement when he thought she wouldn't notice.

Colt cleared his throat but took his time speaking. "I hate to be so much trouble."

Bethany swallowed. "You have to do what you have to do."

"But, like Frisco said, babies are lots of work."

Bethany couldn't deny that. "I know you're trying to find Alyssa's mother. I hope you will before long. In the meantime..." She left the sentence incomplete, not wanting to encourage him to slack off in his search but wanting him to understand that she was willing to give him more time. For the baby's sake, she told herself, and not because of this cowboy's.

"I thought I'd start stringin' wire pretty soon. Maybe over in the East Pasture."

"Good idea. Time to get that fence up."

"Yeah. With this drought, you could use the extra grazing land. You think it's likely to rain anytime soon?"

"I haven't a clue. We can hope so."

The silence spun out between them, but it wasn't uncomfortable. It seemed odd to have company out here on a night like this one; usually she'd be at the house, working on the ranch accounts, watching television or getting ready for bed. She stole a look at Colt, saw that he was studying her, and felt her cheeks grow hot under his inspection. She wondered what he thought of her—really. Beyond the respect that he accorded her as his employer, did he think she was easy to get along with? Intelligent? Pretty?

Sexy?

She shivered, though it wasn't cold. One thing for sure, she shouldn't be thinking about sexy. She shouldn't be sitting here alone with Colt. It only invited ideas, opened up possibilities.

She rose and stretched elaborately. "Guess I'd better get back to the house and see how Dita and Eddie are managing with Alyssa."

He spoke quickly—too quickly, Bethany thought. "I'm sure everything is fine."

Bethany didn't reply, and Colt followed her silently through the underbrush to the driveway. Overhead a slice of pale moon swung in a starry sky. Cicadas chirred, an owl hooted and a coyote in the hills south of them wailed to the moon. Their footsteps were quiet, muffled by dust. Colt had something he wanted to talk to her about, and he figured the best way to bring up the topic was to just come out with it.

"Bethany," he said, then stopped until she glanced at him inquiringly.

He drew a deep breath. "I heard about the feud between you and Mott Findley in town today. Some guy at the drugstore asked me if I expected to be paid for my work here, and he let me know a little bit about what's going on."

Bethany's head shot up. She looked angry, defiant. "You'll be paid. Don't worry."

"I wasn't."

She went on looking annoyed anyway. "That's a rumor Mott started. That I couldn't pay my ranch hands. It's his way of undermining and demoralizing me."

"Why's he so nasty?"

"He wants the ranch, pure and simple. He's willing to do anything to get it."

"You sound bitter."

"Who wouldn't be? But I'm not going to let him have the Banner-B. I promised Justin."

They walked on a few steps while Colt digested this information. He understood now—or thought he did—why Bethany worked so hard to keep the ranch going.

"It can't be easy," he said.

"It isn't. Especially with Mott doing everything he can to wear me down. Boy, the things he says sure have made it hard for me to get help here."

"Well, you've got help now."

"I appreciate it. I really do," she said, looking straight ahead and walking with her arms crossed across her chest. She seemed calmer now, more centered. Maybe it was because he had reassured her.

Ahead of them the house looked comfortable, peaceful, with lights in the downstairs windows. It was the kind of home Colt had always dreamed of having, but in all his thirty-five years, he'd never been that lucky.

The lights from the house cast a gentle glow on Bethany's face. "You know, Bethany, I've got no inclination to go anywhere," he said evenly.

She shot him an assessing look. "Eventually?"

"Well, maybe, but not anytime soon. I expect I'll be movin' on when it's time for me to start my business."

"I guess Gompers isn't the kind of place most people from outside would choose to stay for any length of time," she said.

The lift and fall of his shoulders approximated a shrug. She had no idea what it meant.

"What kind of business are you intending to start?" she said.

He seemed to be looking off into a distance that she couldn't see, and when he spoke his voice was firm, sure. "Training horses the way they should be trained. Teaching other people to use my methods. Seems like there'd be a whole lot of happier animals if people knew what they were doin'."

"What a great idea," Bethany said slowly. "You'd be so good at it."

"Yeah. That's what I figure."

As they drew closer to the house, Jesse got up from his customary spot on the porch and loped toward them wagging his tail, his tongue lolling out of the side of his mouth.

"Watch out," Bethany warned, expecting the dog to lift his leg on the nearest object, which happened to be Colt's boot. But Colt bent and scratched the dog behind his ears. To Bethany's amazement, Jesse stood quietly as Colt's big hand moved to the top of his head. The dog allowed Colt to stroke him.

"Jesse must like you," Bethany said. "He never lets strangers touch him."

"I guess I'm not a stranger anymore."

This was true. He wasn't.

"I can work with Jesse, if you want," Colt said. "Get rid of some of his worst habits."

"That would be nice. Maybe then I could grow those sunflowers around the house."

Colt straightened and grinned. "Maybe."

Eddie came out of the house, his round face glowing in the yellow light from the porch bulb. "The baby has been sleeping for a long time. Mom's here, and we've been watching TV."

Bethany smiled at him. "That's great, Eddie. Colt and I will be here from now on. You two can go home if you like."

Jesse trotted back to his station beside the rocking chair, and Bethany preceded Colt up the back porch stairs as Eddie went inside to get Dita. The screen door slammed behind him, leaving Bethany and Colt on the porch. The light here was harsh; too bright, Bethany thought. She'd rather be walking along the driveway, talking quietly with Colt. She liked talking with him.

"Bethany," said Colt. She recognized something urgent in his tone, something disturbing.

She turned her head, not realizing that he was standing so close behind her. In that moment she didn't dare look into his eyes for fear of what she might see there. But she couldn't *not* look, and when she did, a curious heat swept through her, and she couldn't think. Colt seemed to create his own electrical field, and she was caught in it, and if they touched, sparks would fly. She closed her eyes, opened them, and she *did* see sparks.

But no, those were only fireflies at the edge of the garden.

Colt touched her arm, ran his fingertips along the skin as if he couldn't help himself, and maybe he couldn't. Maybe he felt it, too, this strange sizzling energy that made her feel so alive, so aware.

"Don't," she breathed as his head lowered toward hers. "Don't."

And, brushing against him, she slipped away through the screen door, leaving him outside staring after her through the mesh.

Damn, thought Colt as he realized what he'd almost done. Something could have happened. *Would* have happened.

Whoa! He was shaken by his lack of control. He knew he'd have to be more careful around Bethany in the future. He sure didn't want to jeopardize his position here by compromising his boss. He needed this job, liked it here. He had things he wanted to do. He wanted to help Bethany shape up the ranch. He wanted to straighten out Sidewinder, make a good working horse out of him. He wanted to convert Jesse James into an admirable citizen, teach him to work the cattle right along with him and Buckaroo.

He wanted—

Oh, hell. He wanted Bethany Burke. But he knew good and well that he couldn't do anything about it unless she also wanted him.

Chapter Five

Bethany slept that night as if she were drugged, but she woke earlier than usual. It was still dark when she stumbled out of bed and pulled on a robe. She paused to listen for sounds from the guest room, but Alyssa must not have awakened yet, and if Colt was awake, he wasn't stirring. She tiptoed downstairs and started the coffee.

She spent the next hour or so going over accounts, becoming so involved in computer spreadsheets that she was surprised to hear a car pull up to the house shortly after dawn. She looked out the window and recognized Loreen Thaxler climbing out of her little sedan. Colt had said that he'd asked Loreen to baby-sit, but he hadn't mentioned what time she would arrive. Evidently he had told her to show up early.

Bethany switched off the computer, smoothed her hair and went to let Loreen in.

"Mr. McClure said to come at seven," Loreen said when Bethany expressed surprise. "He said you needed somebody here so you could get to work."

"Make yourself comfortable in the den," Bethany told her. She turned on the TV for Loreen and went to wake Colt.

She hesitated outside the door of the guest room. The question was, if she knocked loudly would it wake Alyssa? Better to let the baby sleep rather than wake her up, even if Loreen was there to take care of her. Loreen could wash a load of baby clothes before Alyssa woke up if she didn't have to see to the baby's feeding. Bethany tapped lightly on the door. No sound from within. She knocked more loudly. Nothing.

Clutching her robe in front, Bethany pushed the door open slightly. It didn't squeak as she'd thought it might, so she nudged it a bit more until she could slip inside the room.

Colt was lying on his back, his chest rising and falling gently. Alyssa was asleep in her cradle. Both were dead to the world.

She tiptoed to the bed. Colt lay under the sheet, and his chest was bare. She wondered if he slept naked. A lot of men did, she knew. Or maybe he wore shorts.

His tan contrasted sharply with the white sheet, and his eyelashes were surprisingly long and full. The scar on his cheek seemed paler than it had in the light of day. She wondered, not for the first time, how he had gotten it. It bespoke a violent past, or at the very least, an accident. Maybe he'd fallen from a horse or been injured by one, but her instinct told her that this wasn't the case.

She wanted him to start stringing that barbed wire today. She bent over the bed. "Colt?" she whispered.

His eyes opened, and he stared up at her for a moment before comprehension dawned in his eyes. Comprehension, and swiftly following it, apprehension. "Is anything wrong?" He sat up in bed so suddenly that it startled her.

She put a finger to her lips, forgetting for the moment

that she was supposed to be holding her robe together. It gapped, and she grabbed for it, fumbling for the snap that held it and deciding that it must have fallen off. Alyssa made a few muffled noises and began to wail.

"I was trying to wake you without waking the baby," Bethany said. "Loreen's here."

Colt, unaware of the time, glanced wildly at the clock. "I thought the baby would wake me up earlier. I didn't think she'd sleep this late." He started to get out of bed, then pulled back. "I'm not decent," he said.

Bethany blushed furiously. Despite his embarrassment, Colt was amused that the idea of his nakedness under the sheet could have such an effect on her.

"I—um—well, I'll take Alyssa with me so Loreen can feed her," she said, backing away from the bed. When she bent to pick up the baby, her robe opened at the top and he could clearly see one firm round breast through the gap before she managed to lift the baby up and out of the cradle. He felt a sudden surge of longing; he wanted to touch Bethany in the most intimate way a man can touch a woman, to feel that creamy skin beneath his lips, to hold her in his arms and revel in her womanliness. He most certainly could not get out of bed now, not with her standing there.

"I'll have breakfast ready when you come down."

"I'd better get over to the barn, take a shower and clean up."

"You can do that here at the house," she said curtly. "No reason to go all the way over there." If she knew the state of his arousal, she gave him no clue. But she did leave, closing the door firmly behind her.

Colt waited for his anatomy to calm down and headed for the shower. A very cold one.

COLT KNOCKED OFF WORK shortly after noon. He'd been so involved with stringing wire that he hadn't stopped for dinner, and when he got back to the barn, he was hungry. He stopped by the foreman's house and let Eddie rustle him up some leftovers before heading back to the barn. Afterward he spent the better part of an hour in his own apartment, repairing a hackamore that he intended to use on Sidewinder. When he came downstairs to return the hackamore to the tack room, he heard a noise and looked over toward Dancer's stall.

Bethany was in the stall grooming her horse, and she greeted him when she saw him. She would have gone on working, but he stopped to talk.

"You noticed any problem with the feed? Something's been gnawing holes in the bags."

"It's probably mice. We had a problem with them here once before."

He sauntered closer, leaned against the edge of the stall. "You got grain around, you're gonna have a few mice for tenants. You need some cats."

Bethany straightened and shook her hair back. "We had some till Jesse scared them off."

"I'll set a few traps, and I better get started teaching Jesse his manners, too." He paused, sure that she didn't want to continue the conversation and equally sure that he did. "How's Loreen working out as baby-sitter?" he asked.

"I checked with her about an hour ago. She was giving Alyssa her bath. She knows what to do—she has several young cousins that she's been taking care of ever since she was about ten."

"Sounds like I was lucky to find her."

Bethany spared him a tight smile. "Yes."

He went over to Sidewinder's stall, and the horse

rolled his eyes at him. "Good boy," he said approvingly, letting Sidewinder get used to the way he talked. If you let horses hear your voice at times when you weren't asking something of them, they were more likely to perform when you wanted them to.

Bethany snapped the lead off Dancer's halter. She closed the stall door and latched it before coming over to where Colt stood.

"You going to work with Sidewinder today?"

"Sure am."

"I'd like to watch, but I need to get back to the ranch accounts."

"You do all the bookkeeping here?"

"I'm afraid so."

"It's a hard job you've set for yourself," he said.

"I know. But I like it. Most days, anyway." She let out a rueful little laugh, kind of sad in its way.

"Do you mind if I ask you something?" he said, watching her face.

"I might." She glanced up at him as if to gauge his seriousness. He was plenty serious, and he figured it showed in his expression.

"How does a woman like you stand living in a place like this?"

She blinked, bit her lip and decided that he wasn't being a smart aleck. "I can't imagine living anywhere else," she said slowly. It was true; she hardly remembered her life in Wichita. She simply wasn't the same person she'd been in those days.

"Is your promise to your husband all that keeps you from packin' it in? Sellin' out to Mott Findley and spendin' the money to move to someplace nice?"

"That's right," she said.

His eyes pierced through her. "Justin's gone. It's time for you to be thinkin' of yourself."

Agitated, she walked to the other end of the barn and stood looking out the open door at the wide cloudless sky. Colt followed her, but he didn't say anything, just tipped his hat back and balanced his hands on his hipbones.

"You see my ranch foreman's house?" she said, gesturing with her head.

Colt, unsure what point she was trying to make, nodded.

"That's where Frisco has lived for forty years. He brought Dita here twenty-three years ago, and they had Eddie, who was born in the back bedroom because there was no time to get to the hospital in Lubbock. Where would Frisco and Dita and Eddie go if I closed down the Banner-B?"

"Frisco's an experienced ranch foreman. He'd find work."

"He's old and sick and tired, Colt. I can't boot him out, no matter what. He and Dita have been my mainstays. They taught me everything I know about running this place. And Eddie—he needs the work he does here. It gives him self-respect to know he's earning his keep, making a valuable contribution."

"It's admirable of you. To take care of all of them." All of us, he'd almost said.

Bethany said nothing, but her smile was bleak.

He shoved his hat down on his head. "Well, guess I'd better get on the phone. Once Alyssa is gone, there'll be one less of us for you to worry about." He went up to his little room over the barn to get his address book, and when he came down, he saw that Bethany was mucking out stalls.

"Hey, I'll do that," he said, already feeling bad that he hadn't been able to get to it yet.

Bethany looked up and blew a stray strand of hair off her forehead. "You go ahead and make those phone calls. Anybody can do this," she said, and went on with what she was doing.

Colt strode toward the house, chastened by her dedication and her vigor. What was he supposed to do about a woman who refused to act like a woman? She looked like a woman, that was for sure. She had breasts and soft skin and a backside that would just about fit within the curves of his two hands. She had tremendous sex appeal. And the worst thing was that none of it was for him.

He was tired of aching with longing as he lay in bed at night, and he was flat-out disturbed at the way he thought about his employer all the time. Tonight he had a good mind to drive into town, drop by the local watering hole and see if he could find him a woman he didn't care about. There ought to be someone who could turn him on and make him stop thinking about Bethany Burke.

"FRANKIE DOBSON HERE." The husky male voice was muffled because of a lot of background noise, but Colt stuck a finger in the other ear to block out the sound of Loreen talking to Alyssa in the other room.

"This is Colt McClure," he said. "I've been lookin' for you."

The man on the other end of the line said nothing at first, then, cautiously, he said, "You're the guy Marcy visits at the prison?"

"Was. I got out." He clipped the words off sharply.

"What do you want from me?"

"Marcy's whereabouts."

"I got no idea where she is. And I don't want to talk to you." Frankie slammed the phone down.

Furious, Colt lost no time before punching out the number again. This time Frankie didn't answer the ring. Instead it was a sweet female voice. "Biggo Burgers. How may I help you?"

"You can put Frankie Dobson on the phone," he growled.

"I'm sorry, sir, but Mr. Dobson is unavailable."

"He was available a few minutes ago. Tell him to get himself over to the phone."

"I told you, sir—"

"And I'm tellin' you, ma'am, if Frankie doesn't talk to me, I'm callin' his supervisor in Salt Lake City. And his supervisor's supervisor. Not to mention the president of Biggo Burgers. So are you goin' to put him on the phone or not?"

A shuffle, a muffled curse, and then Frankie said, "Yeah?"

"Either you tell me where Marcy is, or I call the police."

"About what? I ain't done nothing."

"I've got something that belongs to you here. A cute little package by the name of Alyssa."

"You've got the kid?" Frankie's surprise was genuine.

"Yeah."

"The baby's not mine."

Colt did a slow burn but managed to remain calm. "You lived with Marcy Ryzinski for a year. You took advantage of a teenage girl who had no place to go. And by the way, you want to talk to the police about domestic abuse? I saw that black eye you gave Marcy. It wasn't pretty."

"She ran into a door. I didn't hurt her."

"That's not what Marcy said. I personally think you ought to be shut up behind bars—"

"Like you were?" sneered Frankie. "Listen, I'm no murderer."

"Watch it, Frankie. All I want is Marcy's address. I'll leave you alone if you tell me where to find her."

Silence. "She might not want you to know where she is."

"You might not want me comin' to look for you. And I will. It wouldn't be hard to find you, Frankie. You're flippin' burgers at the only Biggo Burgers in Greenleaf County, Arkansas. I promise you, if I show up there, you'll have more than a black eye to show for the experience."

Another silence, this one shorter. "Okay, okay. I heard Marcy went to stay with a girlfriend in Oklahoma City. She took the kid with her."

"You know the name of the girlfriend?"

"It was Casey or Kelly or something like that. She used to live in Tallequah, Oklahoma. Casey was going to go to beauticians' school in Oklahoma City."

"Do you know her last name?"

"Nah. No clue."

"All right, Frankie. But before I hang up, let me tell you this, you scum—if you so much as get within one city block of Marcy Ryzinski again, I'll come lookin' for you. Got that?"

The answer was having the phone slammed down in his ear again, but Colt didn't care. At last he had a lead, a real lead. He had something to go on, and he'd follow it as far as he could.

BETHANY, SITTING ON THE porch rocker after dinner, held Alyssa in her lap. Jesse James snuffled around the steps, looking for crumbs of any kind. The baby was bright-eyed and cheerful, cooing and gurgling. Loreen had fed her before she left and had said how much she enjoyed baby-sitting.

"This is so much better than working in a discount store," Loreen said. "Babies are fun."

Bethany had to agree. She had hardly been able to wait until Loreen was gone so that she could hold Alyssa herself. Now she counted ten little fingers and ten little toes, and she played "This Little Piggy" until Alyssa chortled with glee.

Hearing the noise, Eddie came over from the garden toting a large basket of green beans and a smaller one of tomatoes.

"Does Alyssa like green beans?" he asked.

"She can't eat them yet, but I bet she will before long. Go put those on the kitchen counter, will you, Eddie?"

Eddie disappeared inside momentarily. When he came back out, he sat down on the top step of the porch at Bethany's feet. "I always did want a baby sister," he said, tickling Alyssa's toes.

Bethany knew how keenly Eddie had longed for a sibling, but Dita couldn't have any more children.

"I have a new brother, too," Eddie said.

This caught Bethany off guard. "You do?" she asked, puzzled.

"Sure. Colt's like a big brother. He wants me to teach him to make tacos, and I said I would. And you know what?" He patted Jesse on the head, and the dog wagged his tail a few times.

"What?"

"Colt's going to take me to a movie sometime." Eddie loved going to the movies over in Lubbock, and lately Frisco and Dita hadn't had time to take him.

"Wonderful. That sounds like fun."

"It sure will be. Hey, Bethany! I just had an idea!" Eddie was flushed with enthusiasm.

"Well, shoot. Don't keep me in suspense."

"Maybe you could go with us to the movies."

"Maybe," Bethany said, but she was doubtful that this was a good idea.

"I better get back. Dad said not to be too late." Eddie got up and dusted off the seat of his jeans.

Eddie had scarcely left when Colt rounded the corner of the barn. He hailed Bethany and strode over. He was carrying a small paper bag.

"What's up?" Bethany asked. Jesse got up and ran to meet Colt, his whole hind end shimmying with the wag of his tail. Colt fed him a treat out of the bag, and Jesse wagged even harder.

"I stopped by to tell you that the session with Sidewinder went well today," he said. "I rode him for a few minutes."

"Amazing!" Bethany stared up at him.

"I'll ride him again tomorrow. Maybe you can watch."

"Did you show Frisco?"

"I don't think he wants to hear about it."

"Of course he does. That horse has been a thorn in his side for months." She paused. "It doesn't sound like you and Frisco are hitting it off."

"He's okay. He may even like me a little now that he sees that I like Eddie and Eddie likes me."

"About Eddie," Bethany said, and then stopped.

"What about Eddie?"

"I'm glad you get along with him."

"What's not to like? He's a good kid."

"Have you ever been around a Down's syndrome adult before?"

Colt shook his head. "Nope."

"You seem to have a natural affinity for working with him. And with horses. And with dogs."

"Maybe. There was a kid at a ranch I worked at once. He didn't trust many people, but he learned to trust me. He was..." His voice trailed off. He hadn't ever talked about Rusty before, but he owed him a lot.

"Yes?" Bethany was looking up at him inquiringly.

"He was a friend. The best. People didn't give him a chance. Everyone should have a chance." He got up, walked a few feet away and called Jesse. Jesse just looked at him and flailed his tail around in the dust.

Colt held out a dog biscuit. Jesse lifted his head, sniffed the air and got up and trotted over to Colt, who gave him the biscuit. "We're establishin' rapport, Jesse and I," Colt explained. He straightened. "Come on over to the barn with me, Jesse James," he said. "We'll indulge in an etiquette lesson or two."

Colt and the dog were almost out of the yard when Bethany called Colt's name. He turned around, taking his time, since the last thing he needed to see was Bethany looking all motherly and happy with the baby in her arms. He found motherhood attractive and appealing, especially on her. Never mind that she wasn't Alyssa's mother. He thought of her that way somehow.

"If you have time this evening while you're in town, I'd be most appreciative if you'd pick up some baling wire. Fred Kraegel said his store will be open late tonight."

"I was plannin' to go to town anyhow. Mind if I stay a couple of hours, get myself a bite to eat?"

She studied him curiously, and he thought she might comment. But all she said was, "Stay as long as you like. No problem."

The baby's tiny fist clutched reflexively at Bethany's rounded breast. Colt's mouth went dry. He was suddenly reminded of why he wanted to go to town tonight and what he hoped to accomplish while he was there, which was a sight more than picking up baling wire.

COLT BELLIED UP TO THE BAR at Pug's Tavern. It was a dive, and it was full of cowboys throwing money around after payday.

The bartender brought him a bourbon and water, and he downed it right away. He'd had his qualms about stopping in here. Earlier Kraegel's employees had loaded the baling wire into the pickup, even throwing in some extra at Kraegel's orders, and afterward Colt had wandered around Gompers for an hour or two trying to muster enthusiasm for what he was about to do.

The town didn't show him much. It consisted of a string of stores lined up along Main Street, their windows mostly fly-blown and covered with dust. A squat little courthouse sat smack in the middle of the town square, complete with rings in the walls where you could tie a horse. There was no fast-food place, no fancy restaurant and only one gas station. Rubye's Beauty Box sat at one end of the town, the Gompers Café at the other, and in the middle were a gift shop and the barber shop where he'd had his hair cut. To sample the local nightlife, people dropped in at Pug's Tavern. It had taken Colt a while to make up his mind to step inside and scout around for signs of intelligent life. So far, he hadn't seen any.

Everyone at Pug's Tavern tonight seemed to be wearing some combination of denim and silk, and the women all, every last one, had big hair. Country music, loud and twangy, blared from a jukebox. Still, there was a pool room in the back and a long shiny bar out front, and he figured that was enough for him. Would have to be, come to think of it. Colt leaned on the bar and, through a haze of tobacco smoke, tried to summon a modicum of interest in the pool game in progress.

The women came up to him about midway through the second drink.

"Howdy, cowboy," said the first one, a blousy bleached blonde with a husky, smoke-wasted voice.

"You're new around here, right?" asked the other, a redhead fast closing in from the other side.

He'd come here to meet women, hadn't he? So why was his first impulse to bolt and run?

"Reckon I am," was all he said.

"I'm Cindy. She's Jasmyn," said the blonde.

"I'm Colt McClure," he said easily. The blonde wasn't his type, and anyway, when he looked at her, all he could see in his mind was Bethany, her long pale hair switching around as she turned her head to look at him, her well-rounded derriere as she scrambled up and over a fence, and the way her laughter sounded like Little Moony Creek purling in the shallows.

The redhead seemed the most interested in him, and soon she was leaning possessively in his direction, her breasts only a fraction of an inch from his arm. They were nice, but they put him in mind of Bethany's robe and how it had fallen open this morning when she'd picked up the baby from the cradle. He actually ached when he thought about how much he'd wanted to touch her as he watched her from the bed where he lay.

"Most people call me 'The Duchess,'" the redhead said with a wink. "Can you guess why?"

Colt didn't want to play guessing games. He didn't even want to talk to her anymore. "No," he said gruffly.

"Because," she said confidentially, moving closer and hugging his arm so that her breasts pressed full against him, "Some folks think I look like the Duchess of York." She offered this last bit in a fake English accent.

"The Duchess of York," he repeated, unable to see any resemblance other than the red hair, which was kinked into tight ringlets.

"Yes," she said, whispering the word in his ear. His head jerked backward in reflex avoidance, which is how he happened to spot a short squat man with ivory-colored teeth and scraggly gray hair swaggering toward him. The man seemed puffed up with his own importance, though Lord knew why. He sure didn't look like much.

"Hello, Mott," said Cindy with an ingratiating smile. "This is Colt McClure. Colt, Mott Findley. He about runs everything around here."

So this was the Mott Findley who was making Bethany's life miserable! Colt studied him and decided that Mott was an unfriendly cuss without a shred of warmth to his personality. Mott said, "How do?" but didn't offer his hand, and neither did Colt.

"Maybe Colt could join all of us for the evening," Cindy said brightly. "Jasmyn and me, we were hankering to ride to Lubbock and go to a few clubs over there."

"Not tonight," Mott said dismissively. "McClure, I'd like to see you for a minute. Alone," he said, jerking his head toward the door.

Great. Colt wasn't sure what this was about, but he had an idea it had something to do with the Banner-B. There was no other reason for Mott to request a private audience.

He thought of trying to wiggle out of this, but if nothing else, going outside to talk with Mott would provide an escape from the two women. Cindy's pout convinced him that this was a good plan, so Colt slid off the bar stool and followed Mott outside.

Mott lost no time in parking his backside on the fender of a black pickup parked at the curb. Mott looked Colt over as he fished a frayed toothpick out of his shirt pocket. The erratic blue neon light from the drugstore flickered across his teeth, which were bared in a semblance of a folksy grin. Colt didn't trust it, not one whit.

"You know, The Duchess is pretty good at what she does best. You want her? I'll give her the word."

"Not interested," Colt said, unsure where this was leading. He did know one thing: Mott was letting him know that he controlled things around here, all the way down to the town's wild women.

Mott nodded, pretending as if he were giving Colt's refusal some thought. Finally he spoke. "I won't beat around the bush," he said abruptly. "I'm offering you a job working for me. Starting tomorrow."

"Why?" Colt said, deciding that bluntness was the only way to handle this unexpected development.

Mott's toothpick worked at something between his bottom front teeth. "Because I could use another hand. I heard you signed on at the Banner-B."

"That's right."

"The work's easier at my place than at the Banner-B. There's more men to share it because I've got more ranch hands. I'll pay you double what you're getting now."

Colt thought about making more money; he thought about how he was going to have to dip into his investments to start his business when the time came. Overriding these considerations was his responsibility for Alyssa and how kind Bethany had been to let her stay at the ranch. He liked working for Bethany, he really did. She had a lot of spunk. That made this choice a real no-brainer.

"No, thanks," he told Mott.

"Wait a minute. Do you realize what I'm offering? The Banner-B's a lost cause. You can see that, man."

"I don't agree," Colt said.

Mott narrowed his eyes. "Beth Burke can't keep that place afloat much longer. The bank's gonna call in her loans, and she owes money to 'most everybody in town."

Colt shrugged. He didn't want to get in an argument. All he wanted was to get back to the Banner-B, to his comfortable bed with Alyssa in her cradle nearby, and to Bethany sleeping in the room across the hall. Stopping at Pug's Tavern had been a bad idea. He started to walk away, but before he'd taken two steps, Mott had positioned himself squarely in front of him.

"You better take this chance while you got it, boy," Mott said in a tone of quiet menace. "I'm not likely to offer again."

"Excuse me, I've got things to do," Colt said, and he started to sidestep Mott.

Mott's hand snaked out and gripped his upper arm with surprising strength. "I'll get you, boy," he said, his voice grating close on Colt's ears. "One way or t'other."

Colt skewered Mott with a look and wrenched his arm away. He hated little guys who thought they could throw their weight around and get what they wanted. He wanted to stomp Mott out, crunch him under his boot heel like a cockroach. But that wouldn't do him any good, and it certainly wouldn't help Bethany. He couldn't be of any use to her from a jailhouse cell, and he had no doubt that, in a small town like this one, he could land in the slammer overnight if he so much as looked at Mott Findley cockeyed. He didn't care to tangle with the cops. The last thing he needed was to lug the baggage of his past along with him to Gompers, Texas, the place he'd chosen, more or less at random, to start a new life.

Colt stalked back into the bar to get his hat. Inside was smokier and murkier than he remembered it, and someone had turned up the volume on the jukebox. As he realized that his hat wasn't hanging on the rack by the door where he'd left it, Jasmyn slithered up to him. She was wearing his Stetson on her head, and a big grin was plastered across her face.

"Cute, don't you think?" she said, spinning around to model it for him.

He'd come here in the first place with the idea of finding a warm body to comfort him after a long time without a woman in his bed, but it was the last thing he wanted now.

He snatched the hat off her head. "Give me that," he said tersely.

"We thought you might like to come over to our apartment," Cindy said, poking her chest out in his direction. "Have a nightcap. With both of us."

"Can't," said Colt. He left Cindy and Jasmyn staring openmouthed as he marched out the door.

"Stupid cowboy," Jasmyn called after him.

"Slimeball."

"Welcome to Gompers," said Mott, who was still leaning on the fender of his truck and still working on the toothpick. "You might as well know that I intend to make you a mite uncomfortable around here, McClure."

Colt climbed into the cab of the ranch truck, impervious to insult. Why should he care about this two-bit small-town jerk? He'd served time in prison. Mott Findley was nothing compared to his fellow inmates in the pen.

Mott waved him off with what on closer inspection proved to be an ungentlemanly gesture, but Colt ignored it. All he could think about was that he was going home. He was on his way back to the ranch and to the people who lived there, each and every one of whom knew what it was to respect another human being. Where he came from, that was no small thing.

BETHANY WAS IN THE KITCHEN when Colt came in. He stank of smoke, and she smelled liquor on his breath.

"I guess you stopped off at Pug's Tavern," she observed without rancor.

He wanted to tell her that it had been a bad mistake. He wanted to compliment her on how pretty she looked wearing that blue knit jersey instead of those oversize shirts she usually wore, and he wanted to say again that he was grateful for the kindnesses she had shown to him and Alyssa.

But his responses were tempered by those months in

prison, and before he thought he said, "You got a problem with that?"

She raised her eyebrows slightly. This was her ice princess look. He'd grown familiar with all her expressions since he'd lived at the Banner-B; there was the go-eat-roadkill one, and the one he'd privately labeled the beep-beep, because it was how she looked when she'd decided to turn tail and run. He liked the ice princess one, though. It was kind of classy.

Bethany slammed a baby bottle onto the countertop. "What you do on your own time is of no concern to me," she snapped. "You want coffee? To help you sober up?"

"I haven't been drinking all that much," he objected.

She looked as if she were going to contradict him, but she didn't. He went over to the coffeepot, where there was about half a pot left, still hot, and poured himself some.

"How is Alyssa?"

"She drank all her formula at her last feeding. She's asleep in her cradle."

"I want to see her. I've been thinkin' about her."

"Go on up, but I expect you'd better sleep in the barn tonight." She closed the dishwasher door and rinsed her hands off in the sink.

Oh, so she was kicking him out, was she? He pondered this new and revolting development as he took the coffee with him and climbed the stairs two at a time. The hall boards creaked as he made his way to the guest room, where Alyssa was sleeping on her side, her little mouth a perfect rosebud. He leaned over the cradle and studied her. He wondered if the emotion he was feeling was the same kind that new parents felt, and if this was the way they felt, how could any of them ever hurt their children? How could a parent abandon a baby like this one?

But Marcy had had a hard life. She was, perhaps, driven by a pain that no one else could understand.

He didn't hear Bethany as she slipped up beside him. "She probably won't wake up for a long time," she said in a low voice.

"She sure looks like her mother," he said.

He happened to glance up as Bethany's face went blank. Then he could have kicked himself. Of all the fool things to say! She still thought this kid was his. She might think he was in love with Marcy, although such an idea had never crossed his mind. In that moment he wanted to make it clear to Bethany that Marcy had never been anything to him. Never had, never would be.

"I think I'd better go to bed now," Bethany said in a small voice. She turned and marched from the room.

In the few seconds that it took her to reach the hallway, myriad thoughts chased through Colt's mind. The most important of them was that he was crazy about Bethany Burke and, if it bothered her so all-fired much that he might be in love with another woman, she could have feelings for him as well.

He was across the room and out the door in two seconds, emboldened, no doubt, by the whiskey still thrumming in his veins. He caught up with Bethany as she was about to enter her own bedroom, her hand on the doorknob.

She wheeled around, the look in her eyes that of a cornered doe.

"Just a damn minute," Colt said, grasping her arms. She would have run if there had been anywhere to go, she would have called out if there had been anyone to hear. He knew that, but he did it anyway. He kissed her full on the lips, the way she was meant to be kissed, long and slow and with all the longing and gratitude he felt for her.

She melted in his arms. And then she yielded with a passion that he'd only sensed before, sliding her arms up his, linking her fingers behind his neck, pulling his head down so that she could drink more deeply of the kiss. Her breasts strained against his chest, and his hips ground against hers. When he was finished—and he didn't want to be finished, just needed to come up for air—when he was finished, she gasped.

"There," he said. "I've been wantin' to do that for some time."

"You—you—"

If she was going to fire him, he didn't want to learn about it tonight.

He laid a gentle finger against her lips. They were still moist.

"Hush," he said. "And sleep well."

He left her there, her hand on her throat, her eyes wide, as he headed for his small apartment over the barn.

With almost any other woman in the world, he could probably expect some company later tonight. But that wasn't Bethany's style.

He punched his pillow into shape and lay in his bed for a long time thinking how much he liked listening to Bethany preparing for bed in the room across the hall when he slept in the house.

No telling what morning would bring. But he didn't regret that kiss.

What he regretted was not getting around to it sooner.

Chapter Six

A cricket kept Bethany awake all night long. She heard him in the night, calling to his ladylove from somewhere in her room. He might have been in the wall, or maybe in the closet, or perhaps he was hiding out in the curtains. Wherever he was, it didn't matter. Even if it hadn't been for his lovelorn chirping, she probably wouldn't have slept anyway.

What had ever possessed her to kiss Colt McClure back so forcefully? She could still feel his lips exploring hers, had replayed the kiss over and over again in her mind until she was sure that every nuance was engraved upon her soul forever.

Okay, so he was just a lonely cowboy who had come home half-drunk and had merely availed himself of what she had wanted to give anyway.

But it wasn't right. He shouldn't have taken that liberty.

On the other hand, she'd liked kissing him and he knew it. So where did that leave them?

It left her with a ranch hand who didn't know his place, but she needed him desperately to help her keep this ranch going. It left him with a child who had nowhere to go and who probably wouldn't be welcome in any other place he tried to get a job. It also left a lot of unanswered questions, such as why he'd taken leave of this Marcy person in the first place and why she'd signed her note to him I Love You, Marcy.

"I Love You, Marcy" might be a casual closing. Or it could really mean "love." What kind of love, that was the question. One-night-of-great-sex-and-then-I never-want-to-see-you-again love? This-is-for-a-lifetime love? I'll-take-care-of-you-and-you'll-take-care-of-me-until-we-both-decide-to-call-it-quits love?

The knowledge hit her like a blow to the stomach. She was falling in love with Colt McClure.

No, she wasn't.

Yes, she was.

She couldn't love him. She loved Justin. Love never died, that's what Justin had said, and she believed it with all her heart. So how could she fall in love with anyone else?

She couldn't.

Oh, yes, she could. But she didn't want to fall in love with Colt. She didn't know enough about him. And he was quite possibly in love with someone else.

When Alyssa woke up and started to fuss at the crack of dawn, Bethany dragged herself out of bed and stood looking in the mirror over the dresser for about a minute, which was the length of time it took her to decide that she didn't want Colt to see her looking like something that had been hauled behind a horse for six miles. She staggered into the bathroom, splashed cold water on her face and pulled over her head the first item of clothing that she found. It turned out to be the blue jersey she'd put on after her shower last night.

She carried Alyssa downstairs, murmuring to her. She'd grown accustomed to the morning routine. Even after a rough night, she had energy for this baby, and that was kind of amazing, she thought. It made her think about how she'd always wanted a baby of her own. She wouldn't even mind if this baby were hers—but there was no point in wishing for things that couldn't come true.

There was no sign of Colt this morning. He must have decided to keep to himself after last night.

Loreen arrived right on time, bright as a button and apparently unaware that Bethany wasn't in the mood for talking. "My mom, she said Mr. McClure is one handsome man, all right. Said he asked about getting his hair cut at her place, but she sent him over to the barber shop. She said Mr. Butler couldn't weasel any information out of him. You know, Mr. Butler likes to chat. He said Mr. McClure read a magazine the whole time he was cutting his hair and didn't say one thing about where he was from."

"He's not real talkative," Bethany said, wishing that this were true of Loreen this morning.

"My mom, she said she hopes you know something about him. She said you can't be too careful who you employ these days. She said for instance, that baby. Little Alyssa. She wonders how he happened to come by that baby, she says."

"If you'll prepare Alyssa's bottles this morning, Loreen, I'll be running along. Dita and I have a long day ahead of us."

Loreen seemed not to notice that Bethany hadn't responded to her last comment. "Sure, Mrs. Burke. And I'm not worried about Mr. McClure. He's always been real nice to me. I told my mom—"

Exactly what Loreen had told Rubye, Bethany didn't wait around to find out. She fled.

On the way to the cattle chutes where she was to meet Dita, she couldn't help wondering, though. Where did Colt McClure come from in Oklahoma? And where had he worked before?

Not that it mattered, she reassured herself. He was an excellent worker.

A great kisser, too.

COLT SLAMMED THE PHONE down in frustration.

"Anything wrong, Mr. McClure?" Loreen poked her head around the edge of the den door and favored him with a quizzical look.

"Uh, no," he said, though that wasn't entirely true. After last night's smoke-filled bar and lack of sleep from second thoughts about kissing Bethany, he felt like an elephant was sitting on his head. Not only that, but he had called every cosmetology school in Oklahoma City but had been unable to trace the Casey or Kelly that Frankie Dobson had said Marcy had gone to see.

"Well, is there anything I can do for you?"

He stared up at the ceiling for a moment and expelled a deep breath. When he looked back again, Loreen was picking at a piece of lint on her sleeve and cracking her gum, which made it sound as if the elephant sitting on his head had gotten up and started crashing through the brush.

He tried to ignore it. "Loreen," he said as patiently as he could, "your mother has a beauty shop."

"Right," said Loreen, clearly confused as to where he might be going with this.

"Well, I'm tryin' to track down someone who is a student at a cosmetology school. I've checked several, but I can't find her. Is there some kind of directory that might list all the places in a city where you could go to learn cosmetology?"

"Hmm, I don't know. I do know that you don't necessarily have to go to a cosmetology school, though. Like over in Jefferson, the town ten miles away? The consolidated high school there has a vocational program. You can take beauty school classes right there."

Colt had never thought of trying public vocational schools. He grinned at Loreen. "You're a gem, you know that, Loreen?"

She smiled back. "I hope I helped."

"I'll let you know." He swung around, picked up the phone. It took him all of ten minutes to find out that there was a vocational high school in Oklahoma City and that one of their students was Casey Landers, recently moved there from Tallequah. She lived with her parents, and he was persuasive enough so that the student office helper took his name and number and promised she would pass it along to Casey in case she had a friend named Marcy who wanted to reach him. He knew the gambit might not work, but Colt hung up feeling elated all the same.

"Was your search successful?" Loreen asked, looking up from the pile of baby clothes that she was folding on the couch.

"Maybe," he said. "In the meantime, I'm treating you to a banana split at the Gompers Café."

"Can't do that. I'm on a diet," Loreen said.

"Well, then, name your treat. I'd like to do something nice for you."

"It would be great if you'd let me bring my boyfriend to watch you work with Sidewinder," she said. "I saw you riding him yesterday. The word was out that nobody could ride that horse, and Joey couldn't believe me when I told him what you'd done."

"That's easy enough. Bring Joey over this weekend."

Colt went out to the barn, where he busied himself putting up more wall hooks in the tack room. He hadn't seen Bethany all day, and he knew she and Dita were at the cattle chutes over in East. Thinking about that kiss last night, he wondered what she would say to him when at last they saw each other. A smile twitched at the corner of his lips. At least she hadn't fired him—yet.

"MRS. BURKE, WHO'S MARCY?"

Bethany hoped Loreen wouldn't notice that she stiffened at the very name. She was sitting in the kitchen rocking chair as Loreen prepared to leave, and Alyssa was stretched out in her lap, cooing and gurgling to beat the band.

"Marcy is, um, someone Colt knows."

"Well, he sure is trying hard to find her."

"I know," Bethany said, inhaling the scent of baby and talcum and wishing in that moment that Alyssa could stay with them forever.

"I'll be going now, Mrs. Burke. See you tomorrow." Loreen let herself out the back door and squealed as Jesse jumped up from his nap beside the rocker. "You leave me alone, dog," she said, but not without affection. Bethany thought that maybe she'd better tell Loreen tomorrow that Jesse had reformed, kind of.

Alyssa waved her arms in the air, and Bethany picked her up and cuddled her close. "What happens when Colt finds your mommy?" she asked. "What happens then?"

A shadow fell across the door. Colt.

"Mind if I come in?" he said easily.

"The door's open." She held her breath, wondering how naturally they could talk after last night and the kiss that had fairly taken her breath away.

He closed the door softly behind him. He'd been working with Sidewinder, and there was a streak of dust on his T-shirt, another on his jeans. He tossed a small gift-wrapped box on the table and stood looking down at her, his hands balanced on his hips, his eyes delving into hers.

"The little one's okay?"

"She's fine. Loreen said she drank all her formula today, every bit, and she's already had her bath, and—"

"I guess it's not the baby I'm really askin' about, Bethany." He said her name as if it didn't feel comfortable on his lips, and his eyes searched hers until she thought he might be able to read what she was thinking.

She stopped rocking and held Alyssa up so that the baby's head was resting on her shoulder. She knew exactly what Colt was wanting to know, and she could either pretend she didn't or be straightforward. She wasn't sure what was the best thing to do in this case, so she said nothing.

"I suppose I should apologize for last night," he said. He paused, giving her a chance to speak, but she didn't. She was too busy trying not to feel that kiss on her lips, as fresh as if it had just that minute been planted there. Her lips tingled, and other places, too, and she felt that Colt McClure knew every inch of her even though he hadn't done a thing but kiss her.

"Colt," she began, unsure where she was going with this, but he leaned back against the counter and crossed his arms. The slightest smile tugged at the corners of his lips and was gone almost as quickly, or had she imagined it?

He ran a hand over the back of his neck—he'd had a haircut, and she liked the way it looked—and got a kind of sheepish look on his face. "I—um, well, I shouldn't have come in here so late last night. And I certainly shouldn't have done what I did afterward."

Bethany held his gaze. "Kiss me, you mean?"

"That's what I mean, all right."

Thank goodness for the baby, because she could hide her face while pretending to center the baby in her lap and zip up her little playsuit.

"I know I should apologize," Colt said. "But I don't intend to."

She looked up, saw that he was serious.

"And," he went on, "I hope we can go on as before. That you didn't take offense, I mean."

"I—I didn't," she said. What's more, she wanted him to kiss her again. The realization knocked her for a loop, made it difficult to maintain her composure.

He spared her a sharp nod. "Good. I'll sleep in the barn from now on if you like. Except that would leave you to get up with Alyssa when she wakes up, like we said before."

"You may sleep in the barn or over here. Either will be fine." She could have kicked herself for the way she sounded—so old-maid priggish. But what to say when she was majorly confused about the way she felt? She knew she shouldn't encourage familiarity—she *knew* it—but these circumstances were unusual, the situation was different from any she had experienced before, and she was so off balance because of the way things were going! Now, with Colt in the room, with his eyes boring into her, it was as if she were back in the upstairs hall last night, feeling his lips upon hers, his strong body pressed against her entire length.

"You mean you don't mind if I stay in the guest room? You're not just bein' polite?" The eagerness in his tone surprised her. And the pleasure, too.

"I mean it. That apartment over the barn gets hot and uncomfortable on some of these nights. Alyssa needs more attention than I have energy to give."

"I won't be goin' to Pug's anymore," Colt said. "I'm not a drinkin' man."

She didn't ask him what had driven him to go there last night, and she didn't want to know.

She stood up, holding Alyssa close. "All right. I understand." She didn't, but that was beside the point. Right now all she wanted was for him not to be looking at her like that anymore. She wanted him out of her kitchen.

"I've got plans," he said suddenly. "I told you about them. I won't do anything that jeopardizes my future. Oh, and before I forget—I bought this for Alyssa in town yesterday." He retrieved the package he'd tossed on the table.

"I can't open it while I'm holding her. Can it wait?"

"I'll be glad to do the honors," Colt said. Bethany watched while he tore open the package to reveal a fuzzy yellow toy duck. "It winds up," he said, twisting the key in the side of it. The duck's neck twisted back and forth, and it played "Singin' in the Rain."

"I guess the song about rain is just wishful thinkin', considerin' the drought," Colt said. Alyssa was fascinated, her eyes following the duck's head as it moved.

"There's no rain in the latest forecast. We sure could use some." Talking about the weather was safe and distracted her from Colt's presence.

"Here, you better take this." Colt handed Bethany the duck and turned to go. A glance at the clock over the stove told her it was time for Eddie to set supper on the table over at the Neilsons', and for a moment, Bethany regretted that she wasn't in the habit of eating her evening meal with the others.

"Thanks for the duck," Bethany called out, thanking Colt because Alyssa couldn't. Colt barely acknowledged her with a nod, and Bethany noticed that Jesse James joined him for the walk to the foreman's house. They were getting thick, those two. Colt swore he'd have Jesse cutting cattle before long.

As the duck ran out of music, Alyssa spit up on Bethany's jersey. "Uh-oh," Bethany said. "Guess I'd better go change clothes."

Bethany took Alyssa upstairs and settled her in the cradle with the duck for company. Alyssa's eyelids drooped, her long lashes shadowing her plump cheeks, and Bethany stood and watched her for a few minutes, thinking that she'd never seen a more endearing child.

It was while Bethany was changing into a clean blouse that the idea sprang into her mind full-grown.

She would start a horse training business like Colt wanted! They could do it right here on the Banner-B.

Why, she had the pasture, she had the barn, she had the corrals. She wasn't making much money on her cattle, and the training school for horses would be a new direction for the Banner-B, one that might prove profitable. Furthermore, then Colt would be less inclined to pick up and leave.

But as soon as the thought took shape in her mind, as soon as she realized that it was possible to start a horse training program at the Banner-B, she was caught up short. How could she do this? It wasn't fair to Colt to bind him to her in that way. If he wanted to go to be with Marcy, there was nothing she could do about it. Nothing.

And also, Colt might turn her down. He might not like the idea at all. That would hurt.

There'd been enough pain in her life to last a lifetime. She sure didn't need any more.

AFTER BETHANY FIRST thought about starting a horse training school and just as quickly put it out of her mind, life at the Banner-B got more complicated. The next couple of weeks were busy with rounding up cattle and shipping them to the feed lots, all during a record-breaking heat wave and in the midst of a drought that wouldn't quit. The operation taxed their limited resources, and Bethany, Colt, Dita and Frisco dragged themselves off to bed every night shortly after darkness fell, only to rise again before the sky was even light.

Alyssa began to sleep longer and longer during the night, but she still woke up early in the morning for her first feeding of the day. Colt was the one who got up with her for feedings and diaper changes, and he never complained. True to his word, he didn't come home late again.

Instead he spent his evenings in the barn until Alyssa's bedtime, and then he would show up to give the baby her final feeding and prepare her for the night. Bethany, who usually spent the last hours before bedtime in her office, grew accustomed to seeing the big cowboy in the kitchen rocker with Alyssa in his arms, and she often found herself feeling slightly jealous when Alyssa smiled at Colt. She never stayed jealous for long, though. Alyssa, sweet and sunny-natured, had plenty of smiles for all of them.

Her smiles particularly charmed Frisco. The ranch foreman took to stopping by to see Alyssa every morning before Loreen arrived, sometimes giving her the first bottle of the day.

"We'll have you changing diapers before too long," Colt jokingly told him, but Frisco only shook his head. "Seems to me I'm doing as much as I can do for this here baby," he said seriously, but Colt only chuckled. Bethany found Frisco's attachment to Alyssa rather charming, but she wouldn't ever tell him so. It would only get his back up, make him think that she thought he was getting too soft in his old age.

One morning after the cattle had been shipped, Dita showed up at the house with Frisco.

"We're having a picnic today," she announced. "Twelve o'clock over by the creek."

"A picnic?" Bethany said, thrown off balance. "I thought we were going to burn thorns off the cactus in the High pasture." Sometimes they did this during a drought so that cattle could eat cactus; it provided more moisture in their diet.

"Them cactus will still be there tomorrow," Frisco said. "We've all worked hard, and Eddie says we need a day off. He's going to fry chicken for the picnic."

"Sounds good to me," said Colt, who was sitting at the kitchen table scarfing down bacon and eggs that he'd cooked for Bethany and himself earlier. "What time?"

"I'd say around noon. Bring Loreen and Alyssa, and maybe some bug repellent," Dita said. With a cheery wave, she departed for the barn.

Bethany spent the morning trying to track down the blacksmith for Sidewinder, who needed to be shod. Colt was busy until noon working with the horse, and by the time he arrived at the creek for the picnic, the food was already spread on the table.

"I can't remember the last time we did this," Bethany said.

"Before I got sick last time," Frisco told her. He was setting out plates and cups.

"Speaking of which, I wish you'd sit down," Dita said, fussing at him. "Let me do that." She went and took the cups and plates from her husband, shooing him off to a lawn chair that had been set up at the head of the table.

Loreen was sitting on a blanket spread nearby, and Alyssa was on the blanket, too. Colt eased himself down beside them and plucked a blade of grass that he used to tickle Alyssa's cheek. She responded with a gratifying coo. Colt commenced making funny faces to amuse her until Loreen broke into giggles.

"Here comes Eddie with the chicken," Bethany said, clearing a space for it on the table.

"Hey, Eddie, that chicken sure smells good," Loreen called as he approached.

"It's delicious," Eddie said. "And what's that other word you said last time I made it, Bethany?"

"Scrumptious," she told him. "I said it was the most scrumptious fried chicken I'd ever eaten."

"I bet you make great potato salad, too," Colt said to Eddie.

"Oh, I sure do. I even put green olives in it and everything. Come over here and eat some of it."

They all helped themselves from the bounty on the table: chicken, potato salad, deviled eggs, watermelon pickles that Bethany had made last year, and sweetened iced tea. Dita produced a cherry pie for dessert, and after they had eaten so much food, no one felt inclined to move around.

"I guess I won't be working too much this afternoon," Frisco said. He was holding Alyssa, and Eddie, looking totally charmed by the baby, was dangling a rattle in front of her eyes.

"That's good," Bethany said. "If it takes a picnic to slow you down, I say we should have more of them."

"Now that's a really good idea," Eddie said.

Loreen produced a Frisbee. "Anyone for a quick game of Frisbee?" she asked.

Eddie followed her into the clearing, and with some coaxing, so did Colt. They began to toss the Frisbee around, and finally, after much persuading, Frisco agreed to play, too.

Dita and Bethany packed up the food while keeping an eye on Alyssa dozing in her carrier seat. "I wish he wouldn't exert himself," Dita said with a worried glance in Frisco's direction.

"As long as he doesn't get overtired, I think he'll do fine," Bethany said.

"Who will do fine?" Colt said. He'd dropped out of the game to get something cool to drink.

"Frisco," said Bethany.

Colt glanced back over his shoulder. The game was progressing with much whooping and hollering. "They're having a good time," he said.

"I don't want anything to happen to him," Dita said with a worried look.

"Frisco had a mild heart attack a year or so ago," Bethany explained in an aside to Colt. "We've all been concerned about him."

Dita poured a glass of tea and carried it out to Frisco,

who paused to drink it. Meanwhile, Loreen and Eddie carried on the Frisbee game.

"Look at them," Colt said suddenly. "Dita and Frisco, I mean."

"I know. Isn't it sweet?"

Colt saw that Frisco grasped his wife's hand for a moment and squeezed. He didn't think he'd ever seen anyone look at a man more adoringly than Dita looked at her husband, and for a moment he felt a pang of envy.

"I wonder how they do it," he said before he'd thought.

Bethany treated him to a blank look.

"I mean, I wonder how they manage to be so in love after all this time."

Bethany smiled wistfully. "She's his second wife, you know. His first wife died a long time ago."

"I knew that Frisco was much older than Dita."

"He was forty-three when he married Dita. She was only twenty when he brought her here to the Banner-B. Everyone was kind of surprised. They thought he'd remain a bachelor after he nursed his first wife through her illness."

"He and his first wife had no children?"

"No, and they'd been married quite a while."

Dita kissed her husband on the cheek and came back to the clearing. "Well, I can't talk him into quitting, so I guess I'll just have to put up with that old man's shenanigans," she said affectionately.

"I'll talk to him about slowing down again," Bethany said. "For instance, there's no need for him to be riding around on that bulldozer tearing up mesquite like he was the other day."

"You can't make him take it easy. I know, I've tried." With a long-suffering sigh, Dita hoisted the picnic basket. "Guess I'll head back to the house. You two going to stick around here?"

"For a while," Bethany said. "We'll keep Alyssa with us." The baby was snoozing in her child seat, oblivious to everyone.

After Dita left, Colt went to the blanket and sat down, leaning back against a tree. "Come down here," he said, patting the blanket beside him. After a slight hesitation, Bethany lowered herself beside him and sat resting her weight on one arm, her face partly in sun, partly in shade.

"I think Dita worries about Frisco's getting so sick that someone has to take care of him. She doesn't want him to be a burden to me," Bethany said after a time.

Colt brushed a bothersome gnat away from Alyssa's face. "She worries about you? If Frisco got that sick, it wouldn't be easy for Dita, either."

"Dita isn't worried about herself. She says it's in the contract, that when you marry someone it's for better or for worse. I know she thinks about Frisco's taking care of his first wife all those long months when she was sick. If it happens that Dita's got to take care of him, well, that's the breaks. Of course she knows I'd help her."

Colt digested this for a moment. "You wouldn't have to, Bethany."

"I couldn't have made it this long without Frisco's expertise in running the Banner-B," Bethany said quietly. "I owe him."

He picked up her hand and inspected it, running a finger over the calluses. "Stop it," Bethany said, and she tried to pull her hand away.

"What if I don't want to stop?"

"You're being silly," she said, but she stopped trying to pull away and sat regarding him quizzically.

"I happen to think your hand is beautiful," he said. "Especially since I know it shows signs of hard work that you wouldn't have had to do if you hadn't promised Justin, and decided to take care of Frisco and Dita and Eddie, and—"

Now she did pull her hand away, looking confused. "I don't want Loreen and Eddie to see you holding my hand."

"How about if they'd seen me kiss you?" he teased. "How about if they'd been watchin' last night?"

"We shouldn't be talking about that," Bethany said primly.

Colt laughed. "I like talking about it."

"Well, I don't. And you've got a strange idea of beauty if you think my hand is beautiful." Bethany tried to get up, but he hooked an arm around her shoulders.

"For your information, I can find beauty in lots of things. What you told me about Dita makes me see how beautiful she is."

"Because she said she wants to take care of Frisco if he gets sick?"

Colt nodded. He was truly touched that someone could care about another person so much that she would care *for* that person during times that were hard. In his life, there hadn't been any people who honored commitments like that.

"And you're beautiful, too, Bethany. Not just externally, but inside as well." It was the first time he'd ever paid anyone a compliment that went beyond the superficial. He hadn't ever been able to express his feelings so clearly before this, nor had he ever wanted to.

Now Bethany truly looked confused. "I think maybe

I'll go join the Frisbee game," she said, and this time he let her scramble to her feet without trying to stop her.

"I meant it," he called after her. "You're a beautiful woman, Bethany Burke." And she was, with that bountiful blond hair and those cool eyes as blue as the sea and a figure that never failed to put him in mind of something he'd gone without for much too long.

Bethany didn't look back, and she kept on walking.

From the way she was acting, Colt figured she didn't want to hear what he thought about her. Yet.

Chapter Seven

It was one evening a week or so after she'd shipped her cattle to the feed lot that Bethany had a chance to pore over the figures she'd posted in her records. As usual at the Banner-B, there were more funds going out than there were coming in.

After she wrote a few big checks, Bethany closed her checkbook and breathed a big sigh. The Banner-B was still hanging on—but barely. She had enough money left to cover Colt's salary after paying other bills, but she could forget repairs to the barn. It needed painting, and termites had taken up residence in the door frame of the feed room. Frisco said if the termites stopped holding hands, the barn would fall down.

What she needed was a surefire way to raise funds. She buried her head in her hands, trying to think of some way to accomplish it. She'd already sold most of the valuable antiques out of the ranch house, and she wouldn't be selling any stock for a while. The only thing she could think of was to sell her diamond engagement ring, and she hesitated to get rid of that.

Nevertheless, she'd better consider it. She reached into the back of the middle desk drawer and withdrew a green box from the compartment where she'd always kept it. She held it in the palm of her hand for a long time before she opened it. From its nest of velvet, the diamond solitaire winked back at her, shimmering through her tears.

Justin had been so proud when he gave her this ring that night in Wichita. They'd been out to dinner and were walking in the garden behind the small house where she'd lived with her roommates, and he'd carefully led her to a small rosebush that he'd planted for her a few months before. They'd been admiring the large pink blossoms, and suddenly she'd looked down and seen the ring tied to one of the branches with a white satin ribbon. She'd reached with trembling hands to untie the loop, and Justin had scooped the ring up and placed it on the third finger of her left hand.

"Of course I'll marry you!" she had cried as he swept her up in his arms and whirled her around the quiet, sweet-smelling garden beneath a moon so fine and full that it hurt her eyes to look at it.

"I'll do everything I can to make you happy," Justin had sworn, and she had cried with joy until he said that if she really wanted to water that rosebush, they should go get a watering can, not try to drown it in her tears.

And they had been happy throughout their brief marriage. She didn't want to sell this ring. It had great sentimental value, and she could hardly bear to part with it.

"Bethany," said Colt from the doorway. She hadn't heard him come downstairs; she'd thought he was with Alyssa.

She swiped at her eyes, hoping he hadn't noticed that she was crying. It didn't work; of course he noticed. He always noticed everything.

"What's wrong?" He was across the small room in two strides.

"I—I—" Her first impulse was to deny that anything was amiss, but he'd already seen the tears.

"You can tell me," he said encouragingly, and from the way he said it, from the kindness that he displayed, she knew she could talk to him without embarrassment.

She slid the ring over her thumb, considering. Colt was looking at it with a great deal of curiosity, and she knew there was no point in telling him less than the truth. Anyway, Colt knew the situation at the Banner-B, how there was never enough money and how hard it had been to keep going all this time.

"I think I'm going to sell my engagement ring," she said, trying to infuse her words with a dispassionate briskness that she certainly didn't feel.

His eyes fell to the diamond, then rose back to her face. "Is it the bills? Is that why?"

"Yes. I've been trying to avoid reality, and it's time to face up. I don't need a diamond ring, but I do need to feed my stock."

Colt sank down on the couch and stared at the floor, elbows on his knees. He seemed taken aback.

"I should be able to get a good price for it," she went on. "It's an almost full-carat diamond, a classic brilliant cut." She thought she sounded sensible and matter-of-fact, not looking for sympathy. She didn't want Colt McClure to think of her as some poor unfortunate pathetic creature who was floundering around, not knowing what to do.

Colt lifted his eyes to hers. "You don't have to sell your ring, Bethany," he said gently.

"I've made up my mind. I'll see about it the first of the week." She slid the ring from her thumb and inserted it into its velvet slot, then shut the box with a brisk click.

"No, you don't understand. What I'm sayin' is that I've got some money. You can borrow it, pay me back when you can."

"I can't borrow from you, Colt." She dismissed this idea with the swiftness it deserved.

"Of course you can. Remember what you told me a while back, Bethany? That when one of us has a problem, the others pitch in to help?"

But she hadn't been looking for help. She'd only wanted to talk. Agitated, Bethany stood up and paced to the other side of the room. "I didn't mean—"

"You didn't mean that you could depend on anyone else, is that it? It's okay for everyone to expect you to take care of them, but you won't let anyone take care of you?" Colt's eyes flashed with anger.

"I promised Justin—"

Colt leaped to his feet. He came to where she stood, his eyes blazing. "You promised Justin too damned much, but in my opinion, he wouldn't have expected you to handle everything on your own! From what I can tell from Frisco and Dita and Eddie, he was a wonderful man who took good care of you. He would have been the first to tell you to take help wherever you can get it."

"I—"

Colt grasped her arms, pulled her roughly toward him. "You ride the herd, you put food on the table, you hire and fire and you even, for cryin' out loud, swamp out stalls. I can see that you don't cotton to borrowin', but if I can do one thing to help you, let me do it."

He was so forceful that she sagged against him, unable to look up into his furious face. She didn't understand his being angry with her—what had she done to deserve it other than do her duty as she saw fit? To her embarrassment, her eyes again clouded with tears and she began sobbing into Colt's shirtfront, utterly unable to stop herself. So much for impressing him with her calm and judgment; her crying was belly-deep, a manifestation of her pain and rage and frustration over her circumstances. She didn't pull away as he slowly wrapped his arms around her and gently rubbed her back. She inhaled the warm masculine scent of him, not minding at all when he smoothed her hair back from her face the way he might have done with a small child.

"Go ahead and bust loose," he said soothingly in the vicinity of her ear. "Cry all you want. I'm waterproof."

She couldn't help herself; a little giggle hitched itself onto a sob.

"You can laugh if you want, too. I don't care what you do." His arms around her were strong, the muscles taut. She hiccuped.

Colt chuckled and held her away at arms' length. She reached up a hand and brushed away tears. She hiccuped again, and he pulled a handkerchief from his pocket. "Here," he said. "You can mop up if you like."

She did, and when she went back to her desk chair, he sat down on the couch and waited patiently. She regretted breaking down in front of Colt, but on the other hand, it felt good not to have to keep up the pretense of being on top of things. Sometimes she felt worthless, as if she weren't doing her job to the best of her ability. Other times she felt confused. Most times she felt tired. No one knew any of this. She was supposed to be a fountain of strength. People depended on her, not the other way around.

She crumpled his handkerchief up in her hand. It had felt so good to be held by him, to be bolstered by his strength and good humor.

"Colt," she said, unsure if this was a good idea. "I have something I've been wanting to discuss with you."

Colt shifted in his seat. "All right. I'm listenin'."

"Remember how you told me about your dream of opening a training facility for people who want to learn about horses?"

He nodded. She could tell that his mind was racing as he tried to figure out where she was headed.

"Well, you could do that here."

"Here? At the Banner-B?" He sounded flabbergasted and looked totally taken by surprise.

"You'd pay rent. I wouldn't have to take a loan from you. The money you pay me would bring in some income right away. There are plenty of extra stalls in the barn where the horses could stay."

He looked as if he couldn't believe the offer. "You mean it? You'd let me do that?"

"I hope you will."

Colt stood up. "I never thought—I never dreamed I'd ever have a chance like this." He walked to the end of the room, then wheeled to stare at her. "Are you sure? Have you thought this thing over?"

"Yes." She watched him steadily.

"I'd have to make improvements to the barn, paint it, build a solid wall on the trainin' pen."

"All those things need doing, but do you have the money to do them? I wouldn't be able to help out."

"Sure, I've got the money I was goin' to let you borrow."

"Colt, I hate to ask, but where'd you get it?" She

might be getting too personal, she knew that, but she felt that she had to inquire.

"Saved it," he said. "All my life." His eyes met hers honestly.

"You wouldn't mind putting money into the Banner-B?" She asked it haltingly because the repairs would require a considerable investment.

Colt appeared to think about this. "I'd be investin' in myself, wouldn't I? In my future. It's what I've always planned to do."

"It's a chance for you, true, but you know it would help me tremendously, Colt."

"If we decide to go ahead with this, I'd need to get the word out, let everyone know what I'm doin' here. I have some people who could help."

"What kind of people?"

"People who have seen the results of my trainin' methods. There's a large racing stable in Kentucky, I met the owner once. He wanted to know how to teach his trainers my method. I told him I'd work with them, but I never followed up on it. I could get some students in here, let them learn as I train the horses who need help." His eyes lit with excitement, and it was impossible not to soak up his enthusiasm.

She'd already anticipated the problems. "If you had students, they'd need a place to live. The bunkhouse isn't livable in its present state. There's no hotel in Gompers, not even a motel."

Colt answered eagerly. "I heard some talk in the barber shop about two sisters who live in a big old house on the highway. They want to turn it into a bed-and-breakfast."

"That would be Miss Maudie and Miss Claretta Truett. Their family has owned that house since time out of mind, and they're scrabbling around for ways to hang on to it."

"So how many rooms would they have in that house?" Colt was calculating in his head how many students he could muster for the first go-round.

"Maybe seven bedrooms."

"I reckon that's big enough for now. They could house my students."

"Could you bring the Truetts enough business to make it worth their while?"

"I believe so." His mind raced ahead, getting hold of this thing and running with it. "The stable in Kentucky might account for several people who want to learn my methods. That would be enough to get me off the ground." He knew that news would spread by word of mouth, one trainer talking to another. No reason why he couldn't expand after a while.

Bethany looked encouraged. "Let's do it, Colt," she said. "Let's go ahead with it."

Colt was about to answer in the affirmative when they were interrupted by a long wail coming from upstairs. The wail became a series of cries ascending into piercing shrieks.

"Alyssa!" Bethany said, jumping to her feet. The baby seldom woke up so soon after being put in her cradle for the night, and she never screamed quite so loudly.

They rushed for the stairs, thoughts of the training school replaced by concern for Alyssa. Colt was right behind Bethany when she reached the room where Alyssa had been put to bed less than an hour before. "I don't know what she could be cryin' about. I fed her before I came in to talk to you."

Alyssa was doubled up in the cradle, her face red as

a beet as she let out some of the most heartrending screams Bethany had ever heard in her life, bar none. Bethany picked her up, shushing her, cuddling her, but Alyssa only screamed louder.

"Something's wrong," Bethany said over the din. "She usually doesn't cry like this." She considered that she had, over the past weeks, become an expert in types of crying. There was fussy crying, and there was angry crying, and there was hungry crying. This seemed to be none of the above.

"Sounds like a calf bawlin' in pain," Colt said, peering down at Alyssa in the pale circle of light from the lamp on the dresser.

"That's it, I think," Bethany replied, joggling Alyssa. "She's hurting."

Their eyes met over the baby's head. The idea of Alyssa's being in pain hurt them both.

"I got a baby book in town when I bought that musical duck," Colt said. He reached into the drawer of the nightstand and withdrew a small paperback volume. "Don't rightly know what to look under."

"She's eaten, so she won't be hungry." She checked Alyssa's diaper. "Dry as a bone."

"I'm looking under 'crying,'" Colt said. He sat down on the bed in the circle of light from the bedside lamp. "It says maybe she didn't get all the air up when I burped her."

"I'll burp her again." Bethany tried this, but Alyssa went on wailing.

"Okay, so maybe that isn't it. Let's see, it says here to see if the baby looks sick. What do you think?" He laid the book down and came over to look at Alyssa, a worried frown pleating the skin between his eyes.

"She doesn't seem sick to me. I mean, sure, she's got a red face, but that's from all this crying."

Colt laid a gentle hand across Alyssa's cheek. "Yep, I agree with that. All right, I'll see what else it could be." He returned to the bed, sat down again and thumbed through a few pages. "I bet it's colic," he said.

"What's the cure?"

"I know how to treat a horse with colic, but a kid? I've got no clue."

"Read what it says," Bethany said. Alyssa's legs were drawn up, and her caterwauling was earsplitting.

Colt riffled through pages until he found what he was looking for. He marked the line with his forefinger as he read out loud. "It says here that if they've got colic, it can start half an hour or so after a feedin'. That's what Alyssa did. It says sometimes you don't know why a baby gets colic."

"Forget all that—what can we do about it?" asked Bethany, who was almost at her wit's end with the noise. She hated to hear Alyssa crying, couldn't stand the idea of her being in pain. She would have done almost anything to stop it, anything that would help.

Colt read on. "We could lay her in a stomach-down position on a hot water bottle. Do you have one?"

"I'll look. Here, maybe you'd better take over." She deposited Alyssa in Colt's arms and left him rocking the baby back and forth while she ran for her sanity and something that would help.

It took Bethany a while to think about where she'd seen the hot water bottle last. In the end she had to run over and borrow one from Dita, who said that yes, it did sound like Alyssa might have colic, and did Bethany want her to come over and help? Bethany told her that she didn't think so, at least not yet, and she ran back over to the house. Colt was walking the floor with the howling baby draped over his shoulder as Bethany filled the water bottle at the bathroom sink and hurried back into the guest room.

"Here, let's try this."

Alyssa, her little face scrunched into a knot of misery, was crying louder than ever.

"Nothing wrong with this kid's lungs," Colt said, his voice rising to be heard over the racket.

Bethany sat down on the bed and set the hot water bottle on a folded blanket in her lap. Colt gently eased the baby onto the cushion this made, asking anxiously, "Are you sure it's not too hot?"

"It's barely warm," she said. "I think it'll be okay."

Alyssa kept crying, although after a while her wails seemed to be losing their edge. Soon the baby was emitting a tired sob only once in a while. Colt massaged her little back, and after a while the sobs tapered off.

"She's asleep," murmured Bethany.

"Will you look at that," Colt said in wonder. "She's dropped right off."

"I don't dare move," Bethany said. "I might set her off again if I jostle her around."

"Mmm," Colt said. "Maybe we should have put her in her cradle."

"Oh, I don't think so. I like holding her."

Colt kept rubbing Alyssa's back, and the baby sighed.

Bethany thought about Colt's kindness to her earlier. She angled a look at him. "You've had your hands full tonight with weeping women."

He smiled, a twinkle in his eyes. "As Frisco might say, 'It don't make no never mind.'"

In that moment Bethany wondered how she could have ever thought him hard. Sometimes you had to get to know a person, that's all there was to it.

But *was* that all there was to this? Perhaps she'd only grown accustomed to Colt, used to his ways. Or possibly she had incorrectly perceived him as harsh or hard at first when he had actually been neither.

They sat in silence for a time. It was companionable, this sitting up with the baby when everyone else at the ranch was asleep.

Colt took a pillow from the head of the bed and wedged it behind Bethany. "Looks like you'd be more comfortable if you had support for your back," he said.

She smiled her thanks.

"Want me to go? Leave you alone with her?" Colt looked reluctant, as if he hadn't really wanted to ask.

"This is your room," she managed to say. "As long as Alyssa is here, I mean."

He rose and walked to the window, where he stood looking out at the oak trees in front. The cricket that had disturbed her sleep last night must have connected with his significant other, because the house was quiet and still around them.

"You know, Bethany, I want to tell you something."

"Mmm?" she said. She smoothed Alyssa's gown, wondering if the baby was finally asleep.

"I grew up in foster homes," Colt said abruptly. "That's why I wouldn't let Alyssa go to one."

Bethany quickly lifted her head. She hadn't expected such a revelation. She studied Colt's back, noting the rigidity of his neck, the tension it implied. "So that's why you triggered when I mentioned foster care for Alyssa on the night she arrived?" she ventured.

"Damn right. It's not a good way to grow up."

"You must have had a hard time."

"You better believe it." He turned so she could see his face, and she was surprised at the anguish she read in his down-turned lips, the tic above one eye.

"What was it like, Colt?"

"It was awful. That's the only way I know to describe it. Broken promises from one home to the next. When I was six, one family wanted to adopt me, and then they decided not to. So I went on to the next home, where they'd promised me my own room. I ended up sharin' a room with two other kids, older boys who liked kicking me in the stomach for fun. After I was removed from there for my own safety, the social worker promised I could live in a group home, then reneged and put me in another foster home even worse than the others. And so on."

"I thought somebody screened foster homes."

He walked back to the bed. "They're supposed to, but you have to wonder how some of them were ever approved. There was the place where they locked me in a shed for misbehavin' and passed my food through a hole in the door once a day. And the house where kids weren't allowed to talk at mealtimes. One of the worst was the home where they kept us home from school to work on the farm. I missed most of fifth grade because the school authorities didn't bother to check on my absences."

Bethany tried not to think about the sad and lonely little boy that Colt must have been. "Colt, doesn't it bother you to talk about it?"

"I don't mind. Could be I need to talk. Back then, I made animals my friends, learned how to communicate with them. So it wasn't all bad. Those foster-care experiences made me a strong person, gave me special abilities."

"You developed those abilities on your own, Colt. You should be proud of yourself."

He let out a rueful laugh. "Well, I'm not. But I have a chance now—a chance to make something of myself. I'm not sure we actually finished our discussion earlier tonight. You sure you don't want to change your mind about that trainin' school?"

She didn't have to think long. "I say we might as well go for it," she told him.

For a moment he looked elated. The elation was supplanted by a sincerity that she knew wasn't faked. "I told you about my childhood and how I grew up because I'm grateful to you, Bethany. I don't want you to think I'm doin' you a great big favor by savin' the ranch. I swear you'll never be sorry. Never."

She didn't think she would be. She trusted him, knew that not only she would benefit, but lots of horses and trainers as well. She smiled her confidence at Colt, and he grinned back.

He leaned over the bed, one arm on each side of her. He was so close that all she would have to do is move slightly forward and her forehead would be resting on his chest.

"You know what I like about you, Bethany?"

She shook her head, unable to speak in that moment and unsure why.

"You keep your promises."

She thought about their previous conversation when he'd tried to convince her that her promise to Justin was no longer important. She swallowed. "Isn't that slightly contradictory?" she managed to say.

He straightened and stood looking down at her.

"Maybe it sounds that way, I don't know," he said slowly. "For the first time in my life, I've met someone who thinks a promise is important."

"Don't you? Think promises are meant to be kept, I mean?"

"I never did before, but you've given me something to think about." He paused, clearly in better spirits now. "Something else I'm thinkin' about is that I could use a snack. How about you?"

It had been several hours since supper, and perhaps they were in for a long night if Alyssa woke in pain again. "Sure," she said, glad for the lightening of Colt's mood.

"Well, what do you say we celebrate our optimism about the new trainin' school? There are cupcakes that Eddie made in the kitchen. How about if I go downstairs and see what I can rustle up?"

When Colt came back, he carried a tray laden with goodies; in addition to the cupcakes, there was a hunk of Gouda cheese and some crackers, a dish of orange-roasted pecans and half a ham sandwich.

"It's not much of a feast, but it will have to do."

Bethany had to laugh at the idea of this motley assortment of leftovers becoming a feast, but she accepted her share of the sandwich, and Colt sat cross-legged at the head of the bed as they both munched away.

"The little one is sure sleepin' soundly now," Colt observed. As if on cue, Alyssa's mouth worked as if she were sucking on a nipple, but she didn't awaken.

"Do you think we should put her in the cradle?" Colt wanted to know.

Bethany shook her head. "I'm afraid it would wake her," she said. So instead of laying Alyssa back in the cradle, they propped themselves up with pillows and waited for her to be ready for her next feeding.

There was only one lamp lit, and it cast a pool of pale yellow light across the bed. Bethany closed her eyes and let Colt talk about his plans. She couldn't help but feel that everything would fall into place when she listened to him; it had been a long time since she'd felt so encouraged about the ranch.

Bethany dozed off somewhere in between telling Colt what color she wanted him to paint the barn and his plans for advertising for business. Colt watched as she fell asleep, bemused. He understood why Bethany was so tired. He was tired, too. He felt emotionally drained after having told her things about himself that he'd never discussed with anyone. Still, he hadn't revealed everything about his life. But what he'd told her had been enough to convey his gratitude.

All along he'd thought that if Bethany really knew what he was like, she wouldn't like him at all. He knew she still thought Alyssa was his. Well, he wasn't ready to spill that part of his story. But, he thought as he dozed off, the odd thing was that instead of building a wall between them, it was as if his revealing his miserable childhood had broken down barriers. At one time he would have thought that revealing anything about himself would have driven them further apart than they'd been in the first place. Funny, he thought as he became drowsy and eventually drifted off, maybe relationships didn't work that way at all. Who would have thought it?

WHEN BETHANY WOKE UP the next morning, the first slender beams of sunlight were filtering through the tree branches outside. Her body was curled protectively around Alyssa's, and the baby had slept through the night. As for Colt, he lay sleeping on his back beside them, and Bethany's hand was tucked protectively in his.

Gently, so as not to wake him, Bethany withdrew her hand from Colt's. She studied him in the pale half light that penetrated the curtains, wondering at the stroke of good fortune that had brought him to the Banner-B. They were all better off for his presence here. The new training school would provide a much-needed shot in the arm for the ranch, and she couldn't wait to tell the Neilsons about it.

Speaking of the Neilsons, she heard Jesse barking over near their house. Bethany swung her feet to the floor. She didn't want to wake Colt or the baby, and she was tiptoeing out of the room when she heard the hum of an automobile engine approaching on the driveway.

Colt heard it, too. He sat up suddenly and blinked, first at Bethany, then at the sleeping baby.

"Who's comin'?" he asked in a low voice. Alyssa stirred, then opened her eyes, too.

Bethany went to the window and lifted aside the curtain so she could look out.

"It's Mott," she said. The all-too-familiar black pickup truck swung halfway around the circle in front of the house before pulling to a stop below.

Alyssa made little smacking noises with her mouth and started to fuss.

"What's he doin' here?"

Bethany dropped the curtain. "The usual. Don't worry, I'll deal with him. I'm used to it." She glanced into the mirror over the dresser and tried to fluff her hair without much success. "I look a fright," she said.

"You look right smart," Colt said. He picked the baby up and shushed her.

"I'll go down to the kitchen and get the formula ready while I fend off Mott. You go ahead and change Alyssa's diaper."

Colt stood up. "That I will do. She's mighty hungry this morning, aren't you, darlin'?"

Bethany left Colt, marveling at how easy their relationship had become. It didn't seem at all strange to be getting up from the same bed where they had both slept, or to be discussing the mundane details of child care with him. There was a spring in her step as she made her way downstairs and into the kitchen.

The bark of Mott's boot heels on boards signaled his presence on the porch. Bethany went to the door and opened it. The hinges were rusty; they squealed. Distractedly she made a mental note to ask Colt to oil them.

Mott smirked at her through the screen. "Good morning," he said. Mott had a curiously high voice, and Justin had once said that he sounded like a cartoon character. But there wasn't anything funny about him or about his designs on the Banner-B.

"There's nothing good about a morning that starts out with you on my porch. What do you want, Mott?" She glared at him. His sparse hair, the color of clothes-dryer lint, was worn in a ponytail, and strands of it straggled across his forehead under his hat. But it was Mott's eyes that Bethany hated most—they were like two chunks of pale amber and glittered with a feral light.

"I like me a feisty woman," he said, ignoring the question she'd asked.

"I said, what do you want?"

"I guess you could say I just want to talk to you."

"We have nothing to discuss." Bethany turned her back on him and went to the counter where she opened a can of formula.

"I thought maybe I could offer some help. I hear you've got a small mouth to feed around here." Uninvited, Mott opened the screen door and stepped inside.

"I didn't say you could come in. And how many mouths I have to feed is of no interest to you," she told him.

"Anything that happens on the Banner-B is of interest to me, since I plan to own it someday."

"Over my dead body," Bethany shot back.

Mott's eyes lingered pointedly on her breasts, then moved downward. "Your body might be a good topic of conversation, and it's very much alive. You wanna show me—"

"Just a damn minute," said Colt behind her. "You got no call to talk to her like that." Bethany swung her head around and saw Colt, the baby in his arms, standing in the doorway. His eyes were as hard as gray agate. He glowered at Mott.

Mott seemed slightly taken aback at the sight of Colt but recovered right away. He looked from Bethany to Colt, then back to Bethany. She was conscious of how she must look to Mott—her shirt rumpled, her hair a tangle, and eyes still bleary with sleep. And Colt—he wore an overnight stubble of beard, and he was barefoot.

Bethany could almost see Mott adding two and two and getting—well, two. Two as in a pair. Two as in sleeping together. Two as in he'd better back off and reassess the situation. "So that's the way it is," Mott said as understanding dawned in his eyes.

Very carefully, Colt set Alyssa in her baby seat and

strapped her in. Then he walked up behind Bethany and stood close enough that she felt the heat radiating from his body.

"Look, Mott, why don't you just get along home? Save us a whole bunch of trouble if you did." Colt spoke in a deceptively slow drawl, but Bethany could feel the tension in him coiled tight as a spring.

Mott laughed. It was a long, hyena-like laugh, knowing and mocking all at the same time.

"Seems like Beth here got herself more than a ranch hand when you came along."

Colt stepped around Bethany. His jaw was working, a vein at his temple throbbing. In that moment she knew that something in him was about to give way to the anger that he was only barely holding in check.

"You don't need to get mixed up in this," Bethany said to Colt quickly in an attempt to defuse the situation.

"Maybe I want to. Maybe someone should teach Mr. Findley here a lesson." Colt's fists clenched and unclenched as if they couldn't wait to grab Mott around the neck and squeeze.

Bethany would have liked nothing better than to watch Mott's eyes bulging out of his head as Colt throttled him, but the last thing she needed was a fight on her hands and the ensuing rumors it would cause. She lost no time in stepping between the two men.

"You'd better leave, Mott."

Mott's beady bright eyes were cold. "I came to talk to you, not him. I'll be back sometime when your good friend here isn't around. Maybe you can show me a little of what you been showing him."

She ignored the insult. "Get off my land, Mott. And don't come back."

"That's exactly what I'll be saying to you one of these days," Mott said.

Before she knew what was happening, Colt had shoved her out of the way and had grasped the front of Mott's shirt in his white-knuckled fists. He spoke with barely contained fury. "You heard what she said. Get out if you know what's good for you."

Bethany was prepared to wrench the two of them apart when Mott laughed low in his throat. He yanked his shirt out of Colt's clutches.

"Okay, okay, I get the idea."

Colt made another move toward Mott, but Bethany put a restraining hand on his arm. And then Mott turned and walked out the door.

"For less than two cents I'd—" Colt wrenched away, frightening her with his intensity.

"No, Colt," she said, going after him and grabbing his shoulder. He shook her off.

"Don't make things worse," she warned. She wasn't yet pleading, but she would if she had to.

Something in her voice, some nuance that made him understand her distress on a deeper level, must have given Colt pause. He blinked, looked back at her and his eyes softened in awareness of her mood. His anger seemed to subside in that moment, seemed to drain out of him. He backed away from the door, steadied himself by gripping the back of a chair.

"What a sorry SOB," he muttered as they heard Mott's truck door slam.

With the situation defused, Bethany sagged in relief. She sighed and tried to make light of the confrontation. "Yeah, well, no kidding. And I hate to be called Beth."

Colt glared at the trail of dust following Mott's pickup as it retreated up the driveway. "Anytime you have trouble with him, all you need to do is call me. I could beat that little runty jackrabbit to a pulp."

Forcing herself to act normally, Bethany went to the cabinet, took out one of Alyssa's bottles and poured in the formula before setting it in a pan of warm water. Alyssa's big eyes followed Bethany as she moved around the kitchen, filling the coffeepot with water, spooning in coffee. There was something comforting in going about the morning's tasks as if nothing untoward had happened, but her heart was beating faster than usual, and it was all she could do to maintain composure.

Colt watched as Bethany gathered Alyssa into her arms after she had finished with her chores. He cautioned himself to cool it, but it wasn't easy. He'd wanted to beat Mott to smithereens, to do something, anything, to keep him from coming around and bothering Bethany again.

"Mott's a bad man, isn't he?" Bethany crooned to the baby as she sat down in the rocking chair with her.

"My sentiments exactly," Colt said, not even bothering to keep the disgust out of his voice. He focused on Bethany, marveling at how she seemed to take all obstacles in stride. Not only that, but in the past few weeks, Colt had observed a new softness in her, as a result, he was fairly sure, of the baby's presence. They made a pretty sight together, mother and child, Colt thought. Then he brought himself up short. He kept having to remind himself that Bethany wasn't Alyssa's mother.

He handed Bethany the warm bottle, and she popped the nipple into Alyssa's mouth. Then he took his time pouring them each a cup of coffee and set one down on the table beside Bethany. He straddled a kitchen chair across from her. "You want to tell me more about Mott and why he wants the ranch?"

Bethany wiped a dribble of milk from Alyssa's chin. "It was an old family feud that split the original property when Justin's father was in charge. Justin would have liked to bury the hatchet—he and Mott were childhood playmates—but you see how Mott is."

"Yeah, I see. No reason to knuckle under to him, though."

"I haven't. And there's no reason to antagonize him, either." She wasn't criticizing him, Colt knew. She was warning him.

Colt ran a hand through his hair. "Mott shouldn't have said those things to you."

"It doesn't bother me, Colt."

"Well, it bothers me." Outside, they heard Loreen arriving for her baby-sitting job, ending their private conversation. Colt stood up abruptly and dumped the dregs of his coffee in the sink. His anger rose again as he thought about Mott and the way he'd walked uninvited into this house, not to mention his insinuations. But what staggered him, what almost knocked him for a loop, was the way he felt about Bethany. He wanted to protect her, to take care of her, to make everything right for her, and after Ryzinski's, he thought he'd never feel that way again about any woman.

He bit off the words sharply. "You might as well know that I don't like bullies. You won't have to take any more of that from him while I'm around." Without waiting for her reply, and, he hoped, without revealing too much about his feelings for her, he stalked from the room.

Chapter Eight

After he left Bethany, Colt was in no mood to get started with his usual work. Instead he cleaned out the toolshed, throwing old tractor tires and broken bridle bits and a rusted trunk bumper into the back of the pickup for later deposit at the dump. It made him angry that Bethany had hurts he couldn't heal, problems he couldn't solve. She deserved someone to look after her, someone to fend off Mott Findley on her behalf. He wished he could be that person, and maybe he could. It was another reason to want to make his training school a success—to be Bethany's protector.

But for now, he felt useless. Well, not entirely. He knew he was being useful by doing things that needed doing, like cleaning this shed, for instance. He worked with a vengeance, wishing that each article he tossed into the truck bed was Mott Findley's head.

"What you doing that for?" Eddie asked. He had wandered over from the Neilsons' house and was munching on an apple.

"It needs doin'," Colt replied. Eddie watched him for a while, then tossed the apple core over the fence.

"You got any more apples at the house, Eddie?" he asked.

"Sure. Come on over and I'll get you one."

They ambled over to the foreman's house, and Eddie disappeared inside. He handed Colt two apples out the kitchen door. "One's for you and one's for Buckaroo."

"Old Buck is goin' to appreciate that, Eddie."

"Did you like the ribs I cooked yesterday, Colt?"

"I liked them, Ed, but they were a little dry."

"You think so? Dry?" Eddie's face fell.

"Maybe they needed more bastin' with that great sauce you made. They were good, though."

"Okay, Colt. I'm fixing spaghetti today. Will you be here for dinner?"

"You bet, Eddie."

After he left the foreman's house, Colt took Jesse behind the barn and gave him a few more pointers about how to get along with people. Jesse was coming along right pert for a dog that had no upbringing; he'd learned to come when called and to heel. Colt was determined that he'd have that fool dog jumping through hoops in a few more days. Even Frisco was impressed when he came over from his house to see what was going on.

"I never seen Jesse go for more than a few hours without lifting his leg on something," Frisco said as he bent over to scratch Jesse at the base of his tail.

"When I worked with him, I showed him there's a right place and a wrong place to do it." Colt tossed the saddle over Buckaroo's back.

"Maybe I can even let this dumb dog in the house one of these days," Frisco said hopefully. "Keep me company since Dita and Bethany don't let me ride out with them much anymore."

Colt was touched by this evidence of Frisco's vulnerability. "Sure, that would be great," Colt said. He bent over and scratched the dog behind one ear. "Old

Jesse James is comin' along, all right. Here, why don't you call him? You can give him a biscuit if he decides to pay attention."

Frisco called Jesse, his face crinkling with pleasure as Jesse walked sedately to his side and sat waiting ever so politely for his treat. "If that don't beat all," Frisco said. "You know, Colt, you're mighty good at what you do."

Colt grinned. Experience had taught him that compliments from Frisco were hard to come by. "Speakin' of which, what do you want me to do today?" he asked as he tightened the saddle's cinch.

"Ride out and check the herd in the Blue Pasture. I'll talk to you at dinner, you can tell me how they're doing."

"Right. Anything else?"

"That's all for now." Frisco stumped toward his house, Jesse following closely.

The praise from Frisco put Colt in a better frame of mind than he'd been after Mott's visit earlier, and he found himself whistling as he swung into the saddle. He wouldn't mind riding Buck out to the Blue Pasture this morning. The ride would give him plenty of time to think—about his training school, the supplies he'd need, and the repairs he wanted to make, not to mention how much the venture would initially cost. He wanted to present Bethany with a cohesive business plan sometime in the next few days before she thought better of things and changed her mind.

Colt still felt a sense of wonder over the opportunity that Bethany had presented to him and the way it made him feel—as if he was important to someone. That was what had made him open up to her last night. He'd never until now had anyone to talk with about the experiences that had formed and shaped his young mind. Bethany was different from anyone he'd ever met—a strong woman. She knew what she wanted, and she went after it. Now that he knew her better, it surprised him that she had a vulnerable side to her; it made her seem more real to him, more accessible.

More lovable, to tell the truth of it.

BETHANY WAS SITTING at the desk in Frisco's office listening to his usual litany of complaints when she saw Colt dismount and come stalking up the walkway to the front door. It was too early for their noon meal; Eddie had barely started chopping fresh tomatoes for the spaghetti sauce. She glanced at her watch and wondered what could have brought Colt back to the home place this early. It was only ten o'clock.

"Something's bothering him," she said under her breath before Colt slammed in from outside.

Colt didn't waste much time telling her what was on his mind. "We've got trouble over in the Blue Pasture," he said tersely.

"Trouble? What do you mean?" Frisco said.

"Somebody's herded those cows into the fence. They're all cut up." His eyes were as hard as flint.

"Why, every once in a while one of 'em will get hung up on the barbwire. It's not a big deal."

"Oh, but this is a very big deal. I'd say we've got twenty or thirty of them with serious cuts. We need to call us a vet."

Bethany rose. "Somebody herded them into the fence?" She was incredulous.

Colt looked her straight in the eye. "That's right."

She read in his eyes what he meant. "Mott," she said. "You think he had something to do with this."

"The Blue Pasture borders on his land. There's a gate from your land to his, so he has access."

"I've been meaning to take that gate out," Bethany said distractedly. "I never had the time to spare." She thought about her cattle, hurt and milling around in fear and confusion. In that moment she hated Mott Findley.

"I'll take the pickup out, find Dita. She can sew up wounds as well as anyone," Frisco said, heading for the door.

"I'll call the vet, too," Bethany said. She reached for the phone.

"It was sabotage, Bethany, pure and simple," Colt said in an undertone as she tapped out a phone number. "It was probably brought on by Mott's visit this mornin'. While you're callin' people, you might want to think about callin' the sheriff as well."

Bethany shook her head. "The sheriff is Mott's brother-in-law. He won't help us."

"Then we might have to help ourselves," Colt said, and before Bethany could spare him even a warning look, he had turned on his heel and left.

It was hot work, sweaty and dusty, but they herded the injured cattle into a corral and held them down one by one while either Dita or the veterinarian sewed them up. The vet gave each one a shot of antibiotic and said he'd done the best he could do.

"Something must have panicked those steers," he said.

"Something did," Colt said tersely, but Bethany didn't want to encourage such speculation in front of the vet or anyone else. She mounted Dancer and rode away before she said something she might regret.

Colt, riding Buckaroo, caught up with her after the veterinarian climbed into his pickup truck and roared away. He reined in beside her. "You goin' to let Mott get away with this?"

Bethany pulled Dancer up sharp; the horse was always eager to get back to the barn after a hard day. "The only thing that will stop Mott is that if I become so successful that he gives up. He's like a vulture, hovering overhead in hopes of good pickings when I give up."

"Fat chance of that. Say, have you got time to talk about our business deal?"

"Sure. I've always got time for that."

"Well, I'd like to get started fencin' in the home corral right away. Then I could paint the barn. I figure I can do it in my spare time. There's plenty of light left in the early evening at this time of year."

"Okay. That's good." Bethany paused. She might as well bring up her concerns about Eddie, but maybe this wasn't the right time. Still, she might not have a better chance, and at least now they could talk privately. She didn't want Frisco to hear what she had to say.

"Colt," she began. She hesitated, trying to figure out how to broach the topic.

If only he wouldn't look at her like that, sitting his horse so easily with his eyes half-lidded and his eyebrows slightly raised. She plunged ahead.

"Colt, Eddie told me you were critical of his cooking."

He seemed puzzled. "What exactly do you mean?"

"You complained about the ribs he cooked yesterday. There's no need to criticize Eddie. He does the best he can."

Colt shook his head. "And he does a damned good job. Eddie asked me how I liked the food, and I said the ribs were a little dry, that's all."

"You wouldn't have had to say that." She didn't mean to sound so accusatory, but she couldn't bear for anyone to pick on Eddie.

Colt turned slightly in his saddle. "Well, it was true. The ribs were dry. He asked me, and I calls 'em the way I sees 'em. Listen, Bethany, there's no need to coddle Eddie. I treat him the way I treat everyone else."

"But Eddie's—"

"I know. Down's syndrome. I think it does him a disservice to handle him with care. Make allowances for his problem, sure. But other than that, he wants and deserves to be treated like any normal person. And that was what I was doin'."

Bethany was so accustomed to thinking in a different way, to sheltering Eddie and protecting him, that what Colt said gave her an entirely new perspective. Maybe Colt was right. Maybe she should take her cue from him.

They rode on in silence. "You goin' to be there when I work with Sidewinder later?" Colt asked her. "Loreen said her boyfriend is comin' to watch."

"Joey? I'm glad to hear it."

"He may be my first customer. He says he's got a horse who won't let anyone near her."

"I've heard about that one. His sisters wanted to work Princess in rodeos, but she refuses to cooperate."

"I'll make her into a good rodeo horse or know the reason why."

Bethany glanced over at him curiously. She felt a compulsion to know more about him, more than he had already revealed. In her desperation to find someone to help her on the ranch, she had chosen not to inquire too closely into his background. But now surely, since he had opened up to her last night, he wouldn't mind revealing more about himself. The words came out before she could stop them. "Where did you work before, Colt? Where did you train horses?"

"No place you'd know," he said, and before she could say anything more, he urged Buck into a gallop, leaving Bethany behind in a swirl of dust.

A FEW DAYS LATER JOEY brought Princess, a beautiful bay mare, over to work with Colt.

"She's part thoroughbred, part mustang," Joey said. "We bought her at auction, but she hasn't lived up to her promise."

Colt squinted at the horse through the haze of late afternoon. "I'll see what I can do," he said, and he got into the corral and started his routine. Joey watched intently as Colt brought Princess into line.

"I've never seen anything like that," Joey said with a low whistle. "Could I learn to do it?"

"Anyone can learn. You could be my helper," Colt told him.

"You mean it? You'd let me?" Joey was clearly surprised and delighted.

"Sure," Colt said. After that Joey stopped by every afternoon, and soon Colt had enlisted his help in painting the barn as well.

One day about a week and a half after Bethany had given Colt the go-ahead to start his training facility at the Banner-B, Colt rode by the house in the ranch pickup. She was in the garden spreading compost when he pulled up beside the picket fence. She looked the most unkempt he'd ever seen her—hair in braids, ratty old sneakers riddled with holes, and up to her elbows in dirt. Damn, she was still beautiful, even when she looked like she'd been rode hard and put away wet.

"You got a minute?" he said.

She straightened, put a hand to the small of her back. He wished she wouldn't work so hard that she got aches and pains, but maybe, just maybe, if things went well with the new training school, she wouldn't have to.

Bethany shaded her eyes with her free hand against the sinking orange rim of the sun. "What's up?"

"Oh, something new. Can you hop in for a minute? Let me show you?"

"I guess so. Loreen's still here with Alyssa." She went over to the spigot at the side of the house and rinsed her hands off in the reluctant trickle of water. During the process he got a good look at the curve of her backside; he'd never seen a prettier one. He cut his eyes away, feeling like he shouldn't be looking. Then he looked back again, figuring, why not? There was nothing to stop him, nothing to keep him from enjoying. Nothing except his own deep-down sense that he wasn't good enough for her, didn't deserve her in his life. He squelched that feeling right quick. He was trying to be worthy. He truly was.

Bethany, who seemed determined to ignore his interest and his thoughts on the subject of her in general, came over, and after he reached across the seat and pushed the door open, she slid in the passenger side. Colt grinned at her as he gunned the pickup up the driveway.

"What are we doing?"

"Surprise."

She sat forward in the seat, her hands gripping the edge, looking as curious as a little kid. "Can you give me a clue?"

"You'll like it," was all he said, and he was rewarded when she smiled.

"I like surprises," she confessed, and it was all he could do not to reach over and touch her cheek in affection.

When they reached the highway, he pulled the pickup over into the tangle of weeds at the side of the road. "Look," he said with a flourish.

Bethany saw a new sign, black letters on white paint. Banner-B Ranch, it said. Home Of McClure Stables. Horse Training By Clayton McClure.

"Oh, Colt," she said. "It's lovely."

"I had it painted by a guy over in Lubbock. And guess what—he wants to know more about how I work. He trains horses himself, says he's had it with the old methods. Says he's seen a good many horses ruined and wants to try something else."

"I'm glad," she said.

"Me, too," Colt said. They sat for a while admiring the sign.

"I don't suppose you'd like to go out somewhere and celebrate. The new business, I mean."

"Tonight?" She darted a look at him.

"No better time," he said carefully. He didn't expect her to take him up on it. For a while he'd halfway thought about asking Frisco, Dita and Eddie to go along, too. But he didn't feel like celebrating with them, and he'd already lined up Dita to watch Alyssa tonight. Dita had agreed, throwing him a speculative glance when she thought he wasn't looking. Colt didn't care what Dita thought. He wanted to look across a table deep into Bethany's eyes. He wanted to hold her in his arms while they did the Texas two-step. He wanted a date with her, that's what he wanted.

"Oh, I don't know," Bethany hedged, and that's when he brought all his powers of persuasion to bear.

"Wouldn't it be nice to go into a restaurant and be served by someone you don't know? To go dancin'? To kick up your heels one night in your life and forget about bills and problems and Mott Findley?"

"When you put it that way, it's hard to refuse," she admitted, sidling a glance over at him and just as quickly looking away.

"Get all dolled up. We're goin' to ride over to Lubbock and find a great place to eat. And then—"

"You mentioned dancing. I might as well warn you that I haven't danced in ages. I might not be up to it."

"We'll see about that."

Before Bethany could answer, a black pickup barreling toward them in the distance began to slow down.

"That's Mott," Bethany said, tension building in her expression.

"Well, he'll be real interested in your new sign," Colt told her.

The pickup tooled by, and the driver *was* Mott. Colt saw that the man's mouth went slack when he read the writing on the sign. He didn't acknowledge them sitting on the side of the road, though they were in plain sight.

Colt started the ranch pickup's engine and threw the gear into reverse as Mott's truck disappeared down the road. "That'll give Mott something to jaw over for a few days," he said, and Bethany grinned.

"More than a few days, I hope," she said.

COLT HAD AN APPOINTMENT to talk with the Misses Truett about supplying them with boarders, and he dropped Bethany off back at the house. She showered quickly while Loreen put Alyssa down for a nap.

Once Loreen had gone, Bethany took a cardboard box down from the hall closet shelf. Inside was a dress she had ordered from a catalog months ago, long before Colt was on the scene, and at the time, she'd had no need for a new dress. Now she would have liked to think that she'd had a premonition that she might want to wear such a dress, but that wasn't true. She got pleasure from ordering things from catalogs, enjoyed getting things in the mail. Hadn't she ordered Colt himself from the *Cattle Rancher's Journal?*

She smiled at that. They were all better off for Colt's being around, and even Frisco would have admitted it. She was feeling a sense of delight at the idea of going out with him, a kind of breathlessness that reached all the way down to the pit of her stomach.

As she unwrapped the dress from its tissue paper, she wondered what on earth had possessed her to order such a feminine-looking style. The dress was of daintily sprigged cotton, finely pleated all over and with a scoop neck. She wriggled out of her oversize shirt and jeans and slipped the dress on over her head. The neck was low enough to show some cleavage, and the bodice cupped her breasts more tightly than she remembered. The dress barely skimmed her body, swirling out into a gored skirt reaching almost to her ankles. The thin fabric showed off her figure to great advantage, but it wasn't a sophisticated style. She held her hair back behind one ear, studying the slope of her neck. With her pearl earrings and a thin gold necklace, the dress would do.

But oh, Lordy! What to do about her hair? The ends were split from being out in the hot dry weather, and she hadn't had it trimmed for—well, was it six months or more? Time tended to get away from her these days. She got on the phone and called Rubye at the Beauty Box.

"Sure, I can work in a haircut this afternoon. Why don't you just shoot on over here, Bethany?"

Another phone call, this time to Dita, produced a pleased agreement to baby-sit. When Dita arrived to pick up Alyssa, she did a quick double-take at the sight of Bethany's dress hanging from a hook on the kitchen door.

"Where'd you get *that?*" Dita asked in surprise. She was used to seeing Bethany wearing old jeans and oversize shirts, and her expression was skeptical at the sight of something so feminine and appealing.

"Oh, from a catalog," Bethany said offhandedly as if it were no big deal.

"You and your catalogs. Well, if you wear that dress, you're going to impress Colt, no doubt about it."

"I'm not trying to impress Colt."

"Don't be silly. Of course you are. There's nothing wrong with that, either. No reason you should live like a nun."

"Would you like a glass of lemonade?" A change of subject, sure, but necessary.

Dita shook her head. "I'll go up and get Alyssa, if you don't mind. Frisco asked me when she was going to be there, can you imagine?" She started for the stairs.

Bethany poured herself a glass of lemonade, trying to figure out how to handle this thing with Dita. She didn't want Dita to think she was all that interested in Colt. On the other hand, if she weren't interested, would she be going to so much trouble to look nice? Of course not, and Dita knew it.

Dita returned carrying Alyssa, who was looking all sleepy and good-natured in spite of being awakened from her nap.

"I've got formula at my place, so I'll feed and

change her there. And Bethany, let me keep Alyssa all night so you and Colt don't have to hurry home. Or if you do, you won't have to worry about coming to get her."

"I'm sure we'll be back early," Bethany said quickly. Too quickly, probably.

She was spared Dita's tart reply when the phone rang. She ducked into the den to pick it up and was surprised when a woman's voice asked for Colt.

"He's not here right now. May I take a message?"

"Oh, yes. Please ask him to call Marcy." And she reeled off a phone number and hung up.

Bethany's heart swooped down to her feet and up again. Just when she was about to go out on a date with him, here was Colt's girlfriend.

"Bethany? Is that Frisco?" Dita, holding the baby close, appeared at the den door.

Bethany replaced the receiver on its base and frowned at the slip of paper in her hand. "No. Guess what—it was Marcy."

Dita looked surprised. "The same Marcy who belongs to Alyssa?"

"Yes, Alyssa's mother. Colt's been looking for her, you know."

Dita dropped a kiss on the top of Alyssa's head. "I suppose this means your mama is going to come get you," she said to Alyssa, who looked more interested in Dita's swinging earrings than in the possibility that she might soon be living someplace else.

"I suppose it does," Bethany said thoughtfully. A pang of sadness jolted her somewhere in the region of her heart at the thought of losing Alyssa. It was hard to imagine life without a baby around the ranch.

"I guess it was inevitable. That Alyssa would have

to go sooner or later, I mean." Dita looked sadder than Bethany had seen her since Frisco's heart attack.

"And I suppose it was also inevitable that Marcy would come looking for Colt," Bethany said ruefully. "Just when—"

"Just when what?" Dita urged gently, but Bethany wasn't about to be trapped into any revelations about her feelings for him.

"I know Colt cares for this Marcy, whoever she is," she said quietly. "I can see that he has special feelings for her whenever he says her name. He gets this look in his eyes, a faraway look. Dita, maybe I'd better tell him I won't go tonight." She turned away.

"Are you out of your mind, Bethany?" Dita cried. "A guy asks you out and you say you don't know if you should go? On the basis of a short little phone call that probably doesn't mean a thing?"

"There's no point in making this—this thing with Colt tonight out to be something that it's not," Bethany said heatedly.

Dita groaned. "Oh, hang Marcy, anyway. *You* are here, and Marcy isn't. That gives you the hometown advantage, right?"

"No point in—"

"In raising your hopes?" Dita said quietly. "That's what this is about, isn't it?"

"Maybe," Bethany said, admitting this with misgivings. She rested troubled eyes on the baby, whom she knew to be Colt's baby and Marcy's, too. Well, she didn't exactly know it, but she was pretty sure. Colt had never denied that he was the father.

"Let me tell you, Bethany, if you don't go out with Colt tonight, I'll get Frisco on your case. Something tells me you wouldn't like that."

Bethany made a face. "You've got that right," she said.

"Go out, have a pleasant dinner, and if you don't have a good time, you don't ever have to do it again."

"Promise, Dita?" Bethany managed a slight smile.

"Promise. And like I said earlier, take your time tonight." Dita's look as she went out the door with the baby was meaningful.

Great, thought Bethany. *Everyone on the ranch is likely to think that Colt and I are sleeping together even if all we do is have dinner.*

But would it be so bad to sleep with Colt? Isn't that what she wanted? Oh, why was everything always so difficult?

Bethany stared at the phone number on the piece of paper for a long time before she laid it right smack dab in the middle of the kitchen table where Colt would be sure to see it if he came in to check for messages. Then she dumped the last of her lemonade in the sink.

She grabbed her car keys off their hook in the pantry and headed out the door. If she were going to go through with this, she'd better get over to Rubye's before the hairdresser decided that she wasn't going to show up and gave her appointment away to someone else.

"I HEARD," RUBYE SAID conspiratorily, "that Mott Findley's got cash flow problems big time."

"Oh?" Bethany replied, trying not to show her interest in this little plum of information.

"The new loan officer at the bank? The one from Arizona? She was in here the other day and I heard her talking about it on her cell phone. Not that she mentioned Mott by name, mind you, but it didn't take too much smarts to figure out who she meant when she talked about the biggest braggart in town.''

Rubye's beauty salon was the clearinghouse for all local news, so Bethany didn't doubt the veracity of this tidbit. Sometimes she heard news at Rubye's before the *Gompers Gazette,* the local weekly paper, got the word out.

"You wouldn't think Mott would keep trying to buy the Banner-B if he didn't have the money," she said.

"You wouldn't think so," Rubye agreed as she whipped the cape off Bethany's shoulders. "Now suppose you tell me about that Colt McClure. Loreen says he's one good-looking man. How do you suppose he got that scar on his face?"

Bethany had no idea, and she certainly wasn't about to speculate, so she paid Rubye for the haircut and fled.

Since Rubye had cut her hair in record time, Bethany had time to spare before she needed to be back at the ranch. She decided to drop in at Murdock's Sundries and Dry Goods to pick up a card of snap fasteners and a spool of thread so that she could replace the missing snap on her bathrobe.

"Well," said Cindy, the girl at the cash register. "Aren't you all dolled up."

Bethany knew Cindy, a former Miss Gompers and an unsuccessful Miss Texas wannabee. Cindy had never forgiven Bethany for coming all the way from Wichita and marrying Justin, the town's most eligible bachelor at the time. However, since Justin had once described Cindy as a couple of bulbs short of a chandelier, it wasn't likely that Cindy had ever had much of a chance with him.

Before she could reply, Bethany heard someone come up behind her and turned her head to see who it was.

Jasmyn, the one who liked to be called The Duchess, had emerged from the back of the store. Bethany had forgotten that they both worked there—double trouble, as far as she could see.

"Should we tell her?" Jasmyn asked Cindy with studied casualness.

Cindy leaned on the counter, carefully inspecting her nails. "Oh, I don't know."

"Tell me what?" Bethany blurted, ashamed of herself for asking.

"We know something you don't know," Cindy said in a singsong voice.

She wasn't going to fall into whatever trap they were trying to set. "That's nice." Bethany put away her wallet and headed for the door, but Cindy jumped in front of her and blocked the way.

"Don't you want to know what it is?" Cindy asked.

"Oh, out with it," Jasmyn said. "No point in beating around the bush."

"Hmm," Cindy said. "Maybe yes, maybe no."

Bethany tried to be patient. "Cindy, I have things to do, so would you mind letting me pass?"

"It's about your ranch hand. You know, that new guy you've got over at the Banner-B?"

Bethany didn't know what this was about, but she was sure that the two women were up to no good. Cindy was a good friend of Mott's and one of his main confidantes. Jasmyn had a reputation for meddling in places where she didn't belong.

"Get out of my way, Cindy." Bethany tried to stare her down, but Cindy only laughed.

"Don't you want to know my secret?"

"I don't think so. Especially since once you tell me

it won't be a secret anymore," Bethany said, thinking that if she pointed this out, she might be spared.

Jasmyn marched up to Bethany. "Don't let her fool you, Cindy. She wants to know, all right."

"Well," said Cindy, moving in closer. "I don't see how you can trust Colt McClure. With a baby around the place and all. And Eddie, of course."

"What Cindy means," Jasmyn said with a malevolent smile, "is that your friend Colt shot and killed a man back in Oklahoma. He's a murderer."

At first Bethany felt her face sagging in disbelief, and then she looked wildly from Jasmyn to Cindy in a rush of uncertainty, searching for a sign that either one of them was lying.

"A murderer," Cindy confirmed with an air of self-satisfaction. "We thought you'd want to know."

Chapter Nine

Colt, a murderer? The same Colt who had so tenderly massaged the baby's back when she had colic? The same Colt who had calmed Sidewinder and turned him into a docile mount? Colt, who handled Jesse James better than anyone? No, it couldn't be true.

But as her car rocketed toward the ranch through waves of heat rippling up from the asphalt road, Bethany thought the accusation had the ring of truth about it, at least in her saner moments. What did she actually know about Colt's past besides his history of growing up in foster homes? She didn't know where he'd come from, other than someplace in Oklahoma. She had no idea, really, why Alyssa had been dropped off with him at the ranch. She didn't know the status of his relationship with Marcy. Where did the baby and Marcy fit into all of this? Oh, yes, there had always been an aura of mystery surrounding Colt McClure.

One thing was certain, she thought grimly as she turned into the driveway past the big new McClure Stables sign. She felt betrayed. And stupid for not having asked for references.

But maybe, she thought as she noted Buckaroo with his reins dropped under the old oak tree, the rumor wasn't true. Maybe it was only that, a vicious rumor. Well, if that was the case, she'd find out for sure. Now.

She got out of the car and stopped short at the sight of a mother cat and two kittens on the porch. The mother cat was licking one of the kittens, a black one, and the other, an orange tabby, was chasing its tail.

Colt came out of the house. "Cute, aren't they?"

The sight of the cats totally discombobulated her. She'd been ready to light into Colt, to find out the answers to her questions, and now here were these cats.

"What—what's going on?"

"Miss Claretta Truett gave them to me for the barn. We can't have mice chawin' on horse feed, not when money's so tight that every bit of grain counts."

"Where's Jesse James?"

"He's turned into a well-mannered gentleman and is keepin' Frisco company at his house."

"Jesse eats cats. We can't have cats." She stomped up the stairs and stood right in front of Colt.

Colt's eyebrows rose. "Jesse has more refined eating habits these days than he did in his lamentable past. Say, is something on your mind?"

She held his gaze for a long moment. "Maybe," she allowed.

"Okay, did Kraegel charge you for that extra balin' wire?"

"No, Colt. It's nothing like that." She brushed past him and into the kitchen. He followed her inside, looking puzzled and faintly worried.

She saw the piece of paper with Marcy's telephone number on it in the middle of the kitchen table where she'd left it, which only made her more determined to have this out with him. She whirled and faced Colt, marshaling her thoughts. Even as she prepared to hit him with the information that she'd heard in town, she almost melted at the sight of him standing there, his gaze warm upon her, his teeth white against a rugged tan, and his eyes, his remarkable eyes, gray lit with silver. No wonder she'd let him into her life so easily. Who wouldn't want a man like this around all the time?

"I heard a scary rumor in town," she said slowly and carefully, hoping that he couldn't hear her heart beating like crazy against her ribs.

A guarded look was his immediate response, but all he said was, "Oh?"

"Maybe you can tell me what it was."

"Maybe," he allowed. But there was nothing cocky in his manner. Instead he seemed sorrowful, worried. She supposed she would be, too.

"Would you like to give it a try?"

"Was it about me?"

"Yes, Colt, it was."

"I don't suppose the rumor was about the new training school."

"No," she said. "It wasn't."

"You want to give me a hint?"

"This isn't a game of twenty questions, Colt." She regarded him calmly although she felt anything but.

"I reckon it must be about something that happened 'way back in Oklahoma."

"Good guess."

He clamped his lips together. "I can explain everything," he said.

"So far," she pointed out, "you haven't explained a whole lot about anything. Alyssa, for example."

"Alyssa," he said, looking confused. "Is that what you're talking about? Was the rumor about her?"

"No, but something tells me it's all tied in together."

She steeled herself against his charm and his manipulating, if that's how he chose to handle this. But she couldn't ignore his vulnerability, which she had to admit was part of his charm. She wished she could keep her mind on the problem at hand instead of thinking about his personal attributes, the ones that had made her let down her guard in the first place.

Colt looked slightly sick, as if he couldn't bear to have this discussion. "Yes," he said quietly. "They're all part of the same problem—Alyssa, Marcy and what I figure you heard in town."

She drew a deep breath. "So I gather. Would you care to enlighten me? I'm here, Colt. I'm waiting. So let's get on with it."

From the way he looked, she knew this was serious. She'd been hoping that there was nothing to that rumor, that he'd laugh everything off and reassure her. But she sensed from the expression on his face, the guarded reticence and its almost undetectible underlying sorrow, that Colt had secrets he didn't want to discuss. Things that he couldn't tell her.

Colt inhaled a deep, steadying breath. "I called Marcy back, Bethany, a few minutes ago. I'm going to go see her in Oklahoma City."

"Great, just great." The very mention of Marcy's name made Bethany want to throw up. She couldn't understand why, with the larger question of murder looming, she was jealous of Alyssa's mother, Colt's former girlfriend. Or maybe Marcy wasn't all that former. Maybe she was still involved with Colt. Bethany didn't know. She didn't know anything at this point. It didn't make sense to be thinking of Colt and his girlfriend when what she wanted to know was if he had actually killed someone. But then, maybe it was easier to focus on the smaller issue, Marcy, rather than the larger issue that should have been more important.

She pinched the bridge of her nose between her thumb and forefinger, trying to think through the jumble of thoughts that filled her head. Suddenly she was exhausted. Facing Colt across her kitchen like this wasn't the way she had expected to end the afternoon. Her dress was still hanging on the door, the lovely dress that she had anticipated wearing for him when they went out later. Now she couldn't imagine going anywhere with him.

Colt didn't say anything, just stared at her across the empty space between them. There was a white line around his lips, and in the depths of his eyes she saw raw pain. Pain at what? At the doubt and distrust that he saw in her eyes?

"Will you go with me to Oklahoma City?"

For a moment she couldn't believe she was hearing him correctly. "Go with you to see—to see Marcy?" she blurted.

"Sure."

Outraged, she walked across the kitchen, gathered her thoughts. She wheeled around. Was he purposely trying to make her angry? "Let me get this straight. You want me to accompany you to see this—this girlfriend of yours?"

"She's not my girlfriend, I swear it." His voice had thickened, and an air of desperation had settled over him.

"Look, I don't know what you and Marcy are to each other, and I don't care. All I know is that I'm tired of this. You show up on my ranch, and then your baby ends up on my doorstep, and I hear rumors, and—oh, I can't stand this. Maybe you'd better get your things and leave. Permanently." She couldn't bear to look at him in that moment.

"You mean I'm fired?" He sounded incredulous.

Suddenly cold despite the afternoon's heat, she wrapped her arms around herself and cupped her elbows in her hands. "Yes, that's what I mean."

"We've made plans for training horses here. I thought you wanted—"

"What I wanted was more than I got," she said, biting off the words, and if he took that the wrong way, then so be it.

"Bethany," he said, "I pegged you for someone who kept her promises. Always, and no matter what." His words were bleak, his expression more so.

That stung, but she made herself ignore the pain. By this time, she believed that she had read in his eyes all she needed to know. Whether or not he had done the terrible thing that Cindy had told her about, he had been evasive ever since he came to the Banner-B. He was being evasive even now.

"Alyssa isn't my baby, Bethany."

"Prove it." Her eyes locked with his, and she hardened herself against whatever he might say.

When he spoke, it was softly, the words belying whatever emotion he might be feeling. "I doubt that I want to be talking about this any more than you do right now. Some things are better if you let them be. At least until the time is right for the telling."

She lifted her chin. "You're the best judge of that." In that moment, she knew she could have asked the defining question, *did you really murder somebody?* But in her heart, she already knew. She could tell from the anguish that she sensed in Colt, from the hollow look in his eyes, that there was more to this than his baby, more to it than Marcy. So she didn't ask. The words wouldn't shape themselves in her head, wouldn't come out of her mouth, probably because she was hurting. She'd let this cowboy into her life, into her house, had trusted him and yes, she'd cared for him. She wished he'd just go to Marcy, get out and leave her alone.

Colt seemed to be struggling for words. "You know, I could explain," he said finally in a strangled tone. "I could tell you everything right this minute, but it wouldn't be as effective as if I brought Marcy around and let you meet her."

"Bring your girlfriend here? To the Banner-B? You could at least spare me that." She bit her lip so that she wouldn't cry in his presence. Blindly, with tears stinging the back of her throat, she whirled and headed for the hall and the stairs and the blessed sanctuary of her own room.

Colt was right behind her. Before she had reached the first step, he grabbed her from behind. She supposed that she should have been afraid, only it was just Colt, the same Colt she had come to know and to love.

Love? That was a joke. How could she love him? She couldn't love someone who hadn't been straight with her.

He wrested her around to face him so that she had a close-up view of the fire blazing in his eyes.

"I already told you that Alyssa's not my child. How many times do you want me to say it? And Marcy's not my girlfriend."

"Oh, right." There was no point in trying to keep the skeptical edge out of her voice.

"I swear she isn't. I love Marcy, sure, but like a sister."

"I don't want to hear this. Get out, Colt."

His words were as sharp as hammer blows, falling one after the other. "I'm leaving the Banner-B, but not because you kicked me out. I'm going to get Marcy. And when I come back, I hope and pray that you'll understand. Got that?"

She closed her eyes against him, blotted him from her sight.

"In the meantime, here's a little something for you to remember me by."

She opened her eyes in alarm only to see his head bending down, down, and then the heat from his hands seemed to sear the flesh of her upper arms. She heard the roar of her own blood in her ears, tried to breathe but couldn't for the life of her force air into her lungs.

Was it possible for bones to dissolve beneath the skin from sheer wanting? Could she be immobilized by desire? Because she couldn't move. She couldn't speak. All she could do was stare at Colt and wish he'd kiss her, kiss her as she had never been kissed in all her life.

His hands slid upward to the bottom curves of her breasts and cupped them lightly. Her lips trembled, her eyelids fluttered closed, and then his lips took hers. She heard moaning—was it hers?—and stars exploded somewhere in her head, finding their way to her lips, sizzling there, scorching, but no, it was his lips, Colt's lips, that brought the heat. She swirled up and into it, surrendering to him.

He released her lips. His voice was close to her ear, deceptively soft. "You see how it is, Bethany. I'll come back. That's a promise." And he kissed her again, more exquisitely this time, engendering a crazy wild response as her head fell back and she opened to him. The kiss grew deeper, wilder, tongues tangling in haste. She felt the strong muscled strength of him pressing against her, pushing her into the wall as her knees went so weak that they might not have held her up had she not been clinging to him.

Mercifully he let her go. She stared at him, her body a confusion of sensations.

"I *will* be back," he said softly, and then he turned on his heel and marched out the front door.

She put a hand to her lips and pushed herself away from the wall. From the table, Justin's picture stared at her.

Before she went upstairs, she very gently turned it facedown on the table so she wouldn't see Justin when she came downstairs again.

FRISCO ARRIVED NOT HALF an hour later and clomped into the house without knocking.

"Bethany?"

She was sprawled on her bed, the slight breeze from the window cooling her hot face, trying to make sense of things. Not the least of her worries was that now that Colt was gone, plans for the training school were all down the drain. This meant a serious loss of expected income for the Banner-B.

"Bethany? You upstairs?"

"I'll be right down," she said. She jumped up and stared at herself in the mirror over her dresser. She looked terrible, her hair in a bodacious snarl despite her visit to Rubye this afternoon, lipstick smeared across her cheek. She quickly refurbished her face the best she could and then slowly descended the stairs to talk to Frisco.

He stared up at her, a kitten peeking out of each shirt pocket, the black patch over his eye slightly askew. If she hadn't been in such a dark mood, she would have laughed out loud at this droll sight.

"Now you've done it," Frisco said without preamble.

"Done what?" She went into the living room and sat down.

Frisco followed her. He took the kittens out of his pockets and set them on the floor. One pounced upon the rug fringe, the other hid under the couch. "You've upset Eddie."

"What do you mean? Sit down, Frisco. You know I wouldn't do anything to hurt Eddie."

"Eddie was playing with the kittens on the porch when he heard you and Colt having it out in the kitchen. He heard you order Colt to leave."

Bethany sighed. Of course Eddie would have been working in the garden right about that time, of course he'd want to see the kittens, of course she hadn't thought to keep her voice down.

"Oh, Frisco, I wish Eddie hadn't heard, but it's true. I did tell Colt to leave."

"Yeah, I know. Colt stopped by and told me he was going. Said he was leaving Buckaroo in the barn and that he'd be back. Said he's going to go find this Marcy person. Guess that makes sense if Alyssa's her kid."

"I don't think there's any doubt about that," Bethany said tersely.

"You mind telling me why you told Colt to get out?"

"Yes. Yes, I do mind." She might as well keep the local gossip to herself. Frisco would hear all about Colt in town before long, the local small-town gossip mill being what it was.

"You're gonna have to explain to Eddie. He's pretty mad at you right now. Says you took his brother away."

"Colt isn't Eddie's brother. Colt is a drifter, a wanderer, that I in my foolishness brought upon us at the Banner-B." She felt bitter, but only about her own naiveté.

"I told you when you ordered that guy from that magazine—"

Bethany was in no mood to listen. "No 'I told you so,' Frisco," she said. "You were right. There, I've admitted it. Isn't that enough?"

"Well, I don't know. At first I didn't think you should take on a guy like that, but I have to admit Colt worked out fine. Since he says he'll be back, I take it you didn't mean to fire him?"

"Yes. I mean no. Oh, I don't know." She tried to think and ended up with, "We have to do something about Alyssa."

"Not much we can do. Dita sure likes that baby. I promised Colt—"

"You promised Colt what?" To her way of thinking, Frisco had no business promising Colt anything.

"That we wouldn't send Alyssa to foster care. If he's bringing Marcy back to get her, I mean."

"Fine. I'm sure we can manage for a while, even if I have to pay Loreen's salary myself." Where she'd squeeze the money from, she wasn't sure, but it wasn't important. She wasn't about to let this baby go to strangers, even if she had to adopt her herself. Now there was a novel idea, one she hadn't considered before, but for now, she shelved it somewhere in the back of her mind.

"Almost forgot." Frisco dug in his back pocket and laid a roll of bills on the coffee table. "Colt left this. To pay Loreen for baby-sitting and to buy Alyssa's diapers and so on."

It was a considerable amount of money. Bethany stared at it and couldn't help wondering how long Colt thought he was going to be gone.

And if he was really coming back.

WITH BETHANY'S BITTER WORDS still echoing in his head, Colt hitched into town with a passing trucker and paid cash for the first car he saw with a For Sale sign in its window. The aging subcompact, a scabrous yellow one with a manual transmission, was parked on Gompers's main street, and the Mexican man who owned it was eager to sell. Even though the fellow said he was moving to Lubbock and needed the cash, he was reluctant to bargain. Feeling that he had no choice, Colt ended up paying far too much money for the car.

By the time night fell, Colt was chugging fitfully out of town, and as he drove toward Oklahoma City, he ruefully recalled what he earlier thought he'd be doing on this night. He'd planned to be having a good time, and he'd thought there was a good chance that he'd be making love to Bethany before the night was through. He'd waited a long time for this woman, longer than he usually waited. Come to think of it, he'd been waiting for her all his life.

The car coughed and died before he had even crossed the Oklahoma state line. It took two whole days to get it fixed in the one-stoplight town where it broke down, and by the time the repair work was done he wished he'd junked it and bought another.

He thought maybe it was a good thing that Bethany hadn't come with him after all. They would have had to spend two days and two nights together in a dinky motel, and he was pretty sure at this point that the last thing she wanted to do was share a room with him. Or even talk to him, for that matter.

"So," Mott said to Bethany, "your ranch hand flew the coop."

"It's no business of yours." She busied herself scooping horse feed into the troughs in each stall of the barn.

"You found out about McClure, what he did in Oklahoma?"

Bethany eyed Mott over the side of a stall. "Maybe. What do you know about it?"

"Only what my brother-in-law heard from one of his deputies who used to work in the Oklahoma state prison system."

"Which was?"

"Same thing you heard, I reckon. Say, you still want to start that horse school?"

"I'm not discussing my plans for the Banner-B with you."

"I was thinking, you and me, we could go ahead with it. You know, Beth, the two of us, we could go a long way."

"I'm not going into business with you, Mott."

"It wasn't business I was in mind of."

His meaning dawned on her, and she narrowed her eyes. "Do I have to get Frisco to throw you off the place, or will you go quietly?"

"You've got this all wrong. I'm not talking about fooling around. I've got something a mite more serious in mind."

She came out of Dancer's stall and closed the door. "I don't think you mean what I think you mean," she said.

Mott leaned against the door of the tack room, arms folded across his chest. "What I mean is marriage. You might want to think it over."

The man was insufferable. She brushed past him. "I'm not marrying anyone, least of all you. Now don't you have something better to do? When you're not running my cattle into the fence?"

"I know you haven't exactly held me in high esteem lately," Mott said.

Bethany threw him a withering look. "The truth is, Mott, I wouldn't spit on you if you were on fire."

"You can think on my suggestion," he said, pushing his hat down tighter onto his head. "You don't have to answer right now. We'd have the biggest spread in the county, the two of us, if we put the Banner-B and my place together."

It was all Bethany could do not to laugh hysterically at Mott's offer as he headed for his pickup, which he'd parked under the big oak. Wait until Colt heard about this, he'd think it was the funniest thing he'd ever heard in his life.

That quenched any further laughter. Colt wasn't here. Colt wasn't around to share her troubles and her joys. And from what Mott had said, the rumor about Colt was true. That deputy sheriff that Mott was talking about might be in a position to know what had gone on in Oklahoma.

Discouraged, she went to look at Sidewinder, who had seemed depressed ever since Colt left.

"Yeah, me, too," she whispered to the horse, who hung his head over the stall door and actually let her scratch him under his forelock. "We miss him, don't we?"

The only answer was the frantic buzz of a horse fly that circled and flew away out the barn door.

THE NEXT DAY, BETHANY SAT on the back porch while Eddie trailed a bit of yarn along in the dust in front of the steps for the amusement of the new kittens. It was the end of a long afternoon at the Banner-B, and Colt had been gone for four days. Bethany, when she sat outside on evenings like this one, tried not to keep looking up the road for Colt. She'd heard he'd bought a car in town; Loreen and Joey had seen him driving it.

"A really funny-looking yellow car," Loreen had told her, wrinkling her nose. "It made a lot of noise and gave out a lot of smoke." Bethany had tried to imagine Colt in such a vehicle and couldn't. He was inexorably tied to the ranch pickup and Buckeroo in her mind.

"You know what I want to name these cats?" Eddie said, pulling her back from her thoughts.

"I don't know," Bethany said. She was fanning herself with one of the catalogs that never seemed to stop coming and wishing it would rain. Today was the hottest in a long time.

"I think I'll name them Taco, Burrito and Spaghetti after my three favorite foods." He beamed up at her.

Bethany was amused. "I suppose I should be glad that your three favorite foods aren't mashed potatoes, liver and turnips."

"Turnips? That's funny. I wouldn't ever name a cat Turnips." He lifted the string so that the orange tabby kitten jumped at it. "The mother's Taco, and this one is Spaghetti. I'll call the black one Burrito because he likes to sleep all rolled up. I can't wait until Colt comes back so I can tell him their names."

Bethany stopped fanning and edged a finger under her collar. "Colt might not be coming back, Eddie."

"He will. He said he's going to take me to the movies again." The simple faith contained in this statement touched Bethany, but she had taken it to heart when Colt had insisted that there was no reason Eddie had to be shielded from the truth all the time. There was, she had decided after that conversation with Colt, much more dignity for Eddie in learning to cope with the way things really were.

"Eddie, sometimes things change," she told him as kindly as possible. "Colt may not be able to come back."

Eddie threw down the string and jumped up. "It's your fault, Bethany! You made Colt leave!"

She wasn't prepared to see tears in Eddie's eyes, and they cut her to the quick.

"Eddie," she began, wondering how to tell him what he needed to know in order to forgive her, grasping for words that would soothe him.

"Don't 'Eddie' me! You made him go away!" And with that he turned his back on her and slowly walked back to the house, his dejection and disillusionment evident in the slump of his shoulders.

Bethany buried her face in her hands. For Eddie to blame her broke her heart. Eddie was seldom angry about anything, and she'd turned him against her.

Some days—some weeks, for that matter—she couldn't do anything right no matter how hard she tried.

After she dried her tears, she went to her special place by the creek and sat on the bench Justin had built for her. It was cooler here, and peaceful. Bird notes hung in the still air; the leafy dome of leaves above provided a blessed respite from the sweltering heat.

"I think I'm doing this all wrong," she whispered into the silence. "I wish I knew how to handle it."

She thought she heard someone murmur, "You're doing fine," but it may have only been the creek frothing in its shallows.

Chapter Ten

When Colt reached Oklahoma City, he checked into a cheap motel room and slept fitfully, tossing and turning and wishing with all his heart that he were back at the Banner-B.

But did he wish he'd told Bethany all there was to know?

Of course not. He had to take care of unfinished business first. And then—

He hoped he'd have the nerve to tell Bethany Burke that he was head over heels in love with her, even though he doubted she could love a guy like him.

He tried to reach Marcy, but a man—he assumed it was her girlfriend's father—told him that she wasn't at home. He tried again the next day, when Casey, the girlfriend, answered.

"Oh, you're Colt? Marcy talks about you sometimes. I'll tell her to call you."

Colt gave her his phone number at the motel, fuming because this was taking so long. Marcy, when he'd talked to her back at the ranch, hadn't wanted to give him her address. He didn't know why.

It was another whole day before he heard from Marcy, and then she seemed unconcerned about his impatience. "I've been busy," she said. "I couldn't call back right away."

"I came all the way from Texas to see you," Colt told her. "Can I come pick you up and take you out to breakfast in the morning?"

"No, no, I'll meet you." Marcy gave him an address, which he wrote down. He didn't like all the mystery, and he didn't see why he couldn't pick her up at the place where she lived with this Casey and her parents. But he didn't want to push it. He knew Marcy well enough to realize that she was skittish and might refuse to see him at all if that's what she got into her head to do.

So, on the fifth day after he'd left the Banner-B, Colt got up, shaved and drove to the restaurant where Marcy had suggested they meet.

She was waiting in a back booth when he walked in, and he recognized her long dark hair before she turned and smiled at him. Before he knew what hit him, she was flying across the floor, flinging herself into his arms.

"Colt! Colt!" she said over and over, and when he let her go, she looked around at the other staring customers and said with a flutter of embarrassment, "Well, hey, I guess I've made a scene."

"You go right ahead," Colt said comfortingly, thinking that he never could have guessed from this warm welcome that Marcy had seemed reluctant at first to see him. But then, she'd always been contradictory.

When he was sitting in the booth across from her, he decided that Marcy was prettier than ever but still didn't look a day over fifteen even though her eighteenth birthday was coming up soon. They ordered breakfast, and Marcy joked with the waitress before telling him that she herself had been working here on the evening shift for three weeks.

"Tips are good," she said. "The work's not too bad. Did you know I graduated from high school in the spring?"

Colt shook his head, wishing he didn't feel so out of touch with her.

Marcy edged forward and spoke enthusiastically. "I got my GED, that's how I met my girlfriend Casey. I want to enroll in a community college here. Casey's parents said I could live with them while I go to school."

"Nice of them," Colt said, sipping the coffee and finding it substandard compared to Bethany's. He forced himself to pay attention to Marcy.

"It's great to have my high school diploma. Are you proud of me?"

"Sure I am," Colt said. "You better believe it." She'd always been good at her schoolwork despite the problems at home.

Marcy brightened visibly. She paused, gauging his mood. "I've decided that I want to study computer science," she said all in a rush. She watched him for his reaction.

He shifted uncomfortably on the hard plastic seat. "Marcy," he said. "What about Alyssa?"

Her expression darkened. "I know, I know, you're probably real mad at me."

"I wonder what in the world you were thinking when you left her on a stranger's doorstep."

"You're not a stranger. You're my friend, my good buddy. I knew you'd look after her."

"Let me see if I can explain this, Marcy, so you'll understand. It wasn't my doorstep. A very kind lady happens to live there, and she didn't know what to think when a baby appeared out of nowhere. She still doesn't know what to think." He thought better of telling Marcy that Bethany thought Alyssa was his child, his and hers.

"But Colt, you live on that ranch. You could—"

"I couldn't. It's my first job out of prison. Do you have any idea what position you put me in? How you jeopardized my job?" It was getting more and more difficult to keep his cool right about now.

The waitress brought their breakfast, and Marcy stared down at her plate. "No," she murmured. "I guess I wasn't thinking all that clearly at the time."

Colt let out an exasperated sigh. "I reckon not. Why don't you tell me a little more about this? I mean, how you arrived at the decision to seek me out and dump Alyssa on me."

"Don't you like her? Isn't she a cute baby?" Marcy looked anxious, and he decided that she really had no idea how she had inconvenienced everyone involved. Or, for that matter, that there were laws against abandoning babies.

He tried to reassure her, though what he really wanted to do was shake some sense into her. "Alyssa is beautiful. She deserves better than what you dished out, Marcy."

"If you're going to be mean about it, I won't talk to you," Marcy said petulantly. She got up and flounced over to the ladies' room, went inside.

Colt reined in his annoyance. He wouldn't make any progress at all if he forced this issue. By the time Marcy returned, he had decided that she still had a long way to go before she understood the seriousness of her actions. Giving birth to a baby at the age of seventeen was no guarantee of maturity, apparently.

"All right," he said as she settled back on the seat across from him. He had an idea that this was going to be a long morning. "Tell me what was going on when you got it into your head to drive all the way to Gompers, Texas, and drop your baby off."

"Only if you won't yell at me." She eyed him warily.

He told himself that this was what Marcy had consistently experienced with Butch: loss of temper, furious rages. "I won't yell. I'll try not to be judgmental."

"You mean it?"

"I mean it."

Marcy took a sip of juice, swallowed, set her glass down. "Well, Frankie and I broke up right after Alyssa was born. He didn't want any part of her. So I went to live with some friends of ours, but the baby cried all the time, and they said I had to find another place. I ran out of money, and I spent a couple of weeks in a shelter, but time ran out there. I'd met Casey in my GED review class, and she was moving here with her parents, and I knew they would bring me with them if I didn't have Alyssa. So I borrowed Casey's car, drove down and gave her to you. And here I am." This last comment was offered brightly, as if she wanted to be commended for handling her situation so brilliantly.

Colt decided he'd remind her of previous promises. "Your note said you would take Alyssa back as soon as you got some money, but I haven't heard from you since you left her. You should have at least let me know where you were."

Marcy shrugged and ladled a dollop of jelly onto her

toast. "It's not like I've had much of a chance. The baby is okay, isn't she?"

"Alyssa's fine. She's growing fast, and she smiles, and pretty soon I bet she'll be crawling around and getting into things."

"Gee, you think so? What age do they do that?"

At least she looked interested in this, and Colt was grateful for any small miracles at this point. He knew from reading the baby book that the age for certain accomplishments could vary from kid to kid. "It depends on the baby," he said.

"Oh."

He cleared his throat. "Marcy, don't you want to see her?"

Marcy rolled her eyes, thinking. "Kind of." She dragged the words out as if she wasn't sure.

"I was hoping you'd come to Gompers and bring her back with you."

"Bring her back to Oklahoma City?" Marcy looked startled.

"Yeah. You're Alyssa's mother, Marcy."

She set her fork down. "I know, but I don't feel much like her mom. I mean, I go out on dates and stuff. What would I do if she lived with me? I don't make a whole lot of money working in this place. I don't even have my own apartment. What if I couldn't live with Casey anymore? We never told her parents I had a baby. And how could I go to school in the fall if I had Alyssa with me?"

"Marcy—"

"I hardly remember what that baby looks like, Colt. I want you to keep her. You're good with her, I know you are."

He fought his anger, barely managing to keep it in

check. "Don't you think I have my own problems? Don't you understand what you're asking? I don't have a home, either. I'm trying to get over the past few years and make a new start for myself!"

After his outburst, tears sprang to Marcy's eyes, and she looked at him across the table with an expression for all the world like a wounded pup's. "You got a new trial. You were acquitted."

"That doesn't erase those years in prison or the fact that something went terribly wrong in my life."

"And in mine," Marcy shot back, and that was all she needed to say to push his guilt button. He'd killed her father. If Marcy was a problem kid, that could be why. It could be all his fault.

"All right," he said heavily. "All right. We'll work something out, okay?"

"Okay," Marcy said. She offered a tentative smile.

He tried to eat, but the food turned to sawdust in his mouth.

"You know," Marcy said speculatively after a while. "Maybe I should come see Alyssa. Maybe I need to do that."

She might be saying that only to please him, but it was enough. "No maybe about it," he told her firmly. "I think you do."

He didn't know why, but he expected that if he could show up with Marcy at the Banner-B, everything would fall into place. With Marcy there, it would be easier to tell Bethany what he should have told her when he first arrived at the ranch. Or so he dared to hope.

BETHANY WAS MOPPING the kitchen floor when the noisy intrusive engine of a strange car died into the silence of a somnolent afternoon. She glanced out the kitchen door, hoping the visitor wasn't anyone too important; she didn't exactly look her best today. Her hair was piled on top of her head in a haphazard twist, and little sweaty tendrils were plastered against her cheek. She wore an old blouse that was too small, and she'd tied it under her breasts in a big knot to expose as much skin as possible to the air on this hot and unusually humid day. She didn't recognize the car, and she certainly wasn't expecting Colt to get out of it.

But he did, and then she remembered what Loreen had told her: yellow car, belching smoke. She didn't see any smoke, but the car was yellow, all right.

Over the past several days, ever since Colt left, her emotions had run the gamut. First she'd hated him. Then she'd missed him, so she couldn't have hated him all that much in the first place. Then she was angry with him for promising to make things better for her and not being able to follow through. Or maybe he would have if she'd given him a chance, so she hated herself for a while, too, for refusing to give him one.

But now that she saw him unfolding himself from that little car, she knew she loved him.

No, she didn't. She couldn't possibly love a murderer.

Well, she'd never asked him about that. So maybe he wasn't. But then there was the fact that Mott knew something from the deputy sheriff, so maybe he was.

Colt wasn't alone. A girl—a teenager—was with him. She looked around the ranch with a kind of bored interest. She didn't seem too impressed, but then Bethany supposed the Banner-B wasn't much to look at with its battered old buildings and everything dry as a bone because of no rain.

Bethany knew who the girl was. She recognized her

from the picture Colt carried in his wallet. She had to be Marcy.

Jesse bounded out of the shrubbery where he had burrowed in to keep cool and started to bark. When he realized that one of the visitors was Colt, he stopped yapping and pranced over to him, doing a little dance of joy. Colt bent and scratched the dog behind the ears, and Jesse's tail beat a rapid tattoo against his knees. Used to be, when he was happy, Jesse peed. Colt had trained that habit out of him, thank goodness.

"Good dog," Bethany heard Colt say. She quickly wrung out the mop and propped it in a corner of the kitchen. Dodging damp spots, she made her way across the floor and waited at the screen door to see what would happen next.

The girl saw her and smiled tentatively. She looked like a pleasant enough girl but hardly old enough to be a mother, and certainly not old enough to be involved with Colt. Bethany narrowed her eyes, considering if maybe she'd made a mistake all along. This girl—woman?—didn't look like anyone to be having a jealous fit about.

Colt took the porch stairs two at a time. "I've brought her," he said without preamble. He looked anxious, frazzled. Bethany merely stared at him. It was all she could do, considering that she wanted to burst into tears. She'd missed him. Lordy, but she'd missed him.

Colt turned to the girl. "Marcy, this is Bethany. She's the one you should thank for letting Alyssa stay here."

Marcy walked slowly up the porch stairs and peered at her through the screen. "Thanks," she said. "I mean, really. For taking her in."

"May we come in?" Colt stared right back at Bethany as if he couldn't get enough of the way she looked.

"I just washed the kitchen floor. Maybe you should go around front."

Colt nodded abruptly, and before she knew it, he was leading Marcy around the house. She heard Marcy say something about the pretty sunflowers growing under the den window, and, distractedly, trying to think, she pushed her hair behind her ears and went to look in the refrigerator. She'd drunk all the iced tea earlier, and she didn't have a thing to offer them. Well, maybe some fruit juice. Colt might want a beer. She didn't have any, but possibly Eddie could run some over from their house.

What was she doing? She was acting like Colt was somebody she had to impress, and Marcy, too. *Get ahold of yourself,* she told herself sternly. *God almighty, you're acting like a fool.*

It was no comfort to remind herself that she wasn't the first woman who had ever acted like a fool for love, and she wouldn't be the last.

She met them at the front door. She held it open and murmured, "Come in" as cordial as you please, and they did come in. They went into the living room, where Marcy chose a big wing chair that threatened to swallow her while Colt sat uneasily on the edge of the couch. Bethany perched on an antique carved straight chair that had little value as an antique because someone long ago had removed the original milk-paint finish. If it had been worth anything, she would have sold it long ago.

"Where's Alyssa?" Colt said.

"She's upstairs. Loreen had to go home early today," Bethany replied.

"Can I see her?" Marcy looked determined and matter-of-fact, not at all excited like you think a mother would be when she hadn't seen her baby for over a month.

"Sure. You want to go up by yourself?" Bethany didn't know quite how to handle this situation. Marcy didn't look exactly thrilled to be here.

"Okay." Marcy got up. Colt didn't say anything, and Bethany told her, "Up the stairs, first door on the right across the hall. The blue bedroom."

"Okay," Marcy said again. She trotted off, leaving Colt and Bethany alone.

"She's very young," Bethany said. It was all she could think of to say.

"Eighteen this month. Don't be too hard on her, Bethany. She hasn't had it easy."

Bethany heard Alyssa waking from her nap. She thought she heard Marcy murmuring to her, but she couldn't hear the words. A lump in her throat threatened to choke off her air. She didn't like to think of Alyssa's responding to another woman's voice, and she couldn't bear the thought of Alyssa's leaving them.

"I'd offer you something to drink if I had anything. I could call up Frisco, ask Eddie to bring over a bottle of beer."

"No, I don't want anything. How's Eddie doing?"

"He took your leaving pretty hard."

"Ah," Colt said, and he stared down at his boots.

"That's my fault. Eddie blames me, and rightly so."

"Look, Bethany, I don't want you to beat yourself up over asking me to leave. As it happens, I had to go to Oklahoma City and I would have been away for a while anyway. If I get a chance to talk to Eddie, maybe I can set things right with him."

"Maybe," she allowed.

"What's the latest with Mott?"

She wasn't sure she wanted to talk about it, but she couldn't be less than honest with Colt. Too bad he didn't feel the same way about her.

"Mott came around the other day," she said.

"What did he want?"

"It was too silly to tell." She stood up abruptly and said, "I'm going to get a glass of water."

She went into the kitchen and took ice cubes from the freezer and put them in a glass. Colt followed her and stood in the doorway looking ill at ease. "You want some water, too?" she asked out of politeness.

"Sure," he said. He watched her for signs of softening, but all he saw was confusion. And something more, something that gave him encouragement. She seemed to have a willingness to listen. Or at least that's what he figured, since she hadn't suggested that he leave.

She handed him the glass of water.

"You going to tell me about Mott, or do I have to learn about it in town?"

She managed what could pass for a shrug. "He came over here the other day. It was the same old thing with an added twist."

"Did he insult you? Say something he shouldn't?"

"He, um, suggested that we get married."

Colt struggled to keep his face impassive. "And you said?"

"I asked him if he preferred to leave on his own or if I should call Frisco to help him along."

"And?"

"He left. It was weird, though. I got the feeling that he was merely going through some ritual that he figured he'd have to try. He must have known I wouldn't even consider marrying him."

"I should hope not," Colt said grimly. He was burning with things he would like to say, things he would like to do. This wasn't the time, he cautioned himself. He'd better bide his time.

Bethany turned abruptly and began to wipe water spatters off the counter. It occurred to her that she shouldn't have told Colt about Mott's curious proposal. He might think she was telling him in order to taunt him or tease him or something, and that wasn't it at all. It was just that she had fallen into the habit of talking with Colt about the things that happened in her life, large and small. She had thought of him as a friend.

Friend or not, it didn't feel right to be engaging in small talk with Colt when there were so many other things to be cleared up. She dropped the sponge into the sink and grabbed the counter to steady herself. With one trembling hand, she pulled aside the weary kitchen curtains and saw through the window that outside, her garden was wilting in the hot sun.

It was excuse enough. She turned around. "I'd better go out and water those vegetables," she said. "Eddie hasn't been here yet today."

He didn't want her to go. "Bethany," he said, then stopped.

She made herself look at him. Upstairs the floorboards creaked as Marcy moved around the blue bedroom above them. "Colt," Marcy called down the stairs. "You want to come up here and change Alyssa's diaper?"

"Nope, and the clean ones are on the closet shelf," he called back.

This announcement was greeted first with a loaded silence, then a spate of muttering. They listened as Marcy stomped back into the guest room.

The old-fashioned schoolhouse clock on the wall seemed to be ticking very loudly into the ensuing silence. "What was it you were going to say a minute ago?" Bethany ventured.

"Seems like you had some questions last time we talked. Seems like you must want them answered. So why don't you go ahead and ask."

"Oh, my," she said helplessly. He was staring at her bare midriff, and she realized that she'd left her blouse knotted up high when what she should have done was untie it and tuck it into her shorts.

"Well?" he said.

She decided not to untie the knot right this minute. She put her wilting garden out of her mind; those plants would have to wait. She thought to herself, *Well, here goes.*

She lifted her head and looked him straight in the eye. He stared back, his lips fixed into a tight line.

"I heard in town the other day that you killed a man back in Oklahoma. Is it true?"

"Yes. Yes, it is, Bethany."

The words fell into her reality, heavy as stones. Once said, once thrown into the gulf between them, they would not disappear, and she knew it. She heard a great roaring in her ears, and the world seemed to recede a tad or two into a great misty void. "Would you mind elaborating on that?" was what she thought she said, but she wasn't sure. But why her violent reaction to the truth? When she had already suspected that there was something to the rumor?

All the world for her in that moment was concentrated in his eyes. Colt said, "I want to tell you all about it. But—" and he glanced briefly back over his shoulder into the hall "—not while Marcy is likely to walk in and ask a question about the baby. What do you say we go for a walk?"

This took her by surprise. "Walk where?"

"Along the driveway. Over yonder under the trees where it's likely to be cool."

She fought for composure. "All right. We can do that."

He called to Marcy, said they'd be back shortly, and then the two of them stepped out of the house into the scorching west Texas afternoon. The heat slammed into them, made Bethany's throat dry. As if it wasn't already dry enough.

Jesse James jumped up from beside the rocker and wanted to come with them, but Colt told the dog to stay, and he did. Bethany was so numb that she didn't even object when Colt wordlessly took her hand in his as they walked. And after he started telling his story, his terrible story, she forgot that he still held it.

Chapter Eleven

Colt told her that he'd arrived at Ryzinski's place on a cold morning one February. It was a big dusty horse ranch in the Oklahoma panhandle, land that rolled and dipped until it met up with a fence, then rolled and dipped some more until it butted up against the horizon. He'd heard that Butch Ryzinski needed a hand, someone who knew horses, and so he'd caught the first bus out of Tulsa, where he'd been working in construction and hankering to get back to horses somehow, somewhere.

When Colt presented himself for the job, Butch Ryzinski ambled out of the barn, looked him up and down with those slitty eyes of his and shifted the plug of Red Man from his right lower lip to his left.

"You start today, kid," he'd said before spitting a gob of tobacco juice across Colt's boots.

Colt had been heading toward the trailer that served as a bunkhouse when he noticed the girl hunched over on the top rail of the corral. She was slight, her figure barely starting to fill out, and she seemed unsure of herself like a lot of kids were at that age.

"Hi," she said, looking shyly out from under a thatch of dark hair.

"Hi," he replied, and that was how he first met Marcy.

She was a tenacious little thing, following him all over the ranch, and he made it a point to josh her and tease her at every opportunity. He felt sorry for her. The other hands told him that Marcy's mother had run off long ago. There'd been a housekeeper once, an anything-but-motherly woman who had something going with Butch at the time, and when she'd left after an explosive argument during which all the kitchen crockery at the Big House got broken, no one seemed to care much, least of all Butch.

Colt had been hired to break horses. As a bronco buster, he was supposed to have hands of iron and heels of steel. As a human being, he thought the usual way of breaking horses was all wrong. He'd already taught himself a new training method, and he'd inserted his ideas into Ryzinski's program quietly, without fanfare. He liked to gentle horses, not terrify them. The other hands were awed by his skill, and Colt had shown a few of them how to do what he did. Unfortunately Butch disagreed with Colt's philosophy right from the first, but as long as Colt produced good riding horses, he didn't say much.

The first time Colt found Marcy crying in an empty stall of the barn, bruises on her legs where Butch had whipped her with a yardstick, he confronted Butch in his office and tried to talk with him about it.

"You stick to breaking horses, I'll stick with breaking my kid," Butch told him. Colt had argued that kids weren't like horses and that there were other ways to discipline a young girl, but Butch would hear none of it.

"Get out of here," Butch said dismissively before

picking up the telephone and rapping out a number just to show Colt how unimportant he was around there. Seething, Colt had clamped his hat on his head and walked out, furious with Butch. Later that day, he'd shared a strawberry Popsicle with Marcy and got her talking about herself.

Marcy, it turned out, was terrified of her father. "He whips me 'most every day," she said sorrowfully, and when Colt asked what kind of transgressions merited a whipping, Marcy told him that anything could set Butch off. Phone calls from her friends at dinnertime. Not changing the toilet paper when the roll ran out. Giggling.

The other hands at the ranch had noticed how Butch treated Marcy, sure, but they said he didn't treat anyone well. If you worked at Ryzinski's, you were subject to the boss's tirades and tantrums, and the only thing to do was ignore them. They cautioned Colt not to interfere between father and child. "Butch has a terrible temper," they said. "Don't cross him if you want to keep your job."

The job meant a lot to Colt. He was saving his money to start his own business, a ranch where only his training methods would be used. Some days, when he had endured as many insults as Butch could dish out, when red dust hung heavy in the air and all he wanted to do was pull up stakes and leave, he had to remind himself why he was still hanging in there. He was on the way to a good life. Just one more year, he reminded himself, and then it was only nine months, and then six. Colt had invested his money in mutual funds here and there, and his nest egg had grown along with the booming economy. His dream was almost a reality.

And then he'd stumbled into a situation that convinced him that he couldn't ignore how Butch was treating Marcy any longer.

It had been late at night, and Colt had roused himself from his bed to go to the barn and check on a fractious quarter horse gelding he'd worked with that day. He heard arguing in Butch's office, and he knew right away who the participants were.

"You get back in the house and don't let me hear anything more about going out on dates!" Butch raged.

Marcy had turned into a beautiful fourteen-year-old, tall and shapely, and lately the son of a neighboring rancher had been driving over to see her every day since he'd gotten his driver's license.

"But Tiffany goes out with her boyfriend all the time," Marcy pleaded. "It's not like you don't know Jason. He's a good driver, real careful, and—"

"You don't know squat about what a guy really wants," Butch shouted. "You get in a car with a boy and you might as well kiss your virginity goodbye."

Marcy gasped. "Daddy, all we want to do is drive into town and go to a movie," she said, her voice rising.

"Yeah, and all *he* wants to do is run his hand up your leg and check out what's under your skirt."

Colt let himself out of the gelding's stall. He heard a chair scrape the floor, and Marcy flung the office door open. She saw Colt standing there, and she stopped in the doorway, her eyes wild. That's when Butch grabbed her from behind and hauled her back into the office.

"Daddy, you're hurting me! Let go!"

Colt couldn't stand any more of this. He followed them into the office with no clear plan in mind. He only knew that he had to do something.

Butch let Marcy go when he saw Colt.

"What do you want?" he snarled.

"Leave Marcy alone, Butch," Colt said firmly, putting the girl behind him. She cowered there, her breathing punctuated by little sobs.

"Get back where you belong, McClure."

"Why don't you cool off, Butch? Think about this and make up your mind tomorrow."

"I already done made up my mind, and I'll thank you not to interfere between me and my daughter. Marcy, come over here."

"No," Marcy said. Colt could feel her fear; it was almost palpable.

Butch moved toward them, menace oozing from every pore. "What did you say?" he said quietly.

"I said no, and I want to go back to the house."

"You're not going anywhere, young lady." Butch unbuckled his belt and ripped it from the loops. As he flexed it, the pupils in his eyes contracted.

"Butch, you better put that belt away," Colt said. This was one time that Butch wasn't going to hurt Marcy. He'd made up his mind when he'd crossed the threshold of the office that Marcy would be safe. He'd stood on the sidelines long enough, and he had saved almost enough money to leave. If he got fired for protecting a child, then so be it. It would be worth it.

"Stand back, McClure," Butch said.

"Don't touch her, Butch. Or you'll be sorry."

Colt spoke softly to Marcy, using the same tone of voice he employed when he was talking a horse through a difficult training situation. "Go, Marcy. I'll take care of this."

At first he thought she wasn't going to do it, that she was too frightened to bolt. But then she broke for the door, running scared.

Butch was quicker than Colt expected. He grabbed Marcy and caught her in a neck hold.

"Colt!" Marcy managed to cry before her father cut off her words with a swift tightening of his arm.

Colt had never been so furious in his life. He was so incensed that he actually saw everything as if through a red lens. All the slights, all the insults, all the nasty things that Butch Ryzinski had done to him and to everyone else flashed before his eyes in one swift fast-forward. He bunched up his fists and took a pot shot at Butch's jaw. Butch's head snapped back, but Colt's knuckles had merely grazed him. The blow was hard enough to make Butch release Marcy, who screamed.

"Run, Marcy," Colt said as Butch lurched behind his desk. Colt went after Butch, intending to punch the daylights out of him.

"He has a gun!" Marcy screamed, and sure enough, Butch reached in a desk drawer and withdrew a shiny nine-millimeter semiautomatic pistol, the one he kept there in case robbers ever showed up late at night when he was working.

"You think you can talk to me like that and get away with it?" Butch said. "Well, you can't." He aimed the gun at Colt's feet and fired. The bullet narrowly missed his right boot and dug a hole in the plank flooring.

"Put the gun away, Butch," Colt said.

For an answer, Butch fired another shot, this one into the ceiling.

It didn't take long for Colt to figure out that he was dealing with a madman. And it didn't look as if he could talk Butch into a peaceable ending for this surreal scene.

Marcy was frozen in front of the door, her face ash-white, her eyes reflecting her shock. If she could have moved, he reckoned, she would have. So there was no escape that way, and the office had no windows.

So far, talking to Butch hadn't worked. It might buy him some time, however, until someone else decided that it was right peculiar to hear shots coming from the barn and decided to investigate.

"Butch, counselors could help you and Marcy deal with your family issues," Colt said in a reasoning tone. "Put the gun away, and you can look into getting help tomorrow."

"People like you make me sick," Butch retorted. "Always trying to make things nice. Don't you understand that power is the only thing that really works? Not talk, not psychology, not anything."

"You're wrong," Colt said. He knew. He'd been in foster homes where he'd been beaten to within an inch of his life, and all he'd learned was resentment.

"Ranch hands," Butch said, "shouldn't watch *Oprah*." He seemed to find humor in his own pronouncement, and he chuckled, but it wasn't a normal kind of laughter. Colt pegged it as slightly maniacal, kind of crazy.

"So why don't I just shoot off your ear, and you won't be able to hear anything? Or your eye, and you won't be able to see anything?" Butch waved the pistol in a kind of an arc, and that's when Colt made his move. He tensed and jumped, hoping to knock the gun out of Butch's hand. But Butch must have anticipated his move, because he dodged sideways, and the gun went flying.

They struggled, grunting and cursing, and Butch pinned Colt over the desk. Colt rolled across to the other side, and Butch jumped on him so that they both fell to the floor. During the struggle, Colt thought, *Where is the gun?* and then he saw it near the door. He reached for it, and as his fingers closed around cold metal, Butch slammed his hand down on Colt's fist. Colt was aware of Marcy's sobbing somewhere, but he couldn't see her, where was she? Colt gripped the gun tighter, tighter, as he rolled through the open door out into the barn, and Butch pulled at his hand until the gun was between them, and Colt was gasping, struggling as Butch's weight pressed him into the hard floor, and then, suddenly, Butch relaxed his fingers and let Colt have the gun.

Colt pushed Butch off him and slowly stood up. Butch did, too, his chest heaving from the exertion of the struggle.

"Get out of here, McClure," Butch said. "Clear your stuff out of your bunk and don't let me see you around here again."

It was what he'd expected. "I'll leave," he said.

"Give me the gun." Butch held out his hand.

"Not until I take out the magazine." He wanted to protect his back as he left, just in case Butch got any ideas.

Colt knew his way around firearms, and he knew that if the gun's magazine was removed, it couldn't fire even if a round was left in the chamber. He started to snap out the magazine, keeping a sharp eye on Butch, who stood in front of him.

"I think—" said Butch, but Colt never found out what Butch thought.

Because as he was removing the magazine, the gun fired, and Butch Ryzinski took a bullet in the gut.

"He died, Bethany. Right in front of Marcy. Butch looked at me, rolled his eyes back in his head and died."

Bethany stared at Colt in horror. "How did it happen?"

"A bullet was in the chamber. The gun wasn't supposed to go off when the magazine was removed, but it did. No one believed me when I told them. The safety manual says it can't happen that way."

"Then how? Why?"

Colt shrugged. "After I went to prison, long after my trial, a policeman found a design flaw. The same thing happened to him while he was in a firearms-training session. Turns out that slight pressure on the trigger while you're removing the magazine can cause the gun to fire."

"How awful for you," Bethany said, her voice low.

"I'll say. The whole scene was terrible. Me standing there with the gun, not understanding why it fired. Butch bleeding to death in front of our eyes. It was bad for me, but it was even worse for Marcy. All I was doing was trying to protect her, but I only hurt her in the end."

Bethany stared off into the distance beyond the grove of trees where she'd found a place to sit on a fallen log. Colt sat beside her on the ground, his arms looped loosely around his knees. Somewhere a squirrel chittered, but other than that there was only the sound of the nearby creek.

"What happened to Marcy after—after—?"

"After her father died, she became a ward of the state. They put her into foster care, which about killed me. I was a foster kid, and there's no way I'd wish that on anyone. The ranch was sold to pay Ryzinski's debts. And I went to jail."

Now Bethany understood what that look in Colt's

eyes had meant: a secret tragedy. All along she had mistaken it for so many other emotions, but she had never guessed the worst.

"What about the gun? Why it misfired?"

"No one cared about that enough to check it out. Everyone believed I shot Butch on purpose."

Bethany swallowed. "How—how long were you in prison?"

His eyes didn't leave her face. "Three years. Three years of pure hell until I got out. I picked me up a little souvenir, this scar on my face, as a result of an inmate fight."

"Was that the sentence? Three years?"

Colt shook his head. "No, it actually was longer than that, but I about tore up the prison law library looking for a loophole, trying to fight my way out of there. In the end, a witness came forward. Someone was in the barn that night, but he was afraid to say so. His conscience finally got the best of him, and he went to the sheriff and told everything he saw."

"Who was it?"

"We had a guy at Ryzinski's, a helper. He cleaned out the barn, did the worst jobs, things no one else wanted to do. His name was Rusty, and he wasn't the smartest guy in the world. We all liked him a lot, razzed him a bit, but we would have done anything for him. He was kind of quiet, never wanted to draw attention to himself, and he was terrified of Butch Ryzinski. He saw and heard everything from an empty stall right next to me that night, but he didn't say anything at the time, so no one knew he was in the barn."

"Didn't the sheriff talk to him? Wasn't there any kind of investigation?" She felt her voice rising on a tide of disbelief, but not at Colt. She couldn't believe that someone had seen a shooting and hadn't tried to set things straight from the beginning.

"When the sheriff talked to Rusty, he just hung his head and said he'd been asleep. He'd been forbidden to be in the barn when he wasn't working, see, and he had his own little shack at the edge of the property where he slept, so none of the other hands questioned it when he said that's where he'd been. I sure didn't know he was in the barn that night."

"How'd you find out about it?"

"After the ranch was sold, Rusty found work with a local minister who needed him to sweep out the church, that kind of thing. Rusty was torn up pretty bad by what he'd seen, and he knew I'd gone to jail over it. He liked me, I treated him better than most of the guys. The minister urged him to go to the sheriff with his story, and on the basis of what Rusty said about peeping through a knothole in the stall that night, I won a new trial. By that time, police ballistics experts had discovered the design flaw in the pistol. That, along with Rusty's testimony, got me sprung."

"Marcy was a witness. Didn't she testify at the first trial that you didn't mean to shoot her dad?"

"Well, Marcy," Colt said with an exasperated sigh. "She testified, all right, broke down on the witness stand. She would have been a credible witness if she hadn't busted out with the news that she'd loved me ever since I came to the ranch, that she couldn't stand it if I went to prison. Her testimony turned some of the jurors against me. They thought I'd been fooling around with a fourteen-year-old kid."

"Oh, no!"

"I never had anything to be ashamed of where Marcy

was concerned, Bethany. I tried to help her, listened when she needed a friend. Later Marcy got counseling, that's one thing the state provided for her. She apologized to me over and over when she realized that what she'd felt for me was a simple crush, no great love or anything."

"But the damage was already done," Bethany added softly.

"Yeah, it sure was." Colt ducked his head so that Bethany could only guess at the emotions expressed on his face.

She said, "I'm surprised you don't hate her."

Colt stirred, rustling the dry leaves under his feet. "I can't hate Marcy, Bethany. I identify with how she feels, and I'll never forget that I'm the reason her father died."

"You didn't mean to kill him," Bethany pointed out.

"I know. That doesn't keep me from feeling guilty and responsible for the things that went wrong in Marcy's life after Butch wasn't around anymore."

"So you came here, and she followed you and left Alyssa?"

"That's the short version. We'd kept in touch, and I always let her know where I was." He paused, assessing her mood. "When I first started working here, if I'd told you everything I've talked about today, would you have let me stay?"

Bethany had to think about that one. "No," she said finally. "Probably not."

He let out a sigh. "When Marcy first brought her baby here, when Alyssa appeared on your doorstep out of the clear blue, I hoped that maybe Marcy would soon come and get the baby and be gone. And then I wouldn't have to explain anything. I could do my job and do it right, and you'd see that I was an okay guy. I know Frisco didn't like me, didn't trust me, that was one strike against me. The baby was another. I sure didn't want you to find out I'd served time in prison for murder.''

"I thought Alyssa was *your* baby," she said helplessly.

"I know. She's not."

"Why did you let me go on thinking—?" she said, in exasperated dismay.

"If I told you that," he said, and he stopped, watching her.

"Told me what?"

"If I'd told you that Alyssa wasn't mine, you'd have wanted to know whose she was. I'd have had to let the cat out of the bag, tell you everything."

"Would that have been so bad?"

His eyes were fierce now. "You're the first person I've ever talked to about being a foster kid. About how I felt 'way back then. I've never opened up to anyone the way I've opened to you, Bethany, and I was not capable before this of telling you that I killed a man. I wanted—I wanted you to think well of me."

Bethany swallowed. "Well, if Alyssa's not yours, whose baby is she?"

"We're going to talk to Marcy about that directly after we go back." He picked up her hand. She was still ashamed that it was callused like a man's, and she tried to pull it away, but he kept hold of it and pulled it to his lips. He kissed the palm, and she felt a tremor race up her spine.

She stood up, and Colt did, too. She didn't expect what he did next, which was to pull her into a big bear hug and hold her for a long moment. There was something soothing and calming about his embrace, and although the sexual tension was still there, it was not the uppermost thing in her mind.

"So, Bethany," he said, his breath warm against her ear. "Now you know everything about me. Once this thing with Marcy and the baby is settled, you can decide what to do about me. I'll leave, if that's what you really want."

He let her go, and she didn't speak. Couldn't, that was the truth about it, because her throat was clogged with unshed tears. As a survivor of her own tragedy, which she'd thought was the worst possible kind, she felt a kinship with Colt, who'd had to endure more than most. Losing her husband was awful, and she'd grieved and raged and suffered over it, but Colt had suffered, too. Was still suffering. It gave them more in common than she'd ever imagined.

Only one thing he'd said had struck her as false: that now she knew everything about him. Colt McClure had depths she could hardly imagine, and it might take most of a lifetime to learn them all.

"THE WAY IT WAS WITH ME and Frankie," Marcy said carefully, "was that I didn't have anywhere to go. Frankie wanted somebody to take care of him. He didn't like to wash clothes or clean house or cook. 'I been cooking all day at the Biggo Burger,' he'd say. So—" and she shrugged lightly "—I moved in."

"You weren't even seventeen years old," Bethany said, hardly able to believe that this girl had been so foolish.

"I thought I knew what I was doing. Till I got pregnant, that is. At first Frankie was happy. We'd get married, he said. Well, he never found a convenient time to go get a license. Or to find a preacher. So I got bigger and bigger, and Frankie started staying out all night, and then I had the baby.''

''And he still didn't want to get married?'' Bethany asked gently.

''No, and he hated having a kid around. He wanted me to go out with him and party, but we didn't have money for a sitter, so I'd stay home and he'd go. He came home drunk, and he'd hit me, and I finally left. I thought it was the right thing to do since I didn't know if he might hurt Alyssa or not when he got mad.''

''You must have loved him,'' Bethany said. She couldn't look at Colt right then, didn't want to talk about love where he might read the feelings for him that she was sure she could no longer hide.

Marcy's head shot up. ''I never loved Frankie,'' she said. ''He was somebody to take care of me when I couldn't take care of myself. I'm learning how to do that. Maybe I can even take care of Alyssa, who knows?''

Impetuously Bethany got up and crossed the room. She leaned down and put her arms around Marcy.

''I'm so sorry, Marcy,'' she said.

Marcy managed a smile. ''You don't have to feel sorry for me. I'm going to make it. Somehow.''

It was then that the phone rang. It was Dita calling to tell them that she had plenty of chili and would be happy if they all could come over for dinner.

Colt stood up. Marcy did, too. He slid an arm around her shoulders. ''Reckon you can handle a big bowl of Eddie's best chili right about now?'' he asked her.

''Reckon I can,'' she said right back, and then the two of them smiled at each other.

Bethany went upstairs to get Alyssa, removing the

baby from the cradle with even more tenderness than usual.

She cuddled Alyssa for a long moment after the requisite diaper change. "I'm going to miss you," she said. "I'm going to miss you a lot."

If Alyssa understood, she gave no sign. She merely settled down against Bethany's shoulder, and Bethany pushed away the thought that this was where Alyssa belonged, in her arms. The baby had a mother, a mother who had, it looked like, come to claim her.

Supper was a haphazard affair. Marcy, who seemed emotionally flattened by the day's events, retreated into a shell. Dita, after a cursory glance at Marcy, remained strictly nonjudgmental, for which Bethany was thankful. Frisco was his normal distrustful self, and Colt was especially considerate of Eddie, who was overjoyed to see his idol again. Bethany watched the others and wondered where they would go from here. These people were her family. They were unrelated by blood, but they were still the most important people in the world to her. Except for Marcy, of course, and for her, Bethany felt only compassion.

Alyssa was passed around like a sack of potatoes, since everyone assumed that she'd be leaving soon with Marcy. Bethany wasn't so sure about this. Marcy still wasn't acting particularly maternal. She was more interested in smoothing her eyebrows, staring into space, and avoiding Jesse, who annoyed her by trying to lick her hands every time one came within reach of his long pink tongue.

Colt decided that he would move back to the barn and that Marcy should sleep in the house in the guest room with Alyssa. Bethany knew that he was trying to promote bonding between mother and child, but Marcy said, "You mean I have to get up with her at night? Can't *you* do that?"

"Marcy, she *is* your baby," Colt said patiently, a statement that provoked a stony response from Marcy.

After they went back to her house, Bethany showed Marcy where to hang her clothes and told her that she could use a couple of drawers in the dresser, but Marcy didn't seem happy about the idea.

"I'm not going to be here all that long. I didn't bring many clothes," she said, and it was true. She'd only carried a small overnight bag in from the car.

"Did Colt say when he plans to drive you back to Oklahoma City?" Bethany asked.

"Oh, I'm taking the bus. I don't expect him to drive me." This announcement was delivered airily while Marcy studied her image in the mirror and fussed with her hair.

"Marcy," Bethany said, and then she cautioned her that it wouldn't be easy riding a bus while carrying a baby and a diaper bag and a supply of formula and a child seat.

"How would you know?" Marcy retorted, and that's when Bethany gave up.

She made sure Alyssa was settled for the night and left Marcy sitting disconsolately on the guest room bed pretending to read an upside-down copy of *True Romance*. Bethany had things to do, accounts to straighten out, but once she was sitting at her computer, she couldn't concentrate. She moved around the house with a strange restlessness that she couldn't explain, feeling distracted and unfocused.

She attributed her unsettled mood to the hot weather, the humidity. It was hotter than she'd ever known it to be, which was saying a lot for this part of Texas. Finally, after peeking into the guest room and seeing that Marcy was lying on her side with her eyes closed and that Alyssa was asleep in her cradle, she decided to walk over to the barn. Colt had removed the mother cat and her kittens from the porch to the barn earlier, but he'd left the cat food in the kitchen, and he'd need it soon.

She picked up the bag of cat food and stepped out into the sultry night air. Even the cicadas were quiet, and Jesse James wasn't anywhere to be seen. She thought she saw scudding clouds in the distance, but it was too dark to tell if they were thunderclouds. For a moment she thought she smelled the fresh scent of rain but decided that she must be mistaken. But oh, how they needed it. Frisco had told her yesterday that he was worried about their water supply. He'd said the well was drying up, and if that happened, he predicted a disaster, especially since the creek was low.

When she arrived in the barn, Colt was in the tack room checking out a new bridle under the bright overhead light. The mother cat was bedded down in a box in the corner nursing the kittens. Colt looked up, surprised to see Bethany, and in that moment she felt a rush of understanding and excitement and, yes, a thrill that this man could care about her, that he wanted her. She saw it in his eyes, that wanting, and it touched her so deeply that she hardly knew how to talk to him.

But she did. Mundane things would do.

"I brought the cat food over," she said, setting the bag down on the stairs that led to his room. It was hot in here, hotter than the house even, so hot that her shirt stuck to her skin.

"Thanks. I was going to come around later to see

how things are going," he said. "Everything okay over there?"

She leaned on the edge of the door, watching his big hands as they hung the bridle in its place. The light in here was too bright, and it hurt her eyes. "I don't think so," she said. "Marcy's not responding to the baby. How she couldn't, I don't know, especially when the baby is as cute as Alyssa."

Colt sighed. "Maybe this forced togetherness will help."

"I don't know if forced togetherness ever makes anyone feel anything," Bethany said doubtfully.

Colt came and stood before her, his eyes sparkling. "Doesn't it? Maybe you should be thinking that one over again."

She figured out his meaning as a roll of thunder shook the barn to its foundations. "Why, I do believe it might rain," she exclaimed, turning away from him in confusion. Her skin fairly itched with wanting him to touch her.

As if he could read her thoughts, he reached out an arm, drew her back. "I think you're right," he said. "Those might be the first drops we hear right now."

She tried to breathe normally as his hands curved around her waist and pulled her close, snugging her up against him. "We sure need this rain. Frisco said the well might run dry. He said—"

Colt chuckled. "I am not one whit interested in what Frisco has to say about anything unless it's you and me."

"I should get back to the house before it starts really coming down hard," she murmured. The scent of him filled her nostrils, and she closed her eyes.

"Don't go," he whispered. "Not yet."

She opened her eyes as a jagged bolt of lightning rent the air. Thunder followed immediately. "Marcy might be scared. She might worry."

"Marcy isn't the least bit scared of thunder and lightning. We used to have some real thunderboomers back in Oklahoma." He nuzzled her cheek, sank his face in her hair.

"Colt, what's going on here?" she said, trying to bring rational thought into this situation.

"Oh, I'd say it's something right special," he said in that teasing tone of his.

"Colt," she said, but he turned her in his arms and pulled her close.

"Remember I said I'd be back? Remember I said I was giving you something to remember me by? Well, I've been remembering, too. Don't you want me to kiss you again, Bethany? Say you do."

She gazed at him, unable to speak.

"Say it!" This time his voice was rough with passion, and his eyes burned into her like coals.

"I do," she said. "Oh, yes, Colt."

His eyes never left hers. "You do what?"

She swallowed. "I want you to kiss me."

He did, his arms going all the way around her, his lips moving upon hers with unerring skill. My, but he knew what he was doing in the kissing department, and she gave in to it. Before she knew it, she was kissing him back, rising to her tiptoes so that he could kiss her more thoroughly. She had no idea how long the kiss lasted, but she counted several rumbles of thunder and one big clap of it before he was finished.

"I'd say we're getting pretty good at this," he drawled, and she smiled against the front of his shirt.

"Not that we've had all that much practice." He kissed her again.

In one of the stalls behind her, a horse whinnied. Colt stopped the kiss, pulled away. "That's Princess," he said. "Maybe I better see how she's doing."

She nodded, grateful for a chance to regroup, and he walked the length of the barn to where Princess was hanging her head over the door of her stall. Colt patted the horse's nose and talked quietly to her for a minute or so while Bethany looked out at the rain spattering dark pockholes in the dust. She figured that now would be a good time to split and run for the house, run for her life—but she didn't want to. She wanted to stay right here with Colt.

He came back and switched off the tack room light, leaving only the dim light on in the barn. The darkness settled in around them as he slid an arm around her shoulders. "It looks like this storm will have to move through before the rain stops. I was thinking we could go up to my room. At least it would be more comfortable."

She was grateful for the darkness that concealed her expression, which she knew must reflect all the doubt and confusion and longing she was feeling right then. It wasn't as though she didn't know the implications of going with Colt to his apartment upstairs. She did. She knew what was likely to happen if they were alone and in this mood.

But she wanted it to happen. She wanted Colt to make love to her. It seemed to her that their lovemaking was long overdue, that she had waited quite long enough. That Justin—

She had almost thought that Justin wouldn't mind. Well, Justin was gone. He would never be back. And he would have wanted more than anything for Bethany to be happy.

Colt offered his hand. Bethany took it and followed him upstairs, her heart beating in triple-time. Once they reached the door at the top, Colt swung it open and stepped to one side for her to enter.

It was hot in his apartment, but not unbearably so. She saw right away that he'd changed things considerably since she'd been here last. He'd moved the bed so that it caught more of a breeze from the window, and he'd wedged the table and chairs into a corner so there'd be more room. He'd even found a pretty blue plaid bedspread somewhere, and everything was clean and free of dust.

"You've done a great job in here," she said.

He lit a candle and set it on a saucer on the dresser. "Wait until you see what I'm going to do next," he teased, and he turned and tipped a finger under her chin. "Why, Bethany, I do believe you're blushing." The flickering candlelight washed his features in gold, accentuated his deep-set eyes.

She looked away. "I expect I am," she said. "I'm not used to going to men's rooms."

He sobered at that. "Do you mean that there's been no one since your husband died?"

"No one," she said.

"That's a long time for a woman like you to be without a man."

"It was my choice," she said.

"The fact that you have chosen me makes me very happy," he said, sounding strangely formal.

He kissed her and said, "You're not nervous, are you?"

"A little."

"Don't be. I've wanted to do this since the moment I saw you." He kissed her eyelids, each in turn, and pressed his mouth lingeringly to hers. He was so gentle that she ached inside; wanted more. His lips feathered downward along the graceful slope of her neck while his hands lifted her hair. He threaded his fingers through it, spreading them so that her hair fell through them strand by strand.

"You have such pretty hair. It looks like you wash it in sunbeams—smells like it, too."

She hardly knew how to reply to this. She wasn't sure she could have if she had to. She seemed to have no control over herself, her thoughts, her body. For someone who had always prided herself on her own determination and spunk, it felt strange to be so completely in the power of someone else. And not just anyone, but this cowboy whom she'd never even met until a month or so ago.

Slowly he began unbuttoning her shirt and peeling it away from her skin. The air felt good on her bare skin, cooling it. He slid the shirt off her shoulders, circled his hands around and unhooked her bra. When he reached under it to touch her breasts, she shrugged out of both shirt and bra. His surprise and then his pleasure showed in his eyes.

"I knew you'd be beautiful," he said, his voice low and rasping in his throat. He opened his palms over her bare nipples, sending waves of sensation rippling through her whole body. It had been so long since she had felt anything like it that all she could do was close her eyes and ride with it, yearning for more. He bent and took one rosy peak into his mouth, then the other. She let out a soft gasp at the heat of his lips and braced herself against her own flagrant desire by grasping his shoulders.

Then he was kneeling before her as he unbuttoned her shorts, and she was stepping out of them, and everything segued into slow motion. It was as if this was all happening to someone else, and maybe it was. She certainly didn't feel like the same Bethany Burke she had been only a month ago or a week ago or even a day ago. She was someone else entirely, a wanton woman who was urging Colt out of his clothes and who was being swept up in his arms and laid upon his bed.

And then she was crushed beneath him, his hands inflaming her skin as she gasped for breath. He knew how to touch her, how to skim his fingers ever so gently at first until she grew accustomed to their greediness and guided him where she wanted him to go.

Not that she wasn't a little greedy, too. She gripped the tight strong muscles of his forearms, slid her hands around to his back and the hard braided ones there. His mouth found hers, whispered her name once against her lips, then plundered fiercely and brutally.

They kissed again and again, feeding on each others' hungry mouths. Tongue tangled with tongue, teeth nipped and bit until she became delirious with passion. And that's what it was, pure passion, a fierce and savage meeting of bodies and minds and souls that had too long been solitary. It was as though she had found the world again, or at least the only thing that was important in it, and Colt was her lifeline. Her lifeline, and perhaps, she dared to hope, her life.

The window above the bed was open, curtains billowing slightly in the breeze, and outside the rain began to fall in earnest. Past Colt's shoulders, beyond the small room where they lay, Bethany saw lightning as it rent the sky again and again, felt the thunder as it rolled across the land, shaking the barn, rumbling deep in the earth. She saw it, but she could think of nothing but her body and Colt's so ferociously joined together, fused by a power more electric than lightning and more earth-shaking than a few claps of thunder. The rain lashed out of the sky, whipped through the open window, cooled their frantic hot bodies until they were soaking wet. The heat now came from inside, burning her like a flame, searing and torturing her until she arched beneath him, raw with desire. He drove into her relentlessly, ruthlessly, his breath harsh in her ear. She climaxed first, unable to stop herself, unable to wait any longer, and then Colt exploded into her with such abandon that all she could do was clutch him and cry out his name.

They lay spent, neither of them thinking to close the window, neither of them caring what was going on in the world outside the one they had created. After a while, Bethany opened her eyes. Colt, above her, illuminated by the light from the guttering candle, was gazing at her with profound pleasure. She reached up wonderingly and touched her finger to the rain on his face.

"Oh, Colt," she said. "I never knew it would be like this." She gloried in the incredible pleasure of closeness.

"I did. From the first moment I saw you." He settled into her arms, his dark head pillowed on one breast, a hand possessively covering the other.

"You know," he said, "I think the long drought might well be over."

BETHANY SLEPT IN COLT'S arms almost until dawn. She woke up to the glow of the green numerals on the electric clock on Colt's dresser while it was still dark, and at first she had no idea where she was. Then she remembered it all—trailing Colt up the stairs to his apartment, the way he had undressed her, how she had tugged at his clothes, and finally making love as the storm crashed and flickered outside.

Colt's hand curved reflexively around her breast as she stirred. She angled away from him, but he only drew her closer. Was he awake? She wasn't sure. She should get up and go, get back to the house before Marcy noticed that she was gone.

But oh, it felt wonderful to be cuddled up to Colt in the predawn darkness, to take pleasure in their newfound intimacy.

She kissed his cheek, or at least what she thought was his cheek. She couldn't see him all that well in the dark. "Colt? I'd better go."

He tightened his embrace. "Not yet. Let me hold you a little longer."

"This feels so good. I love lying here in your arms. But—"

"But you hope I'll make love to you again?"

She smiled into the darkness. "Yes, I'd like that. When we have more time."

He was caressing her breasts, slowly, gently. "There's time now."

"You know everyone expects me to be in my own bed at the house." Slowly she was giving in to it, to him. His hands moved lower, found her center, touched it.

"Can't you stop bein' responsible for a few more minutes?" His lips moved to the hollow in her neck, nuzzled there, and dreamily she thought that maybe being responsible wasn't all it was cracked up to be. You had to think of others all the time, never yourself, and it was so lovely to have someone who thought about her and what she wanted to do and what she liked. What she liked right now was Colt's fingers circling, teasing, and his mouth moving lower and lower.

"Do you like this? And this?" he murmured, and she answered with a sharp intake of breath.

"Do you want me to stop?" he said, laughter in his voice, and by this time she was a shuddering tangle of nerve endings, all exquisitely primed.

"Lordy, no," she whispered, and he laughed out loud, an exultant sound, and then she felt exultant, too, and uninhibited, and happy.

Which was a kind of miracle, if she wanted to think about it that way, but it turned out that she didn't do much thinking at all.

They were roused later by the sound of a car's engine starting.

"What's that?" Bethany murmured.

"It sounds like my car," Colt said. He sat up in bed and looked out the window as the car jolted in fits and starts up the driveway. "It *is* my car," he said.

"Marcy?" Bethany asked.

"Marcy, for sure."

Colt jumped out of bed and pulled on his jeans. It took Bethany a few more moments to dress, but she caught up with him on the porch of her house. Together they raced through the kitchen and up the stairs to the guest bedroom.

Marcy was gone. And the cradle was empty.

She had taken Alyssa.

Chapter Twelve

The note said, "I always hated goodbyes and I'm not very good at them. Thanks for everything, and I'll do the best I can with the baby." It was signed "Love ya, Marcy."

"We wanted Marcy to take over," Colt said heavily. He sank down on the edge of the bed. "We wanted her to act like she's Alyssa's mother."

Bethany's mind was a-jangle with second thoughts. "What if Marcy can't provide for her? Marcy doesn't have a home of her own. She's going to school, she says."

"She *says*," Colt replied. "She mentioned on the ride down here from Oklahoma City that maybe she could move in with another waitress who works at the coffee shop. Trouble is, she also said that she isn't much good at driving a car with manual transmission, and she just took off in one. Who knows if anything she says is the straight skinny?" He let out an exasperated sigh.

Downstairs, they heard the kitchen door open and close. "Bethany?" It was Eddie, and he sounded frantic.

"Yes, Eddie, I'm up here."

They heard him laboriously climbing the stairs. Bethany started pacing back and forth in front of the cradle, trying to subdue the sick feeling in the pit of her stomach.

Eddie poked his head into the room. "I thought Colt must have left again," he said. "His car drove away."

"That was Marcy. She's the one who left," Colt explained, and he was rewarded by the big grin of relief that spread across Eddie's face.

"Oh, boy, am I glad! I liked Marcy, though." He noticed the empty cradle. "Where's Alyssa?" he said in alarm.

"Marcy took her," Bethany said.

"But she's our baby! How could Marcy take our baby?" Eddie looked bewildered.

Bethany put an arm around Eddie. "Alyssa's not ours, Eddie. She never was. She always belonged to Marcy."

"She liked me! Alyssa did, I mean. She liked me to rock her in her cradle and tickle her to make her smile. Sometimes I got to give her a bottle." He bit his lip, looking from Bethany to Colt.

"Well, Ed, we just kind of borrowed her. You know, like we're borrowing Princess so we can get her ready for Joey's sisters to ride?" Colt stood up and clapped Eddie on the back. "What do you say we go see Princess right now?"

Eddie looked reluctant. "Well, okay," he said. "What are you going to do, Bethany?"

Bethany felt a bleakness settle around her heart. The sight of the empty cradle affected her more deeply than she wanted to let on in front of Eddie. "Oh, I guess I'd better throw in a load of laundry. Clean up around here. That sort of thing."

"You want me to help?"

"No, you go with Colt to see Princess. I'll be fine. Just—fine." She struggled to control the tears that threatened to spill over at any moment.

Colt touched her arm. "You're sure you'll be okay? I'll ask Dita to come over if you like."

"I'm all right." She wasn't, not really. "What about your car?" she said.

Colt shrugged. "I don't know. Marcy didn't ask if she could take it, but if it helps her…" His voice trailed off, and he forced a smile. "I'm going to miss the little one. I sure am." With that he was gone, and Eddie followed.

Bethany let the tears come then, let them slide down her cheeks and dampen her blouse. She would miss Alyssa, too. It occurred to her as she stood in the middle of the room where Alyssa had always slept that she would never hear that first little clink of spoon on tooth that heralded the start of teething. She wouldn't be around for Alyssa's first tiny tentative step or her toilet training. It was awful to think that Alyssa would grow into a toddler and a first-grader and a preteen and a teenager, and Bethany wouldn't be part of any of it.

She tried to imagine Alyssa as a teenager. Would she look like Marcy? Would she be as tall, or would she be shorter? Would she be as flighty as Marcy? Or maybe the question was really whether Alyssa would have a life as fraught with difficulty as Marcy's had been, or as unhappy.

Bethany wished she hadn't thought of that. She'd had a happy childhood herself before her parents died within months of each other shortly after she graduated from high school, and she wanted Alyssa to have a good life. She wanted her to have someone who loved and cared for her, someone who only wanted the best for her, a family like—

A family like hers. Like Frisco and Dita and Eddie, and Colt now that he was one of them.

With Marcy, was that possible?

While Alyssa had lived with them, she'd known that every one of them who took care of her would never let her be uncomfortable, nor would they fail to feed her on schedule. A child who was brought up in that way learned to trust the whole world because the part of it that she knew fulfilled her every need. The parenting at this critical point of Alyssa's development shaped her understanding and expectation of life in general.

Would Marcy be able to provide the same kind of environment?

Of course not.

Marcy was hardly capable of looking after herself yet. How could she take on the responsibility of a baby, too? How could they have encouraged it when Marcy wasn't ready?

Bethany's tears began in earnest then. She cried for Alyssa, who would never know how much all of them at the Banner-B had loved her. She cried for Marcy, who would somehow have to learn how to be a decent parent. She cried for Colt, too, but most of all she cried for herself. She had always wanted a baby. And now Alyssa was gone.

Colt found her that way when he came in later. "Hey, we can't have you looking like the world is going to end," he said.

"I thought I wanted Alyssa to be with her mother. I wasn't prepared to think that we've made a big mistake by encouraging Marcy to take her back."

"Maybe Marcy will grow into motherhood. Maybe everything will be all right." Colt didn't sound as though he believed it, though.

Bethany forced herself to ask about Colt's progress with the training school. "Is there anything new, Colt?"

"I've got a couple of guys comin' from Kentucky next month, and we're goin' to work for a while on how to get a horse to join up. That's when you make him think you're the lead horse and he's supposed to follow you. And that fellow over in Lubbock wants to bring a horse over for me to work with."

This was good news, but Bethany couldn't feel any joy over it. Come to think of it, she didn't feel much of anything. Even her happiness about last night, about making love with Colt, was subdued.

"You know what I think we need?" Colt said.

She shrugged. "I guess you don't want me to say that we need that baby back," she said.

"Well, we might want her, but she's not ours. I hope we'll hear from Marcy in a day or two and that she'll tell us she and Alyssa have found a good place to live. In the meantime, what do you say you and I kick up our heels? We were supposed to have a date the night that I put the sign up on the road. Want to go to Lubbock, have dinner, and I'll see if you've really forgotten how to dance?"

He was being so kind, thinking of something to cheer her up. She didn't think she could be so easily cajoled out of her sadness, but she might as well make an effort.

"I'll pick you up around six-thirty," he said. He glanced over at the dress that was still hanging on the kitchen door. "Wear that. You'll look fantastic in it."

She tried to smile. "Okay, cowboy," she said.

It was the first time in a long time that she'd been

able to leave the house without worrying about a babysitter for Alyssa. That thought, however, was not much comfort.

AS RESTAURANTS WENT, it wasn't luxurious, but candles on the tables gave it a kind of magic. Bethany's eyes lingered on all the little details—the red tablecloths, the fresh flowers, the waiters' white shirts. She hardly ever went anywhere outside Gompers, and she hadn't realized until now that she'd missed some of the niceties that the good life could provide.

She didn't feel ill at ease with Colt. She'd worn her new dress and her hair swept up on one side, and he had on a sport coat that she'd never seen before. He was a handsome commanding presence, broad-shouldered and lean, and she was proud to be with him. He chatted easily, punctuating his words with that slow easy smile that never failed to charm her.

By tacit agreement, neither of them mentioned Alyssa nor Marcy, knowing that thinking about them would cast a pall over the evening. Instead they talked about his plans for the training school, and she suggested some things that he thought were good ideas.

"If we fixed up the old bunkhouse, we'd have someplace for the overflow of boarders from the Truetts' to stay," she told him. "Some simple carpentry—maybe Joey could help—and replacing the front steps would go a long way toward making it habitable."

Colt laughed at this. "You must think I have a chance at succeeding at this," he said. "If you think there's going to be more people than Miss Maudie and Miss Claretta can handle, I mean."

"I do think your school is going to take off, Colt,"

she said seriously. "I'm worried about hiring more help."

"You think that's going to be a problem? Why, I'll be fighting people off with a stick. Everyone will want to work at the Banner-B." He was jovial and expansive, but Bethany wasn't sure he was right. She'd been dealing with the problem of getting people to work for her for too long.

"Where will you find good people? We'll need another hand or two to work the cattle if you're busy training horses, and maybe somebody to help me with the bookkeeping."

"I've got Joey to get the word out. He's been telling folks what I'm planning to do, and when I was in town today, I had a guy walk right up to me and ask if I'd have a job for him."

"Who was it? Anyone I know?"

He named a man that worked for Mott, Chad Murray.

"Chad won't leave Mott. He's been there a long time."

"He said he's ready to leave. Seems he's had enough of Mott. Says he's got a friend who will come with him. Some guy that works the cattle."

This was good news, but for some reason it made Bethany uneasy. Her mood took an upturn, though, and by the time they'd reached the dance hall, she was feeling much more cheerful.

It was the largest dance hall in town, but Bethany had never been there before. A country-western band was featured, and tables were arranged in tiers so everyone had a view of the dance floor, which was three levels below. After they were seated, Bethany took in the brightly colored globe lights hanging from the pillars and the mirrored ball revolving above the dancers and sending rainbow reflections around the room.

"You look like Alice in Wonderland after she fell down the rabbit hole," Colt told her, grinning.

She smiled back. "I'd forgotten how festive a place like this could look."

"Don't you have any hobbies? Things you enjoy?"

"Keeping the ranch solvent," she said wryly, and then they both laughed.

It was early, and the hall wasn't yet crowded. A waitress who was gussied up in a short cowgirl outfit took their order for drinks. "I knew a night out would do us good," Colt said.

As he spoke, two men entering the dance hall caught Bethany's eye. One was short and growing a beer belly, the other was tall and wearing a blue suit. A suit was so out of place in a dance hall like this that she looked more closely. The paunchy one was Mott, but she didn't recognize the man in the suit. Maybe he was from out of town. He certainly didn't look like a local.

She cut her eyes quickly toward the door. "Don't look now, Colt, but Mott just walked in."

Colt spared a glance in that direction. "Just what we need," he said with a groan. "Somebody to remind us about one of the things we're trying to forget."

There were two rows of tables arranged on the tier below. Bethany stiffened as Mott and his companion ambled toward them. Mott was talking so fast and furiously to the man that he didn't see them sitting above him, and when the two men seated themselves at a table, they were screened from view by a large pillar.

"We can move if you like," Colt said in a low tone. "We don't even have to stay here to dance if you don't want to. We could go someplace else."

Bethany shook her head. "I'm going to be living in the same neighborhood with Mott for a long time. I can't dodge him forever, so I might as well get used to running into him now and then."

"You know what I like about you, Bethany? You're a calm woman. You don't get rattled over every little thing."

"Goodness gracious, I have more important things to do," she said.

"Like what?"

"Like planning for the training school. Getting the Banner-B back to the way it's supposed to be."

"We're aiming to do that. For sure."

Bethany sipped her drink. As the band headed for a break, Colt took off his jacket and draped it over the back of his chair. He rolled up his shirtsleeves. "In case I have to teach Mott a lesson," he said.

Bethany narrowed her eyes. "Are you joking?"

"Up to a point. I won't take any guff from him, though. You might as well know that from the get-go."

Mott and his companion were talking loudly, and she couldn't help but hear.

"Bethany," Colt began, but she raised a cautionary finger to her lips.

"Shh," she whispered. "Mott just mentioned his ranch." She leaned forward to listen.

"I can't let you borrow more money," the man in the blue suit was saying. "You're having trouble making payments as it is."

Mott mumbled something about overhead.

"Rubye *said* Mott had financial problems," Bethany whispered to Colt. "I wasn't sure whether to believe her."

"You owe us a good bit of money," Blue Suit said.

"Tell me, Findley, how much do you owe First Bank of Gompers?"

"Well, there's the mortgage, and then there's that other loan I took out a month ago," Mott said. "It ain't my fault our wells ran dry. It's this drought. I had to drill me some new wells, and that took money I didn't have. Plus the new loan officer gal that the bank brought in from Arizona has it in for me." He said more that neither Colt nor Bethany could make out.

"Look here, Findley, it seems to me you have two choices. You can either default on the loans or you can pay them." Blue Suit had adopted a tougher tone.

Mott's voice became whiny. "I can't pay anything right now. You wouldn't want me to sell part of my land to pay off loans, would you?"

"Hell, I don't care what you do. You owe us money, and that's that."

"I'll pay. I'll get the money somewhere." Mott was desperate now, and Bethany could imagine him sweating as he tried to stave off repayment.

"Listen, you'd better have the money in my office by Monday noon." A scrape of a chair on the floor, a shuffle, and Blue Suit got up and walked out. He had a portable phone to his ear and was talking into it when he left.

"Hot damn," said Colt.

Bethany wasn't gleeful over another's misfortune, but she couldn't help feeling relieved now that she knew that Mott really did have money problems. It was clear that he was in no position to threaten her anymore; he must have proposed marriage the other day out of desperation, not only to gain control of her land but for the water on it. The Banner-B had Little Moony Creek and deep wells that, despite Frisco's gloomy predictions, had never yet failed to produce enough water.

"Well," Colt said, "Mott's all alone down there at that table of his. What do you say we go keep him company?" His eyes twinkled at her.

"I think we're probably the last people in the whole world that Mott Findley wants to see now," she said.

"In that case, I propose that we let him see us. As a kind of retribution, so to speak. Bethany, would you like to dance?" Colt said as the band, back from its break, struck up a different tune.

Her voice took on a lilt. "Colt, I would love to," she said.

They started down the stairs to the dance floor. At that moment, Mott rose from his seat. When he saw them on the stairs, he did a quick double take.

Bethany paused. "Hello, Mott," she said sweetly. Understanding dawned in Mott's eyes. His gaze darted back to the table on the upper tier where they had been sitting, and in that moment, she knew that Mott realized that she had heard everything that had transpired between him and Blue Suit. And as his eyes lit upon Colt, he knew that Colt had, too.

"Mott, while I think of it," Bethany went on, "if you ever decide to sell some of your land, I'd really appreciate it if you'd give me first chance at it. We're looking to expand. Aren't we, Colt?"

"Indeed we are," Colt said smoothly. He cupped a hand around her elbow and guided her down the rest of the stairs to the dance floor.

"So much for Mott. Look, he's stomping away." It was all Bethany could do not to laugh at Mott, and considering what he'd put her through, she'd probably be justified.

Colt took her in his arms. "I'd be angry, too, if I were in his situation. I'm sure he arranged this meeting way over here in Lubbock so that no one from Gompers would see him with whoever that man was. That guy's either a banker or a loan shark, but I'd suspect loan shark. And it sounds like he's on a feeding frenzy. I'd say that Mott is one little fish that he'd like to finish in one gulp."

"It sure is a big relief to know that my old adversary isn't in any position to make my life miserable anymore," Bethany said.

Colt chuckled. He glanced down at her. "So what do you say we forget about Mott and all his blustering and empty threats so we can enjoy ourselves?"

She became more serious. "I'll really enjoy it when you get those students out to the Banner-B as well as a few more horses to train, and we can start showing some results."

"Yes, but for now there's just you and me," Colt reminded her, and then she didn't care about Mott's comeuppance or the students or horses anymore. The only thing that mattered—the only thing that counted in the here and now—was that this handsome cowboy's arms were around her and they were dancing.

At first Bethany was unsure of herself and was afraid she'd make a fool of herself with her lack of dancing skill, but as Colt began to lead her around the floor, her uncertainty dissolved. Before she knew it, they were doing a classic Texas two-step.

"You're light on your feet," Colt said so close to her ear that his breath stirred a few loose tendrils that had escaped her barrette.

At that very moment, she stepped on his toes. He only laughed and drew her closer, and she inhaled the rich musky fragrance of his skin as she felt the muscles of his hard stomach press against hers. She couldn't help but think about last night, about how well-matched they had been sexually. Tonight she would invite him into her bed at the house, and they would make love again. She felt a thrill of anticipation at the thought.

"Having fun?" Colt smiled down at her, a rogue's smile, and she knew that he understood exactly the effect he was having on her. His eyes gleamed with pleasure, and she nodded. The music slowed, and he pulled her closer so that his chin rested on her temple. She closed her eyes and leaned into him, letting the music infuse her with its magic.

"Are you ready to give up yet?"

She shook her hair back and tilted her head to look up at him. "Give up what?" She was teasing him, bantering with him, something she'd almost forgotten how to do with a man.

"On dancing. We could sit down, drink our drinks, then dance again."

Bethany assented, but they never got to their table. Halfway there, a man wearing a shirt with the dance hall's logo emblazoned on the pocket came up to them. "Are you Colt McClure?" he asked.

"Sure am," Colt replied and the man handed Colt a slip of paper.

"What does it say?" Bethany asked when she saw him frown.

"It says to call Frisco. I wonder how he knew where to find us." Colt sounded puzzled.

"I mentioned to Dita that we'd probably stop in here. I wonder what Frisco wants." She knew that neither Frisco nor Dita would disturb them if something weren't seriously wrong, and there wasn't much at the ranch that the foreman and his wife couldn't handle.

Colt shook his head. "I don't know. Want to come with me while I scout up a phone?"

She nodded and followed Colt to a pay telephone. He dropped in a coin and waited impatiently while he was connected.

Once Frisco answered on the other end, Colt held the receiver so that Bethany could hear.

Frisco's voice was full of concern. "There's been an accident, Colt. It's Marcy. And the baby, too."

BETHANY AND COLT, terrified at what they'd find when they got to the hospital, drove the rest of the night to get to the small town off Interstate 40 where Marcy had run off the road earlier that day. Marcy's doctor had told them that she'd rolled the car over in a ditch, and a passerby had heard the baby crying and investigated. Marcy had internal injuries, including broken ribs and a ruptured spleen. The baby was, miraculously, hardly hurt at all.

Alyssa was being kept in the hospital pediatric ward for observation, so Colt and Bethany stopped off to see her. She was sleeping peacefully in a crib, her eyelashes casting feathery shadows on her round cheeks, and the nurse in charge said that she had eaten well both last night and this morning.

"She's a lucky child," said the nurse, and they couldn't help but agree.

When they finally dragged themselves away from Alyssa, they went to see Marcy, who burst into tears when she saw them. She was propped up on pillows in her bed, an IV tube leading into one hand. Her face was bruised and cut in two places, and although Colt and

Bethany had been assured by her doctor that the facial injuries were superficial, she looked as if she'd been through a terrible ordeal.

"Oh, Colt, I didn't mean to wreck your car!" Marcy wailed.

Colt brushed her hair back off her face and kissed her swollen cheek. "I know," he said.

Marcy glanced at Bethany. "I guess you hate me. I guess you think I'm a terrible mother."

"No," Bethany said. "No, that's not what I think."

"Well, I thought if I could get back to Oklahoma City, I could talk to my friend who works at the coffee shop with me? Jan? She's got a baby girl, too, and I could maybe move in with her. We could baby-sit each other's kids. But I got to thinking while I was driving, and I thought, why would Jan want me? It's a tiny apartment, not that much room. I've got a good thing going while I stay with Casey and her parents, and now here I'd gone and taken Alyssa with me and had no place to go with her. So I started crying and everything, and I couldn't see, and I'm not used to driving a car with a stick shift, and next thing I knew I was rolling over in the ditch." She began to cry, great gulping sobs.

It was clear to her that Marcy was beside herself with regrets, and Bethany took one of her hands. Colt, on the opposite side of the bed, took the other.

"Marcy, if there's anything we can do to help, please say so," Bethany said.

Marcy wiped her eyes with a corner of the sheet. "I've been doing some serious thinking. Not like before, when I wasn't thinking past the next five minutes or so. No, this time I've really been through hell, and I know I could have hurt her. My baby, I mean. Alyssa."

She began to cry again, this time silently, letting the tears run down her cheeks unheeded.

"What I want is for you to take her. Both of you." She looked from Colt to Bethany, a beseeching look.

"Take her?" said Bethany.

"We can't—" Colt began, but Bethany silenced him with a glance. "Let her talk," she said.

"You have such a nice bunch of people on the ranch. Frisco would be like a grandpa to Alyssa, and Eddie like an uncle. I don't know Dita very well, but didn't she treat Alyssa kind of like she would a grandchild? And you, Bethany, you should be her mother. Not me. I'm not nearly ready to make a home for her. Colt, you're perfect to be Alyssa's father. You've always taken time to help me and steer me through difficult times. Alyssa couldn't ask for better."

"I'm not sure what you're trying to say," Colt said slowly.

"I want you and Bethany to adopt my baby. Give her a happy home like you and I never had, Colt. Will you? Will you take her?" Marcy was painfully direct, and her grip tightened on Bethany's hand.

Bethany squeezed back. "Marcy, the two of us can't adopt Alyssa. Maybe one of us could, but I'm not sure that two people who aren't married can adopt a baby in this state." She wanted to adopt Alyssa; after all, she had already thought about it fleetingly. At that time, she'd thought that Alyssa would be reclaimed by Marcy. She hadn't realized how immature Marcy was and how unready to be a mother.

"You two are in love, anyone can see that!" Marcy exclaimed. "I mean, you could get married." Her words fell into a vast silence.

Colt cleared his throat. "The same thought has occurred to me,'' he said. He'd had plenty of time to reflect that he loved Bethany, that he wanted to take care of her no matter what, that he wanted to be there for her through any kind of trouble as Dita and Frisco were for each other.

Bethany looked at Colt over the narrow expanse of the hospital bed, and in that moment, everything else in the room faded away. There was no hospital, no Marcy, no IV, no sounds of rattling carts being wheeled down the corridor. There was only Colt, only her, and the look in his eyes that spoke the words she had never heard him say.

"Will you, Bethany? Will you marry me?"

"To give Alyssa a home? Is that why you're asking me?" She could hardly speak, and for a moment she thought he hadn't heard her.

"I'm asking you because I love you. I'm asking because you're the best woman I've ever met. I'm asking because I want a future with you, Bethany Burke, and I think you want one with me, too."

In that moment, she couldn't believe that he was actually proposing. Or that she was actually going to accept.

But she did.

Her eyes never leaving his, she reached across the hospital bed and so did he, and he gripped her hand so tightly that she didn't think she could ever let go. Or would want to, for that matter.

"Wow! Does that mean you're getting married? Really?" Marcy looked awestruck, amazed. Bethany couldn't really blame her.

"Yes, really," Bethany said. "As soon as we can." Her eyes filled with happy tears.

"Aren't you two going to kiss or something?" Marcy asked.

Colt let go of their hands and walked around the bed. He placed his hands on Bethany's shoulders and gazed deep into her eyes to her very soul. "I love you, Bethany," he said softly. "I will be a good husband to you." The emotion in his voice warmed her, told her that he meant what he said with all his heart.

She thought about his caring for Alyssa, who wasn't even his baby. She thought about his gentle way with Eddie and how he'd slowly worked Frisco over to his side. She thought about how he'd looked galloping down the driveway on the day he'd arrived and how he'd made her life special. And she thought about how he'd given her something she hadn't had for a long, long time: hope.

"And I will be a good wife," she whispered. Together they would be good parents to Alyssa and to whatever other children blessed their lives.

"I love you, cowboy," she said, words she had wanted to say for a long time, words that she would be saying to him for the rest of her life. There were a lot of other things she wanted to say to him, too, but he hushed her with a kiss.

"Wow," Marcy said. "You're really getting married and all."

Colt wrapped his arms around Bethany and held her even closer. She could hear his heart beating in his chest, strong and steady, and the answering beat of her own heart.

"Yes," Colt said, his voice firm and sure. "I reckon we really are."

Bethany pulled away slightly. "You'll come home with us, Marcy, both you and Alyssa."

"But I'll be starting school soon."

Colt rested a hand on her shoulder. "Stay until then."

"And on vacations," Bethany added, "The Banner-B will be your home place as well as ours."

"My home place," breathed Marcy. "I like the sound of that."

"I do, too," Colt said, gazing at Bethany.

"I think she wants you to kiss her again," prompted Marcy.

"Well," said Colt, pretending to think it over, "I don't mind if I do."

And he did.

Epilogue

It was Bethany's wedding day. In less than three hours, she and Colt would be husband and wife. And she and Colt and Alyssa would be a family.

During a lull when she thought she would have a slim chance of being missed, Bethany slipped away from the ranch house and the wedding preparations and went to her special place beside Little Moony Creek. She lowered herself to the bench that Justin had built for her and sat hugging her knees to her chest. A plane flew high overhead; an ant crawled across the toe of her sneakers. Bethany buried her head in her arms and listened to her heartbeat.

Love never dies, said a voice in her head. She lifted her head sharply, almost believing that she'd heard it out loud. But no, there was no one around, only a blue jay that fluttered down briefly from the cottonwoods and just as quickly flew away.

"I will never stop loving you," she whispered into the peacefulness, hoping that somehow, some way, Justin would hear. "Never. It's just that I have other people now to love, too."

In the moments that followed, a wonderful sense of calm overtook her. She knew that Justin would have understood that she wasn't forsaking him or his memory. She was simply getting on with her life, which would help her keep her promise to him. She would keep the Banner-B Ranch, and she and Colt would make a success of it. Nothing could stop them now, nothing at all.

"Bethany?"

She looked up, and there, as if by magic, was Colt. She held both hands out to him in welcome. "Come sit with me for a minute," she said.

He sat down beside her and slipped an arm around her shoulders. "I told you we should have eloped," he said. "Those women in the house are going to turn this wedding into a circus."

She smiled up at him. "No, they won't, my love. They're so happy for us that they want to make everything go off without a hitch, that's all."

"Even if it doesn't, I'm still a happy man. I've got you, and Alyssa, and the adoption's final in a few months."

"And something else I haven't told you yet, Colt."

"If there's anything I need to know before we go through with this, you better let me in on it now." He was grinning, though, and she bit her lip.

"Well," she began, wondering whether she should just blurt out the news or bring it up in a more roundabout way.

Colt kissed her forehead. "Sounds ominous," he said. "Sounds as if you might be having second thoughts."

She slid an arm across his chest and rested her head on his shoulder. "My only second thoughts are that this is the right thing to do. I love you, Colt. More and more every day."

"I love you, too, my darlin'. So—out with it." He looked down at her questioningly.

Bethany drew a deep breath. "Colt, I'm pregnant. I did one of those home pregnancy tests this morning, and—"

"A baby? You're sure?" He looked stunned.

She pulled away so she could see the expression on his face. "Yes, I didn't want to say anything before, and I thought I was, I think it happened about a month ago when we came back from Oklahoma City and knew that Alyssa was going to be ours forever and you made love to me so tenderly in my bed for the first time."

"You're going to have another *baby?*"

"I never had one before," she reminded him with a twinkle. "Alyssa isn't ours."

"I keep forgetting that. It seems like she's always been our child. It seems like I've been with you forever, and now we're going to have a baby!" He was astonished, and he couldn't believe it. Bethany was going to have his baby!

"Yes," she murmured as he turned to take her in his arms.

He held her close, noticed that their two hearts beat as one. And that would be the way it was from now on, two of them one. Three, counting Alyssa. Four, counting the new baby. He was humbled by the turn his life had taken in the months since he had left prison. Humbled and overjoyed that this woman had made his life worth living again.

"Oh, my sweet Bethany. How much I love you" was all he could say as he buried his face in her hair.

It was only hours later that Bethany, wearing an ivory lace dress that she'd ordered from a bridal catalog, joined Colt in the living room of the ranch house. Rubye played the wedding march on the old upright piano, tuned especially for this occasion, as Frisco, who had done nothing but grouse about having to wear a tie since the moment he'd put one on, walked Bethany down the aisle.

Dita had been thrilled to stand up as Bethany's only attendant, and Eddie was delighted to be given the honor of serving as Colt's best man. Loreen held Alyssa in the front row, beaming her approval along with the others. Even Jesse James, bathed and beribboned for the occasion, was allowed to sit on the carpet beside Loreen, and no one minded that the thump of his tail occasionally punctuated the nuptial proceedings. The only one of their invited guests who wasn't able to attend was Marcy, who had recently enrolled in a community college in Oklahoma City the week before and had sent her regrets along with the signed forms that released Alyssa to them for adoption.

"Dearly beloved," began the minister, and Bethany thought, *yes, these people are all dearly beloved,* catching herself up short as the minister paused and asked her if she would have this man for her lawfully wedded husband.

"I will," she said, gazing deep into Colt's eyes, and she was surprised to see tears in those eyes, tears of happiness.

Colt squeezed her hand, and she squeezed back. It seemed right that they were promising to be together for better for worse, for richer for poorer, in sickness and in health, as long as they both shall live; they were the type of people who kept promises, as Colt said, no matter what.

The rest of the ceremony was a blur to Bethany. It went by too fast. At the end, when the minister directed the groom to kiss the bride, Colt took her in his arms. He looked at her for one long searching moment, a moment of indescribable joy, before he kissed her.

Loreen stood on cue and handed Alyssa to Colt. And then he and Bethany greeted their guests as husband and wife and child—a family.

And a family, people who cared about you, was one of the things, Bethany reflected from within the circle of her husband's arm, that you couldn't order from any catalog.

Announcement from the *Gompers Gazette*, May 2, 2001

BIRTHS

On April 25—To Mr. and Mrs. Clayton McClure (Bethany Carroll Burke) and daughter Alyssa of the Banner-B Ranch, a son and brother, Clayton McClure, Junior. Clay weighed 7 lbs. 6 oz., and mother and baby are doing fine. Bethany says thanks for sending over all the fine casseroles, and she and Colt hope you'll all stop by real soon to meet the newest member of their family.

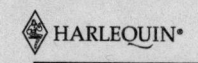

HARLEQUIN®
AMERICAN *Romance*®

JUDY CHRISTENBERRY

is back
and so are the citizens of Cactus, Texas!
Harlequin American Romance is proud to
present another **Tots for Texans** story.

STRUCK BY THE TEXAS MATCHMAKERS

June 2001

TOTS for TEXANS

Dr. Jeff Hausen came to Cactus, Texas, to get away from the harshness of big-city life. Diane Peters returned to her hometown with a law degree under her belt and the hopes of one day settling in the big city. But when the two met, the sparks flew.... And with *a lot* of help from the Texas matchmakers, wedding bells might soon be ringing!

Available wherever Harlequin books are sold.

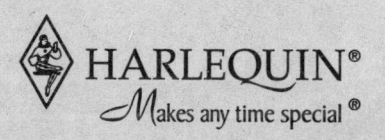

HARLEQUIN®
Makes any time special®

Visit us at www.eHarlequin.com

HARTOTS2

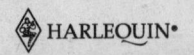

HARLEQUIN
AMERICAN *Romance*

proudly presents a brand-new,
unforgettable series....

TEXAS SHEIKHS

Though their veins course with royal blood,
their pride lies in the Texas land they call home!

Don't miss:

HIS INNOCENT TEMPTRESS by Kasey Michaels
On sale April 2001

HIS ARRANGED MARRIAGE by Tina Leonard
On sale May 2001

HIS SHOTGUN PROPOSAL by Karen Toller Whittenburg
On sale June 2001

HIS ROYAL PRIZE by Debbi Rawlins
On sale July 2001

*Available at
your favorite retail outlet.*

HARLEQUIN®
Makes any time special®

Visit us at www.eHarlequin.com

HARSHEIK

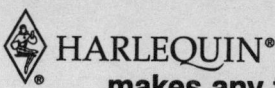

HARLEQUIN®
makes any time special—online...

eHARLEQUIN.com

shop eHarlequin

- ♥ Find all the new Harlequin releases at everyday great discounts.
- ♥ Try before you buy! Read an excerpt from the latest Harlequin novels.
- ♥ Write an online review and share your thoughts with others.

reading room

- ♥ Read our Internet exclusive daily and weekly online serials, or vote in our interactive novel.
- ♥ Talk to other readers about your favorite novels in our Reading Groups.
- ♥ Take our Choose-a-Book quiz to find the series that matches you!

authors' alcove

- ♥ Find out interesting tidbits and details about your favorite authors' lives, interests and writing habits.
- ♥ Ever dreamed of being an author? Enter our Writing Round Robin. The Winning Chapter will be published online! Or review our writing guidelines for submitting your novel.

**All this and more available at
www.eHarlequin.com
on Women.com Networks**

HINTB1R

Harlequin Romance®
Love affairs that last a lifetime.
HARLEQUIN® Presents®
Seduction and passion guaranteed.
Harlequin® Historical®
Historical Romantic Adventure.
HARLEQUIN® Temptation.
Sassy, sexy, seductive!
HARLEQUIN® SuperROMANCE®
Emotional, exciting, unexpected.
HARLEQUIN® AMERICAN Romance®
Heart, home & happiness.
HARLEQUIN® Duets™
Romantic comedy.
HARLEQUIN® INTRIGUE
Breathtaking romantic suspense.
Get caught reading Harlequin.
HARLEQUIN®
Makes any time special®

*Harlequin truly does make any time special....
This year we are celebrating weddings in style!*

A Walk Down the Aisle
WEDDING CELEBRATION

To help us celebrate, we want you to tell us how wearing the Harlequin wedding gown will make your wedding day special. As the grand prize, Harlequin will offer one lucky bride the chance to **"Walk Down the Aisle"** in the Harlequin wedding gown!

There's more...

For her honeymoon, she and her groom will spend five nights at the **Hyatt Regency Maui.** As part of this five-night honeymoon at the hotel renowned for its romantic attractions, the couple will enjoy a candlelit dinner for two in Swan Court, a sunset sail on the hotel's catamaran, and duet spa treatments.

HYATT REGENCY MAUI
A HYATT RESORT AND SPA

MAUI *the Magic Isles*™
Maui • Molokai • Lanai

To enter, please write, in, 250 words or less, how wearing the Harlequin wedding gown will make your wedding day special. The entry will be judged based on its emotionally compelling nature, its originality and creativity, and its sincerity. This contest is open to Canadian and U.S. residents only and to those who are 18 years of age and older. There is no purchase necessary to enter. Void where prohibited. See further contest rules attached. Please send your entry to:

Walk Down the Aisle Contest

In Canada	In U.S.A.
P.O. Box 637	P.O. Box 9076
Fort Erie, Ontario	3010 Walden Ave.
L2A 5X3	Buffalo, NY 14269-9076

You can also enter by visiting www.eHarlequin.com
Win the Harlequin wedding gown and the vacation of a lifetime!
The deadline for entries is October 1, 2001.

HARLEQUIN®
Makes any time special ®

PHWDACONT1

HARLEQUIN WALK DOWN THE AISLE TO MAUI CONTEST 1197
OFFICIAL RULES
NO PURCHASE NECESSARY TO ENTER

1. To enter, follow directions published in the offer to which you are responding. Contest begins April 2, 2001, and ends on October 1, 2001. Method of entry may vary. Mailed entries must be postmarked by October 1, 2001, and received by October 8, 2001.

2. Contest entry may be, at times, presented via the Internet, but will be restricted solely to residents of certain geographic areas that are disclosed on the Web site. To enter via the Internet, if permissible, access the Harlequin Web site (www.eHarlequin.com) and follow the directions displayed online. Online entries must be received by 11:59 p.m. E.S.T. on October 1, 2001.

   In lieu of submitting an entry online, enter by mail by hand-printing (or typing) on an 8½" x 11" plain piece of paper, your name, address (including zip code), Contest number/name and in 250 words or fewer, why winning a Harlequin wedding dress would make your wedding day special. Mail via first-class mail to: Harlequin Walk Down the Aisle Contest 1197, (in the U.S.) P.O. Box 9076, 3010 Walden Avenue, Buffalo, NY 14269-9076, (in Canada) P.O. Box 637, Fort Erie, Ontario L2A 5X3, Canada. Limit one entry per person, household address and e-mail address. Online and/or mailed entries received from persons residing in geographic areas in which Internet entry is not permissible will be disqualified.

3. Contests will be judged by a panel of members of the Harlequin editorial, marketing and public relations staff based on the following criteria:
   - Originality and Creativity—50%
   - Emotionally Compelling—25%
   - Sincerity—25%

   In the event of a tie, duplicate prizes will be awarded. Decisions of the judges are final.

4. All entries become the property of Torstar Corp. and will not be returned. No responsibility is assumed for lost, late, illegible, incomplete, inaccurate, nondelivered or misdirected mail or misdirected e-mail, for technical, hardware or software failures of any kind, lost or unavailable network connections, or failed, incomplete, garbled or delayed computer transmission or any human error which may occur in the receipt or processing of the entries in this Contest.

5. Contest open only to residents of the U.S. (except Puerto Rico) and Canada, who are 18 years of age or older, and is void wherever prohibited by law; all applicable laws and regulations apply. Any litigation within the Province of Quebec respecting the conduct or organization of a publicity contest may be submitted to the Régie des alcools, des courses et des jeux for a ruling. Any litigation respecting the awarding of a prize may be submitted to the Régie des alcools, des courses et des jeux only for the purpose of helping the parties reach a settlement. Employees and immediate family members of Torstar Corp. and D. L. Blair, Inc., their affiliates, subsidiaries and all other agencies, entities and persons connected with the use, marketing or conduct of this Contest are not eligible to enter. Taxes on prizes are the sole responsibility of winners. Acceptance of any prize offered constitutes permission to use winner's name, photograph or other likeness for the purposes of advertising, trade and promotion on behalf of Torstar Corp., its affiliates and subsidiaries without further compensation to the winner, unless prohibited by law.

6. Winners will be determined no later than November 15, 2001, and will be notified by mail. Winners will be required to sign and return an Affidavit of Eligibility form within 15 days after winner notification. Noncompliance within that time period may result in disqualification and an alternative winner may be selected. Winners of trip must execute a Release of Liability prior to ticketing and must possess required travel documents (e.g. passport, photo ID) where applicable. Trip must be completed by November 2002. No substitution of prize permitted by winner. Torstar Corp. and D. L. Blair, Inc., their parents, affiliates, and subsidiaries are not responsible for errors in printing or electronic presentation of Contest, entries and/or game pieces. In the event of printing or other errors which may result in unintended prize values or duplication of prizes, all affected game pieces or entries shall be null and void. If for any reason the Internet portion of the Contest is not capable of running as planned, including infection by computer virus, bugs, tampering, unauthorized intervention, fraud, technical failures, or any other causes beyond the control of Torstar Corp. which corrupt or affect the administration, secrecy, fairness, integrity or proper conduct of the Contest, Torstar Corp. reserves the right, at its sole discretion, to disqualify any individual who tampers with the entry process and to cancel, terminate, modify or suspend the Contest or the Internet portion thereof. In the event of a dispute regarding an online entry, the entry will be deemed submitted by the authorized holder of the e-mail account submitted at the time of entry. Authorized account holder is defined as the natural person who is assigned to an e-mail address by an Internet access provider, online service provider or other organization that is responsible for arranging e-mail address for the domain associated with submitted e-mail address. **Purchase or acceptance of a product offer does not improve your chances of winning.**

7. Prizes: (1) Grand Prize—A Harlequin wedding dress (approximate retail value: $3,500) and a 5-night/6-day honeymoon trip to Maui, HI, including round-trip air transportation provided by Maui Visitors Bureau from Los Angeles International Airport (winner is responsible for transportation to and from Los Angeles International Airport) and a Harlequin Romance Package, including hotel accomodations (double occupancy) at the Hyatt Regency Maui Resort and Spa, dinner for (2) two at Swan Court, a sunset sail on Kiele V and a spa treatment for the winner (approximate retail value: $4,000); (5) Five runner-up prizes of a $1000 gift certificate to selected retail outlets to be determined by Sponsor (retail value $1000 ea.). Prizes consist of only those items listed as part of the prize. Limit one prize per person. All prizes are valued in U.S. currency.

8. For a list of winners (available after December 17, 2001) send a self-addressed, stamped envelope to: Harlequin Walk Down Aisle Contest 1197 Winners, P.O. Box 4200 Blair, NE 68009-4200 or you may access the www.eHarlequin.com Web site through January 15, 2002.

Contest sponsored by Torstar Corp., P.O. Box 9042, Buffalo, NY 14269-9042, U.S.A.

PHWDACONT2